I wondered if the young girl had faked her alarm, to scam her friends or Maddie and me? Or maybe all of the teens had been in on the joke, just because they were teens.

"What makes you think it's not makeup you're seeing?" I asked the girl who was either hyperventilating or a very good actress.

"He's really dead," said a boy who'd gone as far as the bottom step to confirm the report. "It's a dead live man. I mean, a dead dead man." His face was white as he turned and touched the man's forehead. "His eyes are, like, staring, and there's a bullet hole . . . I think it is . . . right here. And there's a gun in his hand, and there's, like, a mess."

The looks on the faces of the teens were enough to convince me, however, that this was no joke, not by the Fergusons, and not by the teenagers.

I saw my quiet Halloween turn into a dead pumpkin.

W9-BLI-733

Monster in Miniature

Margaret Grace

BERKLEY PRIME CRIME, NEW YORK

THE BERKLEY PUBLISHING GROUP
Published by the Penguin Group
Penguin Group (USA) Inc.
375 Hudson Street, New York, New York 10014, USA
Penguin Group (Canada), 90 Eglinton Avenue East, Suite 700, Toronto, Ontario M4P 2Y3, Canada
(a division of Pearson Penguin Canada Inc.)
Penguin Books Ltd., 80 Strand, London WC2R 0RL, England
Penguin Group Ireland, 25 St. Stephen's Green, Dublin 2, Ireland (a division of Penguin Books Ltd.)
Penguin Group (Australia), 250 Camberwell Road, Camberwell, Victoria 3124, Australia
(a division of Pearson Australia Group Pty. Ltd.)
Penguin Books India Pvt. Ltd., 11 Community Centre, Panchsheel Park, New Delhi—110 017, India
Penguin Group (NZ), 67 Apollo Drive, Rosedale, North Shore 0632, New Zealand
(a division of Pearson New Zealand Ltd.)
Penguin Books (South Africa) (Pty.) Ltd., 24 Sturdee Avenue, Rosebank, Johannesburg 2196,
South Africa

Penguin Books Ltd., Registered Offices: 80 Strand, London WC2R 0RL, England

This is a work of fiction. Names, characters, places, and incidents either are the product of the author's imagination or are used fictitiously, and any resemblance to actual persons, living or dead, business establishments, events, or locales is entirely coincidental. The publisher does not have any control over and does not assume any responsibility for author or third-party websites or their content.

MONSTER IN MINIATURE

A Berkley Prime Crime Book / published by arrangement with the author

PRINTING HISTORY
Berkley Prime Crime mass-market edition / April 2010

ISBN: 978-0-425-23390-0

BERKLEY® PRIME CRIME
Berkley Prime Crime Books are published by The Berkley Publishing Group,
a division of Penguin Group (USA) Inc.,
375 Hudson Street, New York, New York 10014.
BERKLEY® PRIME CRIME and the PRIME CRIME logo are trademarks of Penguin Group (USA)
Inc.

PRINTED IN THE UNITED STATES OF AMERICA

10   9   8   7   6   5   4   3   2   1

Acknowledgments

Thanks as always to my dream critique team: mystery authors Jonnie Jacobs, Rita Lakin, and Margaret Lucke.

A special word about my friend and son-in-law, Jim Thomas, owner of JJET Enterprises in Livermore, California. I hope he'll forgive me for turning his wonderful, honest, and upright family business into a den of bad guys. His generous assistance in creating a fictional factory deserves better, but I am, after all, a crime writer. Thanks, Jim!

Thanks also to the extraordinary Inspector Chris Lux for advice on police procedure. My interpretation of his counsel should not be held against him.

Thanks to my sister, Arlene Polvinen; my cousin, Jean Stokowski; and the many writers and friends who offered critique, information, and inspiration; in particular: Judy Barnett, Sara Bly, Mark Coggins, Margaret Hamilton, Judy Olsen (whose twins are nothing like the Ferguson boys), Ann Parker, Ellen Schnur, Mary Schnur, Sue Stephenson, Karen Streich, and Mark Streich.

My deepest gratitude goes to my husband, Dick Rufer, the best there is. I can't imagine working without his support. He's my dedicated Webmaster (www.dollhousemysteries .com), layout specialist, and on-call IT department.

Finally, how lucky can I be? I'm working with a special and dedicated editor, Michelle Vega, and marvelous agents, Elaine Koster and Ellen Twaddell.

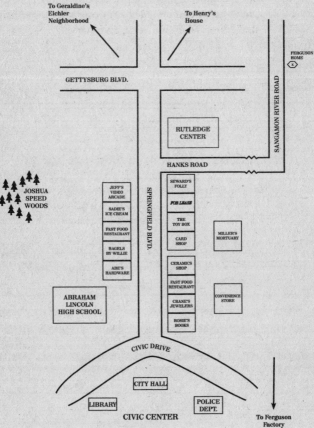

LINCOLN POINT, CA

To Geraldine's Eichler Neighborhood

To Henry's House

FERGUSON HOME

GETTYSBURG BLVD.

SANGAMON RIVER ROAD

RUTLEDGE CENTER

HANKS ROAD

JOSHUA SPEED WOODS

JEFF'S VIDEO ARCADE

SADIE'S ICE CREAM

FAST FOOD RESTAURANT

BAGELS BY WILLIE

ABE'S HARDWARE

SPRINGFIELD BLVD.

SEWARD'S FOLLY

FOR LEASE

THE TOY BOX

CARD SHOP

MILLER'S MORTUARY

CERAMICS SHOP

FAST FOOD RESTAURANT

CRANE'S JEWELERS

ROSIE'S BOOKS

CONVENIENCE STORE

ABRAHAM LINCOLN HIGH SCHOOL

CIVIC DRIVE

CITY HALL

LIBRARY

POLICE DEPT.

CIVIC CENTER

To Ferguson Factory

Chapter 1

It took me nearly an hour to do a few simple tasks around the house: I painted the kitchen and dining room walls a dull gray, laid black shag carpet in the living room and main hallway, and installed torn-up lacey curtains in the bedrooms and the attic. I'd hoped also to rewire the house before lunch, but I needed a break.

I'd always wanted to make a multistory haunted dollhouse for Halloween, and this year the timing was right. My eleven-year-old granddaughter, Maddie, was excited about the project and I was a pushover for whatever enticed her to spend time with me.

Maddie was kind enough to allow me to do the boring parts. "Like, you can glue the shingles onto the roof when I'm not here, Grandma, and I'll help with all the decorations."

"You're a princess," I said, and despite the conditions, she knew I meant it.

I'd bought this newest dollhouse as a fixer-upper at a

miniatures flea market in Sacramento, about two hours from my (life-size) home in Lincoln Point, California. One of my crafter friends, Susan Giles, and I had made the trip together. We'd all gotten used to traveling long distances to find supplies for our hobby since, sadly, so many local doll-house stores had gone out of business.

With only a little more than a week till Halloween, the lawns and porches of our town were lined with goblins and ghosts, shimmering black cats, and lighted jack-o'-lanterns. One street in particular, Sangamon River Road, had become a tourist attraction of late, drawing visitors from all around the county. The residents held a contest every year for the most creative outdoor Halloween scene. Last year's win-ners had converted their one-car garage into a barred, jail-like container for a large green monster that shook his fake cage and bellowed every time someone approached.

"Everybody's using motion sensors this year, Aunt Gerry," my homicide detective nephew, Skip Gowen, had mentioned to me casually. "If you'd like something like that for your lawn, I'd be glad to help."

In other words, the young cop in our family was still trying to drag me into the twenty-first century. Meanwhile, the town's official century was the nineteenth, its citizens sworn Lincoln-ophiles, its government buildings adorned with wise, inspirational quotes from Honest Abe. We cele-brated even the most remote anniversaries connected with our sixteenth president—from his first political speech in 1830, on improving navigation on the Sangamon River, to the day in 1831 when he wrestled his good friend, the rough-and-tumble Jack Armstrong, to a draw.

Miniaturists often recaptured the past, with replicas of Victorian homes being one of the most popular dollhouse styles. The more layers of lace, velvet, and floral patterns, the better. We were admittedly inconsistent: we delighted in furnishing our dollhouse bathrooms with claw-foot tubs and pedestal sinks, but no one in my crafts group would be willing to give up her blow-dryer and real-life Jacuzzi.

Maddie was also angling for a high-tech haunted dollhouse this year. She'd suggested having eerie, screeching sounds come out of the tiny windows and flashing, blood-red lights around the porch.

"I learned how to do that stuff last summer in technology camp, which cost my parents a lot of money," she'd reminded me.

"That doesn't mean I have to adopt all your new knowledge," I'd told her. I accompanied my proclamations with tickling in the right spot, and my granddaughter acquiesced in a burst of giggles.

"Okay, okay, Grandma!" She'd caved easily. "You're wicked."

Which I knew was an endearing term.

I looked forward to a scream-free Halloween.

No one could bring me back to this century like Madison Porter, my only grandchild. I picked her up after school a couple of nights a week—on Wednesdays and Fridays mostly, so she could join my crafting circle. I'd deliver her back to her Palo Alto school on Thursday mornings, but on Saturdays, the time was ours without limit.

According to her parents, I was more rigorous about our schedule than a divorced couple with a custody arrangement.

On the way home this Friday, Maddie and I made a stop at Sadie's Ice Cream Shop on Springfield Boulevard. Maddie put away a hot fudge sundae with extra whipped cream (orange flavored with black sprinkles, in honor of the season) and then asked if I were going to eat the wafers that came with my single scoop of Swiss milk chocolate. If not, she'd be glad to take them off my hands. To look at her skinny body, you'd never know how much food she consumed in a single day. She'd inherited the tall, thin gene from both sides of her family, the only exception in the group being her father, my son, Richard, who ran a bit toward the bulky.

When it was just dark enough for the lighted props on Lincoln Point streets to be effectively spooky, we headed for Sangamon River Road in my little red Saturn.

"I hope Mr. and Mrs. Ferguson have their creature out," Maddie said, sitting tall, buckled into the front seat like the grown-up she considered herself. "Maybe he has some new digital sounds."

I got the message: if her grandmother wasn't going to provide Halloween thrills, she'd find them elsewhere.

As we wound through the darkening streets, taking detours on our way to Sangamon River Road, Maddie played tour guide, calling out the main feature at each residence: a shimmering, black-draped monster hugging a tree; a stiff, long-tailed ghost protruding from a second-story window; an oversize inflatable spider perched on a life-size skeleton. Everything brought an "ooh" or an "aah" from me, as Maddie hoped.

We came upon three stick-figure witches ensconced around a cauldron of boiling . . . something . . . dry ice, I guessed, and not "eye of newt and toe of frog, wool of bat and tongue of dog." I thought of treating Maddie to a discourse on the witches in *Macbeth*. She'd grown weary of the soliloquy in *Hamlet* and had been less than fascinated to hear the context of the phrase "sweets to the sweet," spoken of the dead Ophelia, by Queen Gertrude. Such were the drawbacks of having a retired English teacher for a grandmother. You grew up with Shakespeare whether you liked it or not.

This time I treated Maddie to a passage from *Macbeth*'s witches. "'When shall we three meet again—in thunder, lightning, or in rain?'" I spoke in my best Elizabethan tones, which weren't too bad given my Bronx roots. I answered for the second witch, "'When the hurlyburly's done, when the battle's lost and won.'" I lowered the pitch of my voice for the third witch: "'That will be ere the set of sun.'"

Maddie raised her eyebrows. "There are witches in Shakespeare? Why didn't you tell me? I love witches."

How was I to know? The witches had never impressed my students at Abraham Lincoln High School. I'd done my best to engage them during the nearly three decades I'd taught there before my retirement. Fortunately, there were a few in their number who were sufficiently intrigued to major in English in college.

"We can make witches for our haunted dollhouse," I said.

"Duh."

I took that as enthusiasm.

We turned down Hanks Road and headed far out of town to the east. At one point Hanks became a narrow, rather curvy road, then dead-ended at the Sangamon River homes. Not that there was a river anywhere close. For fans of Abraham Lincoln, it hardly mattered, however; the name was a way to recognize a principal tributary of the Illinois River and a place of note in Lincoln's life.

I pulled over to the curb on Sangamon, a typical tree-lined suburban street that, for the most part, was quiet the other eleven months of the year. Maddie unbuckled her seat belt. She was still in her school clothes, which weren't that different from her hanging-around clothes—jeans and layered tops—simply newer. Today had been short-sleeve weather with temperatures in the seventies, but she'd added a red hoodie now as the late afternoon cooled.

I straightened her sleeve before she jumped out. "When I was your age, it was so cold on Halloween that—"

"I know. I know. You all had to wear long underwear under your little angel outfits. I'd never wear an angel outfit in the first place." I looked sideways at her. She wrinkled her nose. "Except for the time I wasn't even a year old and someone put me in one."

I shrugged, as if I had no idea who might have done such a thing to her.

Maddie's eyes widened as we walked through what looked like a theme park in orange, white, and black. Some of the families dispensed treats remotely, through gumball machines and baskets of candy set out near the edge of their property. I wondered if there would be any left on Halloween night as Maddie popped a chocolate roll into her mouth. Certainly, I thought, and took one for myself.

"That house is lame," Maddie said, pointing to a small green-and-white Cape Cod with only a few pumpkins on the gravel walkway.

"They must be on the judges' committee this year," I said.

I reminded her that the judging rotated each year so no one residence would be permanently disqualified from entering the contest. We found three other lame houses, with minimal acknowledgment of the season.

"I thought there were only three families that did the judging," Maddie said. "But there are four boring houses."

"They must have changed the rules this year," I offered.

"Nuh-uh, it has to be an odd number, like the Supreme Court."

I couldn't argue with that. I acknowledged that there

must have been some other reason why one extra house wasn't participating this year.

Mr. and Mrs. Ferguson lived several houses from the corner on the street of Halloween dreams. Sam and Lillian, pioneers in the high-tech approach, had the same spectacular, though witch-less, scene every year. Their main character, fashioned by Sam, a retired mechanic, was a half-scarecrow half-human figure set out on the wraparound porch of their country-style home. Sam used a lifelike head, probably made of modeling foam, and a straw body with baggy clothes.

We stopped to admire the realistic-looking form, slumped against the newel post closest to the level of the porch and partly surrounded by shrubs. From the street, the figure looked like an adult male relaxing, perhaps sleeping, on the top step. We knew that as soon as anyone got close to it, however, the mannequin would spring to life and stretch his arms wide, Frankenstein-style. His head would wobble, and he'd give out a bloodcurdling scream.

The large lawn in front of the Fergusons' scream-capable figure was filled with nearly as many headstones as the church cemetery on the opposite end of town. Skulls, remote-controlled black critters, headless corpses, and corpse-less heads littered the aisles between the faux granite RIP fixtures.

"There's something new," I said, pointing to an upstairs window in Sam and Lillian's house. "The cat's eyes are blinking."

"Wow," Maddie said. "This whole place is wicked." There was her word of the month again, having nothing to do with Halloween. She draped herself on the old picket fence, leaning in and waving her arms, hoping to get her fingers within range of the motion detector and thus provoke a scream from the floppy, limp form on the porch.

I pointed to the partly rusted latch on the gate. "Look, it's unlocked. Why don't you go inside?" I asked, though I knew the answer. Maddie had never been brave enough to go right up to the Fergusons' scary creature. She always preferred to prod him from a distance and wait until a more courageous soul walked through the gate.

"Nuh-uh. I'm just trying to see what the range of the detector is," she said. "In case I want to build one at technology camp next summer."

"I see."

A group of teenagers, three boys and three girls, happened by. They seemed to be enjoying the start of their weekend as much as released convicts might relish their first day of freedom. I remembered the feeling from having been on both sides of a teacher's desk. The teenagers unwittingly did Maddie the huge favor of crashing through the gate, laughing and prodding one another—who would dare get closest to the figure this year?

Maddie stayed on her perch, watching the action. Soon enough she'd be on her own, traveling with just such a group, I mused. I wondered if she were wishing she could join them now. Or was she relieved to be on the sidelines? For me, I was happy to have a couple more years with her as a preteen.

Eeeeeek!

A human-sounding scream pierced the air. One of the girls had apparently walked within range of the motion detector.

Eeeeeek!

Maddie and I blocked our ears. Sam and Lillian had outdone themselves in verisimilitude.

But something was different—the creature didn't budge. No bobbing head or flailing arms and no wildly kicking legs had been stirred into action.

Maddie came down from the fence and wrapped her arms around my waist. I stroked her red curls as we both sensed something was dead wrong.

Indeed it was. The scream had come from one of the teenage girls. "It's really a dead man," she yelled, in a hysterical voice, running out to the sidewalk. Most of her companions followed.

A prank, I thought. Had Sam and Lillian Ferguson enlisted a Hollywood makeup artist to better their chances at winning a prize? From what I'd read, the prize was nothing elaborate—a modest gift certificate to a store in town, a token gesture to encourage competition.

My teaching wits kicked in and I wondered if the young girl had faked her alarm, to scam her friends or Maddie and me? Or maybe all of the teens had been in on the joke, just because they were teens.

"What makes you think it's not makeup you're seeing?" I asked the girl, who was either hyperventilating or a very good actress. "The porch is not very well lit."

"It is if you're up there." Of course it was. The Fergusons had rigged floodlights with just the right amount of illumination to cover the porch and the steps in an eerie yellow glow. "And, besides, I can tell. I've seen real dead bodies close-up on television," the girl said. If she weren't shaking so much, I'd have laughed.

"He's really dead," said a boy who'd gone as far as the bottom step to confirm the report. "It's a dead live man. I mean, a dead dead man." His face was white as he turned and touched his forehead. "His eyes are, like, staring, and there's a bullet hole . . . I think it is . . . right here. And there's a gun in his hand, and there's, like, a mess."

I knew that if I went up the walkway to examine the scene myself, the teenagers would flee, and on the off chance that there really had been a real gun and a real death,

I needed them to stay. The more I looked at the man's body, the more convinced I became that it was human. The legs of his jeans and the arms of his red plaid shirt were filled out, not drooping over broomstick handles or seeming to be made of straw.

The only downside to believing without seeing for myself close-up was that I'd be embarrassed if I called the police out to investigate a spoof. With all the supplies available at every party and discount store at this time of year, how hard would it be to paint a bullet hole on a fake head?

The looks on the faces of the teens were enough to convince me, however, that this was no joke, not by the Fergusons, and not by the teenagers.

And there was one cop with whom I could take a chance. We had a history of sharing embarrassing moments.

I took out my cell phone and punched in my nephew's number.

I saw my quiet Halloween turn into a dead pumpkin.

Chapter 2

I was enormously and selfishly relieved that it hadn't been Maddie who'd discovered that the Fergusons had been sporting a live—well, once-live—Halloween decoration.

"Do you want to go to the car?" I whispered to Maddie. She shook her head vigorously: *no*. Then she linked her arm through mine in a casual movement, as if she weren't frightened to death.

A quick survey of the house showed no sign of life inside. I was surprised the Fergusons would go out and leave all the decorative lights on but guessed that participation in the contest required it—the more exposure the scene had, the better.

I knew Sam and Lillian Ferguson as well as I knew the parents of any of my former students. I'd known their twin boys, Eliot and Emory, now in their forties, from ALHS, and saw them around town occasionally. My late husband, Ken, had been the architect on an industrial remodeling project that included the twins' manufacturing business,

E&E Parts. That era seemed a lifetime ago, but then, any day without Ken was still too long.

At this distance from the porch I couldn't make out details of the facial structure of the body, but I was fairly sure the victim wasn't old Sam. The Fergusons had had their boys a little older than most parents of that time, and were probably now close to eighty years old. The dead man seemed much younger, around the twins' age.

I felt Maddie shudder and rubbed her arm. I wished I could protect her from anything that brought her shivers, but I felt my duty was to stay at the scene.

What if Sam and Lillian were at home, a few yards away, injured or dead? As much as I wanted to go through the gate, at least to check on them, I felt glued to my spot, with no choice but to wait until Skip arrived. What few passersby I saw were on the other side of the street, and none of them seemed old enough for me to enlist for crime scene inspection.

The teens had gone into a huddle. Not a good sign, in my vast experience with adolescents. I needed to maintain some control over them.

"I'm Mrs. Porter, from the high school," I said, approaching the group. I didn't bother to amend the statement to include the fact of my retirement several years ago. "Is everyone okay here?"

Two of the girls remained silent, moving their thumbs with great speed over a tiny keyboard on their cell phones. The others answered me with murmurings of "I guess" and "Kinda."

"I have some water in my car if anyone needs it," I said. The suggestion spurred no verbal response, but several bottles of water appeared from their backpacks. "I called the police and they'll be here any minute," I continued. "I'm sure they'll want to talk to each of you."

"No way," one boy said, and he and the girl who'd been clinging to him rushed off toward Hanks Road before I could convince them otherwise or even get their names.

Bad start. To contain the remaining four teens, I'd need my strongest teacher voice. "Now, listen to me, please. By all accounts, this was not a death by natural causes, and you can all be considered witnesses after the fact. You can't run away from that." (Sad to say, it wasn't the first time I'd made up an official-sounding phrase to fool a group of freshmen.)

"I have to get home. My mom will be totally worried," said the girl who'd screamed. I sympathized with her sudden need for her mother's comfort, but I had a job to do as an unofficial representative of the Lincoln Point Police Department.

"You can call her and explain that you'll be home very soon. I'm sure you'll be able to get a ride home in a police car, in fact."

"Cool," said one boy. An ally, as I'd hoped for, and one who used an old-fashioned word, I noted.

"Colin!" said more than one of his companions, with accusatory looks.

"What if the dude just killed himself? That's not a crime, is it?" Colin asked, turning to me.

It was not the time to voice my opinion, but I'd always thought it strange that attempted suicide was a felony in some states. As for successful suicide, well, it was a moot point from the point of view of the victim. "Only the police will be able to tell us for sure," I said. I sounded lame even to myself, but so far no one else was moving away.

I was aware of Maddie's arm, linked into my mine, but otherwise, she remained in the background. I'd deliberately taken a position facing the corpse so the youngsters would be looking at me, in the opposite direction. Even so, all their faces had pinched and serious expressions.

The twinkling lights that decorated the lawns and porches of the other houses on the darkening Sangamon River Road took on a more eerie look than even their owners had intended, I was sure. A light breeze swept through the neighborhood and I had the sensation that all the filmy ghosts and stiff bats had come alive for a moment and blew out a breath or fluttered their wings.

I took a breath myself, then got back to matters at hand. I pulled a notebook and pen from my large purse, working my way around glue sticks, tweezers, a sewing kit, and a miniature set of knives I'd forgotten to unload after a shopping trip.

"To speed things up, let me take your names and addresses," I said, as if it were attendance time on a normal day in homeroom.

They responded well, straightening up and preparing to identify themselves, leading me to believe that my guess was correct—they were freshmen, and therefore malleable.

"Ashley Gordon, Two-two-one Lee Street," said the screamer, shivering in a long-sleeved red T-shirt with stamps of the great landmarks of Europe. I took off my unfashionable Irish knit cardigan and put it on Ashley's slight shoulders. She gave me a weak smile of gratitude as she pulled it up past her chin. Thin as I was, my hip-length sweater reached beyond the petite girl's knees.

"Chelsea Sheridan," said a heavy girl with equally heavy makeup in a semi-Goth style. "I live on Merrimac, and I didn't see anything."

"Sometimes we're not aware of what our brains pick up at a time like this, Chelsea," I said, in the best Detective Skip Gowen tradition.

"It's true," Maddie said, surprising me. She'd had to let go of my arm as I transferred my sweater to Ashley, and now she was ready to stand on her own. "Wait till my uncle gets here and starts asking questions. You'll be smarter than you think."

I wished Skip, who was in fact not Maddie's uncle, but her first cousin once-removed, had been present to hear her. The two had had an unbreakable mutual admiration society going since Maddie was born.

I reinforced Maddie's words. "You might have picked up on a detail you didn't think was important but could be a major clue in the case."

Chelsea's face brightened, her cheeks puffing up. The ego of a freshman was no smaller than the ego of a senior.

"I'm Rob Wellington," said the fourth and last teen to speak, through a mouthful of braces. "I saw a boy on a bike at the other end of the street just before we got here."

"That doesn't mean anything," Chelsea said. I had the feeling it wasn't the first time she'd put Rob in his place.

Rob countered. "He was riding really fast and he didn't have any lights on."

Chelsea screwed up her nose and made a gesture of dismissal with her hand. "So?" she asked.

"I still think it could be suicide. The gun is right there in his hand. Just look," said Colin, who did not turn to look. I made a note: Colin was the boy who'd gotten closest to the corpse and had testified to the bullet hole and the gun in the victim's hand. "Oh, I'm Colin McKeon," he said. "I didn't touch anything."

I didn't doubt him for a minute.

"And your friends who ran off?" I asked. "Who are they?" I made it sound as though they'd be considered fugitives, finally captured and sitting outside the principal's office on Monday, while the four exemplary students who'd stayed behind would be honored and applauded at the next school-wide assembly.

They looked at each other. To tell or not to tell?

"Garrett Cox and Amber Frederich," blurted Ashley.

I made a show of writing down the information, flicking my wrist after an imaginary exclamation point. "Were any of you here on Sangamon recently, before this evening?" I asked.

"We came by the other night, but not all the decorations were ready yet," Chelsea said.

"Old Sam was still wiring things up," Rob said. He pointed over his shoulder, not venturing another look at the scene. I was glad of that.

"Did you talk to Mr. Ferguson?" I asked, looking from one to the other, pen still poised over my notepad.

"We just waved," Colin said. His hands were in the pockets of his sweatshirt, and I thought I caught him stifling a shiver.

"Me and my boyfriend, Noah, came by again today," Ashley said, testing my patience with her grammar.

"What time?"

"Lunchtime. We have open campus on Fridays and then we have study hall so we rode our bikes over here."

"Did you look at this house?"

"Uh-huh. It was normal. I mean the straw man was there and jumped around the way he was supposed to. That's not Mr. Ferguson with the . . ."—Ashley touched her forehead—"on the porch. That man is younger," she offered, long after the fact.

"I know it's hard to think about, but just from your brief glimpse, does the man on the steps look like anyone you know, Ashley? You were the first to see him." She shook her head. Once again, I scanned each of the teenagers. "Does anyone here recognize him?"

No, no, and no. The two girls picked up their backpacks. I sensed I was losing them, and I couldn't think of another reasonable question.

An unmarked sedan that I recognized as belonging to the LPPD pulled up behind me. I turned and saw two other LPPD vehicles arriving also.

Leave it to my nephew and his buddies to show up in the nick of time.

Uniformed officers and crime scene technicians, who'd followed Skip to the location, entered the Fergusons' home. They wasted no time waiting for a doorbell to be answered. I assumed this fell under the guideline of "exigent circumstances" and the need to check for evidence or additional victims. I felt a little guilty that I hadn't made an effort to do that myself, but Skip assured me otherwise.

"You did good, Aunt Gerry," he said, as the crime scene technicians took over. "It was important to keep the kids here." He leaned down and kissed Maddie's forehead. "And I hear you were a great partner," he told her. When their heads touched, it was hard to tell where one thicket of red hair ended and the other began, except that Maddie's was curlier.

After administering that compliment, Skip sent Maddie into the care of a female officer I recognized from my trips through the halls of the police department. I expected instant bonding since Maddie made friends easily, and especially with law enforcement. I checked back and saw the two were sitting in the patrol car, engaged in conversation that seemed to involve an examination of the bells and whistles of the vehicle. I wouldn't have been surprised to hear the siren soon and see the lights flash. My granddaughter had negotiating skills far beyond her years.

So far, no neighbors had made themselves known. With all the special lighting, it was nearly impossible to tell which houses were occupied this evening. It was a little too early for returning commuters, and perhaps those who did hear the activity thought the Fergusons had enlisted the LPPD to be part of their contest entry this year.

We all breathed sighs of relief when we learned that there was no one at home, neither alive nor dead, inside the Ferguson residence.

Skip's interviews with the teenagers, though brief, was painful to witness. He took each frightened teen, gently, one by one, as close to the body as possible until he determined that they were all sure they didn't know the man. Then he took their phone numbers (I'd forgotten about that) and the addresses I'd missed and sent them off feeling relieved and important.

When it was my turn to approach the dead man, I took my time and looked (gulping) not only at his body but around the porch, thinking something might jog my memory about the victim or about the Fergusons. When had I last seen any of the family? I recalled that Lillian attended a miniatures show I organized and bought a dollhouse. It had been almost a year ago, but I remembered the enormous Victorian being carried out of the school hall by her twin boys. I hadn't seen Sam to talk to in a while.

I looked at the position of the gun, still in the victim's hand. I hoped the LPPD could do some magic or trigonometry (which amounted to the same thing to my math-challenged brain) and determine whether the man could have killed himself.

Everything on the porch seemed related to Halloween, from the stubby orange battery-operated candles to the fake hay strewn around the floorboards. The two-seater metal swing held rag dolls dressed to look like farmers and farmers' wives and children. Although they were the size of regular toddlers' dolls, I had to resist the temptation to poke them to verify that they were indeed dolls and not more, if tiny, victims.

I walked past the body again, holding my breath all the way. Nothing came to me. Back on the sidewalk, when I finally exhaled, a wave of exhaustion washed over me. My stomach felt nauseous, as if I'd eaten a whole bowl of the chocolate candy.

"It's going to be hard for you to get an investigation going with no identification of the victim," I said to Skip.

"Oh, we know who he is," he said. "The techs gave me his wallet right away. His name is Oliver Halbert. He's a building inspector with the city, lives in an apartment right around the corner on Hanks. Has a wife and two daughters, if you can go by the photographs he was carrying."

I grunted in surprise. "If you already had all that information, why did you put those children though that dreadful rigmarole?"

Skip slapped his notebook against his hand. "For one thing, it tells me something about the kids, who, after all, were at the crime scene. For another—well, you never know what you can learn even when you think you already know it."

Words of wisdom, widely applicable, I thought.

Maddie got out of the patrol car when she saw me back on the sidewalk. Her face had gotten more and more drawn and pale. "Maddie and I have things to do," I told Skip. "Can we go? You know where to find us."

Skip's "sure" was hardly out of his mouth before Maddie headed for my car. A far cry from normal, when Maddie would be clinging to her uncle Skip, offering to help him, and suggesting that she ride home in a patrol car for safety.

Maybe her oft-expressed desire to follow in his footsteps had been squelched at last. Not that I wasn't proud of Skip and his career, but his mother and I both would have preferred not to worry every time he left for work.

If being this close to a corpse was enough to dissuade Maddie from a profession that involved a gun, maybe it was fortuitous that we'd come by when we did.

A call to Maddie's parents when we arrived home was our first order of business. I listened to Maddie's end of the conversation, her tone alternating between matter-of-fact and excited. I could tell she was trying to sound casual, lest she be summoned home, away from the action.

"The victim is no one we know," I told Maddie's mother, Mary Lou. "And Maddie was nowhere near him."

"These things happen, and I know she's in good hands when it comes to the explanations and support you give her," Mary Lou said. "I'm not at all worried."

I was glad I didn't have to speak to my son, the conservative parent who would keep his daughter locked in her room until she was thirty if he could get away with it. I attributed the peculiarities in Richard's and Mary Lou's parenting style to their chosen careers: Richard was an orthopedic surgeon; Mary Lou a professional artist holding to the ideals of her student days at Berkeley.

I thought Maddie was lucky to have both outlooks in her life.

"I wish I could go back," Maddie said, once we were comfortably seated on the couch. I'd put a mac and cheese casserole in the oven, on the off chance that we could have a normal dinner.

"Back to what, sweetheart?" I asked, though I had a good guess.

"Back to when we were in front of Mr. and Mrs. Ferguson's house and I was sort of a little bit scared. Now Uncle Skip probably thinks I'm afraid and I don't want to help him find out who shot the man."

I squeezed my eyes shut. Dreams die hard.

"There's a whole police department in town to take care of that, sweetheart." I tousled her curls. "Your job is to help me get dinner ready."

Maddie rubbed her stomach and made a grimace, as if she'd been told to eat a helping of Swiss chard. "I'm not that hungry. I was hungry, but now I'm not."

This was a first. I could see and feel my granddaughter's struggle. Her desire to be grown-up and a partner in adult circumstances had come up against the fact that she was still a vulnerable eleven-year-old, greatly upset by matters of life and death.

"Would you like me to cancel the crafts meeting tonight? Everyone would understand. We could sit here and chat or watch one of your favorite movies. Whatever you like. I know it was rough this afternoon."

Apparently my proposals were too boring under any circumstances and Maddie snapped to. "Nuh-uh. I'm not that scared."

"Okay, then. We'll go ahead as planned."

"Grandma?"

"Yes, sweetheart?"

"I hate it when people die like that man did, when it's not because they're sick or something." She paused. "I don't like them to get sick and die, either, like Grandpa did. But I guess it's worse if someone hurts you?"

I wished she hadn't made it a question.

My best response was to hold her and kiss her head. I couldn't bring myself to tell her that some things about life would never be comprehensible, no matter how old we got.

Death, whether by suicide, murder, or what were called natural causes, was one of those things.

"Do you think Uncle Skip will need any computer help?" she asked after putting away only a slightly smaller portion than usual of mac and cheese. "I already learned a lot more than I knew before school started." I was glad to know the expensive after-school lessons her parents supported were paying off. "I heard Uncle Skip and the other officers say the man's name. Oliver Halbert. I can Google him."

We'd moved to the crafts room where a considerable amount of straightening up was needed before my friends arrived for a twice-weekly work session.

"If you're so energetic, you can help clear this table so everyone will have enough room for her project." I thought of offering a second ice cream serving of the day as an incentive, but I knew there was an excellent dessert coming with crafter Susan Giles.

"Well, someone has to figure out what happened to the man, right?" Maddie said. She held her palms open, as if to allow the burdens of the world to fall into them.

I sent a loud sigh in her direction. "Would you rather make the witches or the ghosts tonight?" I asked her.

"Okay, Grandma, I get it. Let's not talk about the case right now."

"And there's really no need to bring anything up when the group gets here."

"Bring what up? There's nothing to bring up," she said, singsong fashion, her winning grin filling her face. "If there was anything to bring up, I forgot it."

"I'm glad to hear that," I said.

Chapter 3

I was comfortable with the decision that we should keep to our Friday night routine as much as possible, in spite of the decidedly nonroutine afternoon. The arrival of my crafter friends, and the promise of a scrumptious dessert—an old Giles family recipe from the heart of the South—was sure to give both Maddie and me a welcome distraction.

Karen Striker, who looked ready to go into labor any minute, had chauffeured Mabel, aka the Bead Queen, our oldest member. Mabel Quinlan never met a miniature scene that didn't profit from adding a few beads. As much as we teased her about it, her tray of beads, in all sizes and shapes, came in handy when one of us needed a long (about three-quarters of an inch) bead for a vase or a pile of tiny (less than one-sixteenth of an inch) beads for a bracelet to adorn a miniature dresser.

Karen had already made a beautiful shoebox nursery and was now working on her unborn daughter's first two dollhouses. One was a plain, boxy, unshingled structure with chunky wood furniture, the other a classic Victorian with seven rooms on three floors, two large hallways, and an elegant foyer. The stairways alone had required the use of every tool and bottle of varnish Karen owned.

"This house she can really knock around and play with," Karen explained, showing us a photo from a catalog of the finished house number one. "The Victorian is for a little later when she can appreciate the finer things."

"She'll be sewing mini draperies and bedspreads in no time," Gail Musgrave said. A city councilwoman and a real estate broker, Gail wasn't as regular at our meetings as any of us would have liked. We teased that she'd shown up to-night just for Susan Giles's special cake.

"Whatever you do, Karen, don't teach your daughter about kits," said Linda Reed, the Martha Stewart of minia-turists, who made everything from scratch. Linda gave Maddie and me looks that said it was already too late for the two of us. Maddie was indeed following in my footsteps, preferring the fun of creating scenes with found objects to the discipline it took to craft upholstered furniture by hand, to use one example from Linda's impressive résumé.

Karen had brought the pieces of the wraparound porch of her Victorian dollhouse to work on. Lovely as it was, in the last stages of delicate pink trimming, this evening the miniature porch brought to my mind only unpleasant im-ages of a gunshot victim on the life-size porch belonging to the Fergusons.

I couldn't help wondering about Sam and Lillian. What had they thought when they arrived home to a crime scene? Had they known Oliver Halbert? Did they have a clue why his body was found in the midst of their extrava-gant Halloween contest entry? I hoped Skip would share what he knew.

I looked over at Maddie; I was happy she seemed preoccupied with pieces of glow-in-the-dark green felt that would soon be witches' faces.

"Where's Susan?" Gail asked.

"You mean, where's our pecan praline cake?" Mabel said.

We all nodded.

"She didn't call, so I assume she'll be here. It's only eight twenty," I said.

"This could be a tragedy," Karen said. She rubbed her belly. "Baby Girl Striker is hungry for sweets."

Apparently, even after consulting a shelf full of baby-name books, Karen and her husband hadn't made their choice. Or they simply weren't telling.

Gail pulled out her cell phone. "I'll give her a call."

"If all else fails, I have a new batch of ginger cookies," I said.

"Of course you do," Karen said with a hungry smile, walking over to the cookie jar. She helped herself to a handful of my locally famous staple and brought the container to the table. "You saved my life."

My friends all dug into the jar before I could assemble a civilized presentation on a platter. Crafters will not be kept waiting for dessert.

My kind of group, for more reasons than that.

When Maddie had come upon a materials list for making tiny witches, she'd sweet-talked Colleen, who worked at Sadie's Ice Cream Shop, into giving her a few of their small plastic tasting spoons. True to our respective approaches to making miniatures, while Linda painstakingly fashioned tiny rose petals from polymer clay, Maddie and I prepared to turn plastic spoons into witches. Over the

years, Linda had learned to keep her tsk-tsking to a mini-
mum. This evening she gave us a condescending smile
instead. I gave her one back. It was all good-natured, however, and never affected our long-standing friendship.

Maddie spread six mini spoons on the table in front of
her. The bowls of the spoons would serve as the bases for
the witches' faces; scraps of black and monster-green felt
would be cut into shapes to make the hats and skirts; tooth-
picks and bits of straw would be fashioned into brooms.

"I want a witch in every room, and one coming out the
window like the ghost on Hanks Road," Maddie said.

"Then we'd better get to work," I said.

I didn't know what I'd do without my two (most of the
time) crafts evenings a week. On Wednesdays, we worked
on a common project, which we eventually displayed at a
miniatures show or donated to a charity raffle. The next
show was in February, so (need I say) we were building a
log cabin. Not just any log cabin would do, however—ours
would be one Abe Lincoln could have called home, furnished with what were reputed to be his favorite books (the
Bible and stories by Edgar Allan Poe) and foods (chicken
fricassee and scalloped oysters). We'd divided up the tasks
as usual, giving Linda the ones that took the most time and
patience. Chunky as they were, Linda's fingers could fashion the tiniest bow, the most delicate leaf, or a plate of scalloped oysters.

On Fridays, we each focused on a project of our own.
Both formats provided the opportunity for unbeatable
camaraderie as well as mutual technical help and consul-
tations.

This Friday evening, my crafts room was a comforting,
homey scene: Mabel, who was always a holiday ahead,
glued multicolored beads onto a two-inch wooden turkey
form to make its plume. Gail chatted about her daughter's

engagement while she cross-stitched a miniature pillow for a bridal shower room box. Linda abandoned her tiny roses and searched for an appropriate bead-cum-vase in Mabel's tray. Karen, a bemused look on her face, held a paintbrush in one hand and a ginger cookie in the other.

We missed Susan, a marketing analyst for a cell phone company, and not just for her pecan praline pound cake. She was excellent company, now working on two miniature dorm rooms for her two nieces. She often indulged us by answering our cell phone questions without ever calling them dumb. Gail had left a message for her, but we'd had no response yet.

My crafter friends loved having Maddie participate. On rare occasions, someone might ask her to dish out dessert while we took a minute to bring up a more adult topic, but our conversation was usually kid-friendly, focusing on the intricacies of gluing one piece of material onto another or the latest in containers for organizing our out-of-control supply shelves.

No wonder everyone was surprised when it was Maddie who introduced an adult topic tonight.

"Did you know someone was shot on Sangamon River Road today?" she asked.

The gasps said no one had heard the news. I gave my granddaughter a look—"I thought we had a deal"—but she avoided eye contact with me. We'd have to settle this later.

"Someone was shot? On purpose?" Mabel asked.

"We're not sure," she said, as if she were the spokeschild of the LPPD. "His name was Oliver Halbert." Maddie, now in her element, kept the women's attention with the few details she knew. "He might have shot himself," said the new expert on crime scenes. "We won't know until Uncle Skip figures it all out."

"Did you say Halbert?" Linda asked, reaching through

her beehive hairdo to scratch her scalp. "The name is familiar. It's not coming to me right now, but I know that
name."

"You know everyone's names," Karen said. It wasn't too
much of an exaggeration, since Linda had worked in every
medical facility in Lincoln Point at one time or another, and
now worked as a nurse in the sprawling, upscale Mary Todd
nursing home.

"Everyone's name, and their brother's," Gail said with a
smile.

"Sick or healthy," Karen chimed in.

"Wait," Linda said, increasing the depth of the concen-
tration lines on her forehead. "You said everyone and their
brother."

"You're no slouch, Gail," Mabel said, bypassing Linda's
remark. "You know everyone who's ever bought a house."

"Wait," Linda repeated. "It's coming to me." She seemed
to wave her hands over an imaginary crystal ball.

"Or everyone who ever had to deal with the city government," Karen said, referring to Gail's other persona on the
Lincoln Point council.

"Oh, dear," Linda said, her eyes widening.

"What is it?" I asked her. "Do you know Oliver
Halbert?"

She blew out a loud breath. "He's Susan's brother."

Now all of our eyes widened.

There wasn't much else to talk about besides Susan
Giles and Oliver Halbert. I was commissioned to call the
LPPD to be sure that Susan had been informed about her
brother. Once I got clearance from a former student, Officer
Drew Blackstone, Gail punched in Susan's number and got
her answering machine again. This time the message Gail

left was more specific: "We're all here at Gerry's, thinking of you, and hope to hear from you soon, Susan. We're so sorry to hear about your brother. Please let us know if there's anything we can do."

"I remember Susan's talking about a brother who also relocated to this area from their hometown in Tennessee, but I never met him," Mabel said.

Except for Linda, with whom I'd been close for many years, the rest of us didn't socialize a lot with each other outside the miniatures community. For the most part, our crafts nights were special times, when we took ourselves away from the stresses of our personal and work lives. We considered ourselves friends, but knew each other's families chiefly through anecdotes and an occasional meeting at a fair. And, of course, through the room boxes and miniature scenes we created for them.

I had a flash of memory of a room box we'd watched Susan make "for my only sibling," she'd told us. It was upsetting and sad to think that same brother was now in the Lincoln Point morgue.

Within minutes, everyone's crafts focus changed as we made a sympathy card for Susan out of supplies on the table. Anyone might have thought we were assembly-line workers while we designed and created the card: flowers from Linda wrapped in chiffon from Karen—glued to the best ivory paper from Gail's stack book, topped off with a beaded sticker. Maddie used her newly learned calligraphy to write out a message of condolence.

It was too late tonight, but we all thought of a time when we could stop off and visit Susan. Gail took on the task of calling a friend at the local paper to get advance notice about a service.

Too much in shock to contribute much, I provided a first-class stamp for the handmade card.

* * *

"I couldn't help it, Grandma. I was thinking about it so much," Maddie said, by way of excusing herself for leaking the news about Oliver Halbert. "And now we know something more about the case, right? We know Mr. Halbert was Mrs. Giles's brother." She gave me a sleepy grin from her pillow. "Maybe you should thank me." Even halfway to dreamland, Maddie was making deals. "And it will be in the paper tomorrow, anyway."

"There's no paper tomorrow," I said.

"Well, at Sadie's, then. It will get all over town one way or another. Dad says, 'bad news travels fast.'"

Leave it to my son to give the old negative saying new life. "And you might as well be the one to start the bad news on its journey?" I asked.

She shrugged, causing the soccer balls on her pajamas to roll around on her shoulders. "If we really, really had an important secret, I would never tell, Grandma."

I knew that. I supposed this reaction of Maddie's was better than her having nightmares about the ugly images of the day. Once she got over her philosophical problem with death in general, she seemed to be able to handle the particulars. Did it help that she'd lined up six miniature, somber-looking witches, their glued components drying, on her dresser?

"Are you ready to sleep?" I asked her.

"Uh-huh. Tomorrow I'll do the ghosts. They take a lot of glue, you know."

In fact, they were all glue—gobs of it, piled into a white heap, shaped, and accessorized. "We might have to go to a crafts store," I said.

"Straight," she said.

"What's straight?"

"That's what some of the kids in my school say. It means okay, fine."

Living with Maddie was like having a word-a-day calendar with up-to-the-minute slang.

"Okay, fine," I said and watched her drift off.

I had a feeling Skip would come by as soon as he thought Maddie was asleep. I'd already replenished the cookie plate and put on water for coffee (him) and tea (me) when the doorbell rang.

"I knew you'd be ready for me," Skip said, stepping into my atrium and, three seconds later, popping a cookie into his mouth. "I was waiting until my little squirt would be asleep."

Were all families this predictable? I wondered. Or was I just lucky?

"I can't believe he was related to Susan Giles," I said, as if there had been no interruption in our talk between the Sangamon River Road crime scene and my home many hours later. "Did you see Susan?"

"Yeah, I was the one to give her the news about her brother. She was getting ready to meet all her friends here for the 'girls' night in' crafts session, and instead I had to bring her to tears. I hate doing that. It's the worst part of the job, Aunt Gerry."

His bright mood hadn't lasted long tonight. His handsome young face took on a dispiriting look.

"I'm sure it is."

We took our drinks to the living room since my atrium was too chilly for me this evening. As warm as fall days could be in the Bay Area, nights were always cool. Skip sat across from me on an ottoman, the better to reach the plate of cookies on my dusty mahogany coffee table. I wasn't the only miniaturist who preferred keeping house on a one-inch scale.

I pictured Skip approaching Susan's home, knowing she was one of my friends, preparing to deliver news that would change her life. I thought how good my sensitive nephew would be at a time of sorrow and crisis, as much as he dreaded the task.

Eleven years old—Maddie's age—when his father died, Skip told his mother not to worry, that he would take care of the house from then on. He asked his uncle Ken, my husband, to teach him how to do basic plumbing, since that seemed to be at the heart of many breakdowns in his home, and to help him find a job. He never did master plumbing, but he became the neighborhood errand boy and problem solver.

Seeing him in my living room, in full detective mode, if not dress, I imagined how proud both his father and his uncle would be—he'd gone from serving and protecting his mother to doing the same for the whole Lincoln Point community.

"Where did you go, Aunt Gerry?" Skip asked, waving his hands in front of my face.

"To the nineties," I said. "But I'm back."

"I was asking if you even knew Susan had a brother, since you didn't recognize him at the scene."

"She talked about him and made a miniature for him in our group, but I'd never met him. Maybe the name Oliver should have struck a chord when I heard it from you, since it's not that common, but with a different last name, I never made the connection. Oliver was her baby brother. He moved here a few years ago from Tennessee, after his divorce."

"Yeah, Susan told me that. I guess those photographs in his wallet—the ones of a happy nuclear family—were from days gone by."

"Susan said the breakup was hard on him. Their parents were gone, and Susan was out here." I thought a minute. "And both his girls had come to the West Coast for college. I guess he wanted as much family around him as he could muster."

"That would be why Susan is blaming herself," Skip said. "She's thinking that her brother would have been alive and well if she hadn't moved here and lured the girls here, too."

Poor Susan. Why was it that at any death there was someone taking the blame, usually not the right person? For a moment I found myself thinking, if Maddie and I hadn't taken so long over our ice cream at Sadie's, maybe we would have been at the Fergusons' in time to save Oliver. How, I had no idea. Nor did I want to dwell on the notion that if we'd arrived at the wrong time, we might have suffered the same fate at the hands of a killer, if there was one.

"Do you know yet how Oliver died?" I asked. "I mean, other than a bullet hole to his head."

"It's too soon for an official report, but the ME at the scene said she couldn't rule out suicide. I'm sure that will be hard for Susan to take."

"No harder than murder," I said.

"True enough."

"Have you looked into anything that might suggest her brother was murdered, in case that's the ruling?"

"Yeah, you know we drop everything, even sleep, when there's a murder."

I gave him a sympathetic look, knowing he was only half teasing. "Poor dear."

"As long as you appreciate us. It's only been a few hours, but we found a few things that raised some flags."

"Anything of interest to the general public?" I asked.

Skip gave me a crossways look. I rushed to reassure him. "I'm not going to get involved. Susan's my friend and I'm curious."

"Straight."

"You, too? I thought that was for schoolkids."

"The word's making the rounds. It seems Oliver Halbert was the chief witness in the DA's case against Patrick Lynch."

"The big developer?"

Skip rubbed his palms together as if he were cold, though he usually preferred a little chill in the air. "The same. There's talk that Lynch will be indicted for bribing a city inspector, the guy who had the job before Halbert. That would be Max Crowley, who's also about to be indicted."

I followed local news, but often didn't remember specifics. I tried to be informed at voting time, but wouldn't have wanted to take a quiz on the day-to-day political maneuverings unless they concerned me directly.

"And Oliver was going to testify against both of them?"

Skip nodded and took a deep, loud breath. He rubbed his hands together again, and I remembered the other trigger for that gesture: delivering unpleasant news. I studied his face. There was more to his visit than giving me an update on the body on the Fergusons' porch.

"There's something else you should know about, Aunt Gerry."

My stomach clutched, for no reason other than I knew my nephew's every "tell" and this one was as loud as the ALHS cafeteria on the day before a holiday.

"I'm listening."

"We looked through Halbert's papers. He dug up some stuff, going back a few years."

"How many years?"

"Maybe five or six."

A time period that would include when my husband worked on projects for the city.

Skip's expression grew very serious. "It's one of the main reasons I came over so late."

Now I was really worried. I drew my own deep breath.

"Are all the people who put up buildings crooked?" The question came from a small voice in the hallway.

"Hey, look who's up," Skip said, scooping Maddie close for a hug. He got to her so quickly that I assumed he'd been on cop alert even though he looked relaxed in my living room. Either that, or he'd been hoping for a way to stall giving his announcement. "Were we too loud for you?"

"Nuh-uh," Maddie said. "I just figured you'd be coming by, Uncle Skip, so I tried hard to stay awake. I fell asleep for a little bit, but"—she spread her arms and took a bow— "I'm up now."

"So you are," Skip said. "How did you know I'd be visiting?"

Maddie grinned. "The case and all."

"Why are you asking about crooked builders?" I asked Maddie. Had she been following the local news more closely than I had? I was only peripherally aware of the potential indictments coming up.

"I heard you talking about a developer. He's the person who builds houses and then sells them, right? Aren't they never honest? My dad says you can't trust them."

Too many negatives, but I knew what she meant. Also, I'd have to have a talk with my son. Unrealistic as it was, I wished Richard would keep to happy talk with his daughter.

"What makes you think that?" I asked Maddie. "Your grandfather was an architect, remember, and he worked with people who put up buildings."

Out of the corner of my eye, I saw Skip's head drop to his chest. I swallowed hard. Did I want to know the answer to the question forming in my mind—what was the bad news signaled by Skip's body language?

"I forgot about that. Grandpa was honest. I'll bet he was the most honest person doing buildings."

I thought Skip's palms would smoke if he rubbed any harder.

"You're right, Maddie. But please go back to bed, sweetheart. I need to talk to Uncle Skip," I said, struggling for control of my voice.

"I need to talk to him, too. I want to show him my deep search techniques," she said. "They might help with the case."

I was used to Maddie's wiggling herself into her uncle's cases, offering her newly learned computer skills. Usually I let her and Skip work it out, but not tonight.

Skip sat back, waiting, I knew, to see who'd win. I had the feeling he was rooting for Maddie. I was surprised he hadn't taken the opportunity to slip out of the house.

"Maddie." I gave her a look that said I meant it. She probably hadn't seen this look on my face since she was a toddler. "Maddie, please go back to bed."

Maddie had been about three years old the last time I'd spoken to her so firmly. She'd nearly burned herself climbing up to the stove to investigate a pot of hot chocolate. I'd turned my back for only a moment and she'd made it all the way to the top step of a folding stool, to the counter, ready to dip her hands into the hot liquid. I scooped her up and told her never to do that again. My panic at the time had given my voice a rough tone and we'd both ended up in tears.

I felt the same tone creeping into my voice now. It broke

my heart to see her skulk away, her expression disappointed and confused: *What did I do wrong? What's wrong with Grandma?*

What was wrong was that Skip was about to deliver news that I didn't want to hear.

I closed the door to Maddie's room, having attempted to kiss away the scolding tone. Happily, she'd been tired enough to kiss me back and drift off to sleep.

I returned to my living room, where Skip sat tapping his feet. I took a seat and spoke in a low voice. "It's about your uncle Ken, isn't it?"

Skip's nod sent a shiver through me. He spread his palms. "This can wait, Aunt Gerry," he said.

"No, it can't."

I stiffened against the couch, my hands folded, an ominous shiver traveling the length of my spine.

Chapter 4

Skip walked into the kitchen and stood at my open
refrigerator door with the energy of one who'd had no dinner. "Do you have anything good in here?" he asked.

I was sure he was hungry; I was also sure he was desperate to put off telling me what I needed to know.

"Skip," I said, losing all patience.

"Please, Aunt Gerry. This is hard for me." He gave me his pleading look, the expression I'd given into all his life.

I got up and pulled out a container of cold cuts and half a loaf of rye bread. I had to admit it felt good to be doing something useful. I spread butter on one slice of bread, spicy mustard on the other. The way Skip liked it. "You can talk while I work," I said.

When his phone rang, I was convinced he'd managed to call himself. I gave my nephew two minutes to take the call, which he said was critical to the story he was about to tell. "Test results," he said.

"At midnight?"

"When you care enough."

"I'm not in the mood, Skip."

He disappeared around the corner to the family room and came back to an aunt who was on edge but holding out a plate that was the base for a turkey sandwich with lettuce and a slice of Monterey Jack cheese.

"Let me start from the beginning, okay?" Skip asked, clearly sorry he'd opened the topic in the first place.

I looked at my nephew and spoke without a trace of patience or humor—there might as well have been a stranger, or a representative of another police force from a distant state in my living room. "As long as you get to the point."

"I promise." We moved back to the living room and sat down on the easy chairs at either end of the couch—about as far away from each other as we could be and still occupy the same room. Skip put his sandwich plate on the coffee table and tented his fingers. "Susan's brother, Oliver Halbert, got this city inspector job a year or so ago. He replaced this guy, Max Crowley, that I mentioned. The short of it is that Crowley apparently took bribes from Patrick Lynch and other developers on a routine basis."

"I already got that part."

"The way it worked was Lynch and his guys would cut corners in building specs and Crowley would look the other way when he inspected the building."

"What kind of specs?" I folded my hands, trying to guess where Ken fit in.

"You know, different things. It might be substituting substandard materials, just for a cost break, or not meeting safety regs, which would be worse, because a safety code violation could lead to an accident. Apparently, with the right amount of cash crossing his palm, Inspector Crowley could be counted on to give his blessing to a lot of sins. Or would that be sinners?"

Usually an appeal to a point of grammar would be enough to lure me into a lesson on correct usage or word choice, but not tonight.

"Is that why the inspector's job came open for Oliver Halbert? Because Crowley lost his job when the bribes were uncovered?"

"No. You wish justice were that swift. Crowley had moved on to a bigger and better job."

"He was promoted?"

"In a manner of speaking. After the scandal, he went to work as Lynch's number one man. Only in America, huh? Back to Susan's brother, Oliver Halbert. He was the one who uncovered the bribes. I guess Lynch expected the same service from Halbert that they all got from Crowley, but Halbert would have none of it. He started digging around and eventually the DA was able to make a solid case against Crowley and Lynch. With Halbert's testimony and some data that Halbert claimed to have, the case was a shoo-in."

"And now Halbert is out of the way."

"Yeah, Halbert kills himself just in time to save their hides," Skip said. "Convenient, huh? But that call I just got was from the ME's lab. The preliminary result is that his death does look like a suicide."

My mind was reeling with this background on the victim I'd seen only hours earlier, before I even knew he was Susan's brother. I was torn between hearing how Ken's name came up in this nasty picture and avoiding that subject all together. I chose a delay tactic.

"How do the Fergusons fit in? Whether it was suicide or murder, why would it happen at that house?"

"I don't know exactly, except that the Ferguson twins are renters in one of the worst Lynch facilities, as far as building codes go. They have a small factory on the property, making airplane parts."

I thought again about the Ferguson twins. The policy at ALHS was to separate siblings, so I'd had only one of the twins, Eliot, in my English class. I remembered how Eliot and Emory, both with identical heavy-framed glasses, would set up pranks, fooling classmates and teachers alike, filling in for each other whenever it suited them. Then Eliot had a skiing accident and never fully recovered: he walked with a slight limp. As much as everyone felt sorry for him, we considered ourselves lucky to have a way to tell the twins apart. I hadn't seen either of them in a couple of years but assumed they still looked identical, and that Eliot still limped.

Enough history, I thought. I'd probably never again need to be able to distinguish the men from each other.

"What about the data?" I asked Skip. "You said the district attorney had Oliver's testimony and some data."

"Yeah, about the data." Skip took a huge bite of his sandwich and made a show of chewing thoroughly, just as his mother and I had taught him.

I swallowed hard. "Skip, I need to know how Uncle Ken came up in this investigation. Is there some data that . . . that . . ." I seemed physically unable to keep my throat clear to finish the sentence.

He licked his lips and held up his index finger. "One more little thread first," he said. "Since you asked about the Ferguson twins." Another reprieve. I'd never felt so conflicted. "Remember that fire that broke out in their factory last year?"

The news had been full of the story, though I'd forgotten whose factory had been involved. "A janitor was killed, wasn't he?"

"Right. The original ruling on the fire was 'accidental,' and the twins were cleared of any fault. But Halbert was on a path to a different theory. He was attempting to prove that the Fergusons, or their staff, had forgotten to turn the compressor off when they left the building for the night. Then, a weakness in the hose attached to it caused the hose to rupture, and of course, the compressor couldn't keep up the pressure, so it burned out. The compressor was located under a wooden stairway, and"—Skip waved his hands in a gesture that suggested a burst of flames, losing a piece of lettuce from his sandwich in the process—"the stairs caught fire and burned half the building, plus the janitor who happened to be taking a nap break."

"The twins claim they did not leave their compressor on. They say the problem was with a segment of electrical wiring that had no conduit. That would point the finger back at Halbert himself for not catching that oversight on the part of Lynch. So everyone's blaming everyone else. If the twins weren't so tight with Lynch, they'd probably be suing Lynch for cutting corners on the conduit specs. It's a mess."

"Is the factory so new that Halbert was the inspector, not Max Crowley?"

"Some sections of it are new and some are old, which is another part of the problem. So now the family of the dead janitor is at sixes and sevens, not knowing whom to sue. Exactly who was the negligent party?"

As sorry as I felt for the person who lost his life, I wondered if Skip gave me that complicated story because he wanted to beat around the Ken Porter bush as much as I did. But it was late and I'd waited long enough.

"Uncle Ken?" I asked.

Skip brushed rye crumbs from his hands, then ran his long, freckled fingers through his hair. One half sandwich was down. "There's nothing definite on this. I probably shouldn't even bring it up."

I'd reached my limit. "Skip." My strongest voice, the

one that had sent Richard or Skip to their rooms many a time.

"Okay, here it is. We took a pile of notebooks from Halbert's apartment and we're just starting to go through them. One notebook has a list of what Halbert labeled *Potentials*, which we take to mean persons or line items that he had in mind to investigate."

"That's the data? But you said the district attorney had the data."

"No, I said the DA had Halbert's testimony plus some data that Halbert claimed to have. Big difference."

"But you found the data in Oliver's notebooks?"

Skip made a so-so motion with his hands. "I'm not sure I'd call it data. We have some names, but no specifics. We already know a lot of the people on the list because they've been involved in questionable transactions in the past. Some of them are related to bribes; some are related to accidents where it wasn't clear who was at fault, like at the factory fire. Things like that."

"And?"

Skip sighed deeply. "Uncle Ken's name was on the list."

I tried to reach the arms of the couch, to lean on them. They were far away and I swayed so far to one side, with such a jerky motion, there might have been an earthquake with an epicenter under us. I felt my cheeks burn, my mouth go dry. "Oliver Halbert thought my Ken might have been involved in a bribery or some other unethical activity?"

"It looks that way," Skip said in a voice I could barely hear. "Maybe."

I sat up and forced a breath through my jaws. "Couldn't Ken's name have been on the list because he might have been able to help Oliver prove something against another party? Maybe Oliver didn't know that Ken isn't alive anymore. It hasn't been that long."

It didn't seem long to me, for sure. Why wasn't Ken here now, in fact? Walking through the doorway to the kitchen, eating the last of the ginger cookies, asking for another batch? Defending his reputation.

Skip flinched, just enough to tell me his next words would be suspect. "That's right, Aunt Gerry. Maybe Uncle Ken was down as an expert witness, or—"

His expression told me something different. I shook my head. "No, no. Oliver Halbert thought Ken himself participated in some criminal act, didn't he?"

"Maybe not criminal."

I looked at my nephew. "What, then?"

"Suspicious?" He whispered the questionable word. "But that's just a dim possibility, Aunt Gerry. We haven't even begun to check out what the list really means, if anything."

I put my hand on my forehead. I thought I might have a fever. Could tension bring on a fever? I'd held my breath for so long, I was light-headed. "You just told me that you saw the names of disreputable people on the list. You must know more than you're telling me."

Skip looked as miserable as I felt. "I don't know what to tell you, Aunt Gerry. Uncle Ken was the architect on the new addition to the Fergusons' factory. It was one of his last projects with Patrick Lynch before . . . you know . . . he got sick."

"What does that have to do with anything?"

"There were some problems with the project. I think they were weather-related, or maybe labor, I don't know. But the twins were on a deadline to produce some parts for a company in L.A., and they needed the capabilities of the new wing. There's a good chance they shaved some safety features for the sake of speeding things up."

"*They* shaved? Who?" I didn't give Skip a chance to respond. "Why on earth would anyone suspect Ken Porter of doing something like that? He was the most honest man in the world. You know that." I sounded like Maddie, who, in her innocence, thought everyone she loved was perfect.

Skip had firsthand knowledge of Ken, who'd stepped in when Skip's father died in the first Gulf War. During periods when his mother, Ken's sister, Beverly, was unable to cope, Skip slept in my son's room more often than he did his own.

"Aunt Gerry, in my heart I know Uncle Ken couldn't knowingly do anything wrong. I loved him. Who knows what I would have become without him?" Skip's voice cracked. I was sorry I'd taken him back to a tough period in his young life. "But—"

I waved my hands in his face, now as flushed as mine felt. "No 'buts.'"

"I debated about telling you this. In retrospect, I probably should have waited until things were more clear, but the guys gave me a heads-up when they saw Uncle Ken's name pop up, and I thought I'd do the same for you. Now I think it wasn't such a great idea."

I couldn't think of too many ideas that were worse. I blew out a long breath, trying to clear my head. "I'll bet it's a different Ken Porter. It's a common enough name. I'll bet Maddie will find a hundred of them if she Googles it. Or else you were just looking at someone's Christmas card list."

Skip nodded and made a weak thumbs-up motion. "That's probably it."

Not a convincing gesture, but one that I needed at that moment.

Skip's phone rang. He read a message, clicked it shut, and stood to leave.

"We're not finished, Skip."

"I know, but I really do have to go, Aunt Gerry. I have a feeling my night is just beginning."

"So is mine."

I knew there wasn't much hope of sleeping, so I took a cup of tea to my atrium. After the events of the evening, I seemed to be immune to any conditions of weather or comfort; I was neither too warm nor too cold, neither hungry nor full, neither tired nor fully awake. I counted on the lovely vegetation around the border of the large, skylit entryway, a special feature of my Eichler home, to take my nerves down a notch. My small dogwood, coleus, and hydrangea shrubs provided a pleasant view from wherever I sat.

I switched on the small table lamp by my rocker, and picked up my *Dollhouse Miniatures* magazine. On the cover, miniature pumpkins and ghosts danced around tiny coffins, and the text promised easy instructions for everything Halloween on page fifty-nine. Ordinarily I read every word, from letters to the editor to the frequent "printies" that accompanied some articles. Now I flipped through the pages but couldn't concentrate on anything outside my own head.

Buzzz. Buzzz.

My doorbell rang soon after I tossed the magazine, along with my newest mini knitting project, into the basket by my rocker. I was hardly surprised that I had a visitor. I would have believed that weeks had passed, that it was already Halloween and trick-or-treaters had arrived to collect their candy.

I peeped through the hole and opened the door to a bedraggled Susan Giles. Usually impeccably groomed, Susan was known for wearing a ruffle somewhere on every outfit.

She'd added ruffles at the neck and sleeves of most of her sweatshirts, at the bottoms of some of her jeans, and around the edges of her purses and totes. Her lovely handmade miniature dolls, between one and two inches in length, all sported ruffles on their tiny panties. The branding served her well at crafts fairs when all a customer had to do was ask which booth the ruffle lady was in.

Tonight Susan looked like an overwrought rag doll, her trademark ruffle limp and dingy on the neckline of a worn San Francisco sweatshirt. She wore a pitiful expression, never seen at our fairs.

"I'm sorry I didn't finish baking the cake," she said, as naturally as if it had simply slipped her mind due to an extra busy day doing errands in Lincoln Point. "I was just about to put it in the oven when . . ." She broke down in tears.

I finished the sentence, in my mind: when Skip appeared at her door. Was it only crafters or bakers who responded this way? Was it characteristic of women? Susan's dear brother was dead, and she was concerned about an unful-filled promise of a pecan praline pound cake.

Maybe for her own sanity, she had to think of the unfin-ished dessert.

I always thought it peculiar, what we worried about in times of grief or great stress. An insignificant task or a neglected responsibility could become the most important thing on our minds. While Ken was ill, I'd go for long pe-riods of time not thinking of anything as mundane as gro-cery shopping or watering the lawn. Then out of nowhere I'd get a spurt of needing to do something routine and phys-ically satisfying. I might scrub the tile in the shower, stock the pantry with new spices, pull up every weed in my gar-den, or reorganize my desk drawers. Once I found myself washing the laces from Ken's tennis shoes, as if any of it mattered without Ken.

I pushed Susan's deceased brother's incriminating list to the back of my mind and hugged her until she calmed down.

"I'm so sorry" from me was all it took to bring her to tears again. Susan fell into my arms.

"You have to help me, Gerry," she said, her voice choking.

I patted her back. "I'll do anything I can," I said, leading her to a comfortable chair in the living room.

She accepted an offer of tea. When I delivered it to her, I found her staring into space, seeming unaware of her surroundings.

Susan came to after a few sips of chamomile. "The police think Oliver committed suicide, Gerry. Can you imagine?" I wanted to remind her that I'd never met her brother and had no idea what he was capable of. This was not the time for facts or logic, however, and I let her go on. "He would never do that. Isn't there something you can do? I know we're always asking you to influence your nephew one way or the other, but this is so important, not like a traffic ticket. Oliver must have been murdered," she said, breaking away from me, her voice strong and confident. "I know you can prove it."

By "anything," I'd meant cook her meals, run errands, help with funeral arrangements, contact relatives in Tennessee. Doing her laundry would not be out of the question, nor would finishing the room box she'd promised to donate to her church raffle.

Investigating her brother's death was not on the list.

Within a few minutes, Susan settled down to the business at hand. It was as if she'd spent all the hours since

Oliver's death preparing a case for me to take charge of and solve. She reached into her tote and pulled out a photo album. She opened it at random and placed it on my coffee table.

As Susan turned the pages, I glanced at moments captured at birthday parties, vacations, graduations, and anniversaries. Several photos included Susan's former husband, whom I'd met a couple of times before their divorce and who now lived in Florida near his parents. In nearly all the pictures, Oliver was present—smiling, bouncing a basketball, arms around people I took to be his friends or other family members.

"Look at this one," Susan said. She pointed to a snapshot of four people in a raft, one of them Susan herself. The other two women matched the ages I knew his daughters, both out of college, to be. The fourth was Oliver.

"It looks like a happy time," I said.

Practically every family I knew had a picture like this— usually mom, dad, and kids roughing it on a white-water rafting trip on the Russian River in northern California. Everyone wore red/orange vests. Their hair was wild; white foam roiled up around their raft; smiles were wide. If I lined up on my living room wall all the family rafting photos I'd seen, I wouldn't be able to tell them apart.

Except that this one included a person I'd just seen dead.

Susan tapped the photograph, aiming for her brother's chest. "This was Oliver only a couple of months ago. Does this look like a guy about to kill himself? It was his Jeanine's twenty-first birthday. He had just started looking at property; he was planning to move from his apartment into a house. He joined my church and didn't brush me off when I suggested he join our singles' club."

I wanted to ask Susan how she could be so sure that her brother was happy, no matter what the outward signs were. Often we showed only our best faces to those we loved, not wanting to burden them with deep-rooted problems. I'd read that it was common for people to put things in order and be their most agreeable selves, in fact, just before taking their own lives. That was one of the many things it didn't seem right to bring up, however.

"According to my nephew, the ME is leaning toward—"

"I know what the police think. They called me. With all due respect to the LPPD and the ME, Gerry, how could they determine that so quickly? Oliver didn't own a gun. He hated them. And since when do the police act with such haste? They're all involved in a cover-up. It's no secret how powerful Patrick Lynch is and how he runs city hall and the police station. I'll bet the ME is Lynch's son or something."

I got Susan's point, deciding not to mention that her sweeping condemnation of the LPPD didn't sit well with me or that Lincoln Point's ME was female. There was time for that down the road.

"Anything is possible, Susan. But I think we need to take a breath and let a little time pass." Not that I planned to do that regarding the new cloud over my husband's reputation. That called for a different set of rules.

"The more time that passes, the worse it will be," Susan said. "That's what they all want, for us to relax and forget the whole thing." She brushed her hand in the air, as if she were swatting a fly, nearly knocking the teacup from its saucer.

Susan had reverted to a southern accent this evening; "more" came out as two syllables—"mo-ah."

"They did go through his apartment already, and they

found some papers. I'm sure they'll look into the situation,"
I offered, regretting the choice of word to describe the horrible death of her brother. I was glad her own agenda was
so critical that she didn't notice. For me, it was hard enough
to refer to Oliver's papers without thinking of Ken. It
seemed impossible that my friend's deceased brother might
be the route to the sullying of my husband's reputation.

"Think about it, Gerry. Oliver was about to bring down
that big, disgraceful developer, Patrick Lynch, and that
nasty, crooked inspector for the city, Max Crowley. Oliver
was accumulatin' evidence against them, and he was going
to testify. Then, suddenly he's out of the picture. Doesn't
that smell like last week's catfish gumbo?"

"It does seem . . . uh . . . fishy, Susan, but I'm not sure
what I can do."

"Can y'all at least look around Oliver's house and office
and"—she choked back tears—"and just see what y'all
come up with."

"Don't you think the police will do all that? I told you,
they started already."

Susan gave me a look that asked how I could be so naïve.
"Please, Gerry. You're my only hope. I know how close you
and Skip are, and if you could just make sure he has an
open mind."

Susan was grossly overestimating my ability to influence my nephew. "I'll give it a try," I said.

Susan leaned over and hugged me. "I knew you would."
She reached into her large tote, pulled out a key, and put it
in my hand. She closed my fingers over it as if she were
entrusting me with one of her special, newly minted miniature dolls. "This is the key to Oliver's apartment. It's right
around the corner from where . . . from the Fergusons'."

"This feels like more than talking to Skip, Susan."

"I know, but it's so important, Gerry." She paused. "And, oh, I know this is going to seem so silly, but could you bring me back that little room box I made for him. Remember the one y'all helped me with in crafts group?"

At last, something I could accomplish. I recalled working on a miniature construction scene in which Susan had modeled the interior of a living room undergoing renovation, complete with tiny tools and home improvement supplies. Apparently, that had been one of Oliver's previous professions.

I was so glad to have something easy and specific to do for Susan—return a treasured memento—I didn't even question why she wouldn't just go to Oliver's apartment and retrieve it herself.

"I can do that," I said, meaning, "That might be all I can do."

"Thank you so much, Gerry. I can't tell you how much better I feel already."

I wished I could have said the same. I wondered if I should tell Susan that I had a case of my own to solve, one that might or might not be connected to her brother's death but was most definitely my top priority.

After Susan left, I stayed up awhile longer, going back and forth between two important lists I was compiling. One was of harmless reasons why Ken's name was among those of nefarious Lincoln Point businessmen and -women, and the other was of people who benefited most with Oliver Halbert no longer among the living.

The lists seemed to merge, and I didn't know whether that was a good or a bad thing.

When I finally went to bed, I had a fitful sleep at best. I

found myself in a fantasy world where a miniature list of names came to life, the letters leaping off the tiny page, each name taking the shape of a nasty-looking man or woman who might have killed Oliver Halbert and smeared Ken Porter's good name.

Chapter 5

"Is it okay if I play with Taylor today, Grandma?" Maddie asked at breakfast.

Taylor was Maddie's new best friend forever, "BFF" in text-messaging language, and Henry Baker, her grandfather, was my (here I always paused) friend, I'd decided. If it were up to Maddie and Taylor, in their preteen wisdom, Henry and I would become BFFs and, along with Taylor's and Maddie's parents, we'd all live together happily ever after.

Though I wasn't ready for a major change in lifestyle, the more temporary arrangement of placing Maddie in Henry and Taylor's care was appealing. It would give me time to organize my thoughts and create a plan for putting Oliver Halbert's apartment key to use. It seemed a long shot, but I hoped the key would unlock the mystery of Ken Porter's place among Oliver's "potential" investigations.

"Did you call Taylor to see if she's available today?" I asked.

"She TM'd me already."

"Of course she did."

"She says they're both free all day. And Mr. Baker has a new project to show you. I think it's a gigantic dollhouse. I think Mr. Baker likes you, Grandma." Maddie spooned cereal into her mouth, not easy since her grin made it hard to eat.

I took a sip of coffee and cleared my throat, preparing for battle. "I have some things to do around town. But I can drive you over there whenever you're ready."

"You're not free?" Maddie put down her spoon and looked at me, waiting for my excuse.

I waited her out, busying myself with adding another glob of cranberry and pear jelly to the last of my toast.

A light seemed to dawn. "I get it. I almost forgot. It's The Case, right?"

I heard capital letters in her voice. Maddie had taken to giving simple names to difficult or important things, the better to handle them. Earlier in the year, her family had relocated from Los Angeles to Palo Alto, only ten miles from Lincoln Point, so her father could take a coveted position at Stanford Medical Center. It was a boon for me to have my family so close, but the transition was tough for Maddie. Until she met Taylor, she had a hard time adjusting and missed her L.A. friends terribly. She referred to that trauma as The Move. When she tensed up before a school quiz, she talked about The Test, each time putting equal and unmistakable emphasis on "the."

In my experience, a coping skill was a coping skill was a coping skill, no matter how much sense it made to others.

"What case, sweetheart?" I asked, enjoying a new burst of fruit flavor in my mouth.

"You're going to work on Mr. Halbert's case with Uncle

Skip." Maddie could conjure up a scolding tone equal to that of the best ALHS teachers I'd worked with.

I could honestly shake my head. I had no plans to see Skip. At least not until I'd done some looking around myself. "No, I'm not. I have some errands."

Maddie rolled her eyes. She didn't need to say it: too many times she'd been parked somewhere while I did "errands" she'd have loved to have been included in.

"I'm going to spend some time with Mrs. Giles," I said. I winced at my shading of the truth, leaving out that my errands were for Susan, not with Susan. "She's not feeling very well right now and she needs some company."

Maddie tapped her spoon on the rim of her cereal bowl. When she was little, she'd slap it much harder, smack on the surface of the cereal, and delight in the mess she made. Now she drummed lightly, as if she were doing some heavy thinking.

"Maybe I'll go with you to help cheer her up. She likes me."

"Everybody likes you, but that doesn't mean you're coming with me." My voice was firm, my steps confident as I took my dishes to the sink, walking away from the subject.

I heard a sigh of defeat.

My house phone rang moments after I'd slung my large cloth purse on my shoulder, car remote at the ready. I checked the caller ID display. My best friend and sister-in-law, Beverly Gowen, Skip's mother, was on the line. Usually, I'd drop everything to talk to Beverly, but usually I didn't have any reason to keep something from her—like the fact that her brother's name ended up in questionable company. I knew she'd pick up any strain in my voice, even across town over a telephone line. I'd be better prepared to talk to her once I did my so-called errands, I reasoned, while my fingers clenched around my keys.

I let the phone ring.

"Who is it, Grandma?"

"It can wait," I said, moving Maddie toward the door and out of sight of the telephone number displayed on the small screen.

I hoped this was the only time I'd have to turn my back on Beverly.

At about nine thirty on a bright Saturday morning, we pulled up in front of Taylor's home, a few blocks north of mine. Technically, Henry was the owner of the house; his daughter and her family had moved in when his wife died, not long after I lost Ken. Since Taylor's parents were partners in their own law firm, they worked long hours and benefited greatly from a live-in, retired grandfather. I knew everyone was delighted with the arrangement.

As we'd gotten to know each other, Henry and I had discovered how similar the last years of our marriages had been—each caring for a terminally ill spouse whom we'd loved dearly, trying to hold the family together as well as live up to our responsibilities to our students. Henry was on the faculty of ALHS's vocational program, teaching shop and other trades, while I ran on in my classroom about the prophetic witches in *Macbeth* and poor Yorick's skull in *Hamlet*.

Seeing Henry this morning, in his working uniform— khakis, a heavy denim apron, and a logo-free cap over his thinning brown hair—I was almost ready to give up my quest for justice and spend my day in his workshop. I knew he could help me with a tricky dollhouse problem:

constructing a swinging door between a kitchen and dining room in half-scale (one foot translated to one-half inch).

"How about I make you a mini-size bar stool like the life-size one in my den," he'd offered once. "I have some leftover oak pieces lying around and it would be the perfect use for them. If you noticed, on the real one I shaped it so the tops of the legs form through tenons that are cut flush with the surface of the seat."

"I've done that dozens of times," I'd said, catching him believing me for an instant.

Now, as he came down the walkway to my car, I was tempted to stay and do what retired grandmothers are supposed to do.

Henry leaned into the window of my red Saturn. "You're off? I'd hoped we could hang out, as the kids say."

I thought of Susan's distress, and my own need to learn more about the possible charges against my husband. What I needed was to make up a quick excuse and drive away, and spend a few hours on my own with my confusion and doubts. "I have some errands," I said.

"Anything you need my help with?"

Something in Henry's manner told me his offer wasn't just formulaic. He seemed to sense that my chores didn't involve simply picking up dry cleaning and baguettes and stopping at the post office.

I tapped on my steering wheel. "It's a very long story," I said.

Henry brushed the sides of his head, nearly popping off his cap. "What else are these big ears good for?" He opened my car door and held out his hand.

A helping hand. Just what I needed. I turned off my ignition and stepped out of my car and into Henry's kind offer.

* * *

With Beverly off-limits in a way, and no one else with whom I was eager to share information—"unpleasant rumors" was a more accurate term in my mind—about my husband, I was grateful to have Henry's big ears and welcoming manner at my disposal. It was no trouble to dispatch the girls to Taylor's bedroom where they would work on a dollhouse destined for a raffle at Taylor's Lincoln Point elementary school. Taylor's mother had taught her how to sew, and now Taylor was teaching Maddie a skill she'd shunned when I'd offered her the same lessons a year or so ago. There was no accounting for timing, or for the source of the suggestion. Their goal for the day was to make bedding, pillows, and rugs for every room that needed them.

Henry and I went out back to his workshop.

"You don't mind if I work while you talk?" he asked me.

I sensed the question was rhetorical and that Henry was aware how I preferred it that way. I nodded, then sat on an old chair near his bench while he all but rocked back and forth running a plane over a long piece of wood. The motion itself was enough to relax me. Henry had a calmness about him that I knew I could trust, as surely as he trusted the plane to give him the smoothness he wanted.

"I'm not sure where to start," I said.

"What did you used to tell your students?"

I smiled at the memory and the wisdom. "Once upon a time," I began.

I laid the story out for Henry, shaping it in my mind at the same time. Oliver Halbert had been investigating many people in Lincoln Point who might be called white-collar criminals, including the developer, Patrick Lynch, and the former city inspector, Max Crowley. That fact, plus personal reasons, led Susan to believe her brother had not committed suicide but was murdered.

"So, Lynch and Crowley are the most high-profile suspects," Henry said.

"I'm assuming they would be, if Oliver's death is ruled a murder, but so far that's not the case. The jury's still out. Or, rather, the ME's official ruling is still out, though it's beyond me why anyone would believe a man would walk to a neighbor's porch, arrange himself like a straw man, and shoot himself."

"I see your point. Are there any other likely suspects?"

The question jolted me out of a mental box. I hadn't had the time—nor, truthfully, the foresight—to think about other possible suspects. I tried now to expand my horizons.

"I suppose another possibility would be the family of the janitor who died in the fire at the Ferguson twins' factory. It's admittedly a stretch as far as motive." What about the twins?

"Oliver's body was found at their parents' home, correct?"

"Correct. But Sam and Lillian are close to eighty years old, if not older. Not likely suspects," I said.

Henry took a break from his planing (if that was a verb) and stood straight. He laughed. "Is there an age limit on suspects now? Let me know when I reach it, okay? I have some unsettled debts."

I tried to conjure a picture of Henry swinging into any violent action that wasn't meant to split wood or hammer a nail. None surfaced.

"I know you're trying to cover all bases," I said. "And you're right. We should consider everyone who benefits from Oliver's death."

"Everyone we know of," Henry said.

Henry's simple, obvious comment brought me back to reality—there was no way a civilian could know the extent of the suspect pool in a murder case or for any other crime. The police alone had the resources to delve into a victim's life and search far and wide for the connection that mattered.

"What do I think I'm doing?" I asked Henry and myself.

Henry gave me a warm smile. "Did you agree to help Susan?"

I felt the large key in my purse. "Apparently I did."

"What's holding you back?"

I averted his gaze at first, then met his eyes. "Excuse me?"

"Well, it doesn't seem that tough. You've done this before." I was beginning to like his grin, now spreading across his face as he walked the fingers of one hand across the palm of the other. "Gone snooping."

"I guess I have."

"So, what's different about this case?"

Thud.

A loud noise came from the side door to Henry's workshop. The answer to Henry's question would have to wait. A good thing, since I wasn't ready to share it.

"I knew it. I knew it," Maddie said, stepping over the backpack she'd just dropped (thrown). "You're talking about The Case." She put her hands on her skinny hips, and Taylor followed suit. I wondered if Taylor knew why the gesture was important: Maddie staking her claim to a place on the investigative team.

"Did you show Mrs. Porter the new dollhouse, Grandpa?" Taylor asked.

"I forgot," Henry said.

"I thought you were busy sewing," I said, taking the coward's way out and focusing on Taylor.

"We were, but then we needed some snacks from Maddie's backpack and the zipper got stuck, so we came for help," Taylor said.

"Let's see that zipper," Henry said.

"How come you're letting Mr. Baker help with The Case, but not me?" Maddie asked.

Henry worked on the zipper, head down, leaving me to answer. I'd wait until bedtime to suggest that Maddie be a little less petulant now that she was old enough to sit in the front seat of a car. "Mr. Baker and I were having a conversation, sweetheart," I said.

"It's not polite to eavesdrop, especially on adults," Taylor said.

Maddie shot her a look. I thought I noticed a tinge of defeat in her eyes. That was twice in one day that my granddaughter suffered a loss, and this time at the hands of a little girl with a blond pixie cut, four months younger than she was.

I knew that eventually someone would have to pay.

The plastic bag of ginger cookies that Henry rescued from Maddie's backpack would be enough to keep her happy for now.

Thanks to the arrival of Taylor's parents, who had assumed day-care duties, I found myself at Bagels by Willie (named after Abe's young son, of course) for an early lunch with Henry.

"You two go and have grown-up food and talk and we'll fix something for us and the girls," Henry's daughter, Kay, had said.

When I hesitated, her husband, Bill, had added, "Really, we hardly ever get to do lunch with our daughter, and it will be fun to have Maddie with us."

I dared not look at the fun girl, Maddie, left behind as I walked to Henry's car.

Thinking of Kay and Bill, it occurred to me that now there might be two more people rooting for Henry and me to become BFFs.

Willie's was always among the first to promote the spirit of the season with bowls of Halloween candy on the table. I helped myself to a miniature (loosely speaking) candy bar and bit into layers of chocolate, marshmallow, and caramel. Things could be worse.

"You were about to tell me what's different about this case," Henry said, pretending to look around—for Maddie, I knew.

Then I remembered that things actually were worse.

"It's about my husband."

After the fact, I realized I'd gone on far too long about how Ken's name had appeared on Halbert's "most wanted" list and how Ken would never, ever have been involved in anything the slightest bit questionable.

Henry had managed to finish off two cinnamon bagels and several pieces of orange- and black-wrapped taffy and still listen attentively.

"Since it seems Halbert's death will probably be ruled a suicide, do you think the police will even bother to look into any of those people on his hit list, so to speak?"

I shrugged. "Probably not."

"Which means that they might not be looking into Ken's records or files, or wherever Halbert got his name. The whole project might just go away."

"True, but that doesn't matter." The little I'd eaten of my own cinnamon bagel was not sitting well in my stomach. "Either way, I have to know."

Henry looked at the paper napkin I'd shredded to bits. He pulled another napkin from the metal holder on the table and handed it to me. He pushed my glass of water closer to me, the gesture a suggestion that I take a sip. His gaze wandered to the ceiling and I suspected he was visiting another time, as I often did myself.

"Of course you have to know," he said to one of the fans, unmoving above us. He gave me a serious look. "Let me tell you, if anyone had even hinted that Virginia was less than perfect, let alone had committed a crime, you'd be visiting me in jail after I punched out whoever it was."

Once again, as when Henry had asked me my presumed age limit for murder suspects, I had a hard time picturing this gentle woodworker, who made the most beautiful rockers, cradles, and bookcases, lifting a finger to hurt anyone.

"Thanks" was all I could say. I hoped he knew my gratitude encompassed the new napkin, the water, and the understanding.

"So you have two reasons to investigate," he said. "Where are you going to start?"

"I have no idea."

Henry spread his arms wide. "I'm here to help."

Big ears and a big heart.

"You forget that I've seen your workshop. I know you have so many projects already," I said.

"I don't think of you as a project."

Had Johnny, Willie's manager, turned up the heat? Or was I blushing? Why weren't those ceiling fans working to cool me down?

I cleared my throat, a recovery tactic. "I meant—you're building the dollhouse for Taylor's school, and the toy box for the women's shelter, and the rocking horse for the Christmas drive." I ticked off the items I knew about. He

waved his hands as if to indicate that there was not that
much on his plate. "And all those boxes on shelves in your
workshop. I'll bet each one is a project of some kind."

"Nope. Those are just old files. Records from years and
years ago that I'll probably never look at. It's the hazard of
living in the same house for decades—there's no incentive
to clean things out."

Records? From years ago, never looked at? Incentive to
clean things out?

I spread cream cheese on my bagel and took a bite. Suddenly I had renewed energy.

"I think I know where to start."

I made a quick call to Kay and Bill to be sure they were
still okay with the girls. I could only imagine Maddie's
mood when she'd hear that I'd be away longer than the al-
lotted lunch hour. I hoped her parents and I had trained her
well enough that she'd behave herself with strangers. It was
a lot to ask of a precocious eleven-year-old with a Nancy
Drew complex.

I also had a lot to ask of Henry. I wanted him to help
me get dozens of boxes down from the rafters of my garage
and then go away. I couldn't bear the thought of anyone
else's seeing the contents of cartons that contained Ken's
property. Not even Henry, my new confidant. If, on the
very slim chance that there were something untoward
between the dusty covers, I wanted to be alone when I
found it.

"I'll need you to leave once the boxes are off the shelves,"
I said. Could I have been more blunt? I smiled to take away
some of the sting. "Can you drive home and keep Maddie
away from here?"

"No problem. Shall I maintain custody of Maddie and your car at my house indefinitely or do you want either of them back sometime?"

It felt good to laugh so hard. "I think an hour will do. And I guess we have some logistics to work out."

About twenty minutes later, Ken's ladder was back in its place along the garage wall, and about two dozen boxes were at my feet or on my small worktable.

"Thanks a lot, Henry," I said. "I'm sorry about all the dust."

"I've had worse Saturdays," he said, brushing off his khakis. He waved his arm toward the stacks of boxes. "I'll leave you to it. Let me know if you need anything. I'm a phone call away."

I watched him drive off, feeling lucky that I'd met him. The timing could not have been better.

I turned back to the piles of boxes. Cartons that had once held printer paper or books now presumably held financial records, log books, building plans, and whatever else Artie, Ken's partner, and Esther, their secretary, had found when they cleaned out Ken's office. They'd both driven to my house with the boxes once it was clear that Ken would never recover and return to work. If I closed my eyes, I thought, I'd be able to feel Esther's tears on my cheeks when she hugged me that day.

Though I couldn't throw the material away even after Ken died, I'd never taken the covers off the boxes. Skip had helped me put them at the highest points of the garage, and there they had been until now.

I took a deep breath and cut through the first strip of sealing tape. My shoulders ached as I lifted the top of the box nearest me. I felt as exhausted as if the simple piece of cardboard weighed more than all my dollhouses combined.

My body relaxed as I saw that the first box was filled with nothing I should worry about. I pawed through dozens of books of the same size—long, narrow telephone message books, like the kind used in the ALHS office and probably a large majority of offices around the world. All that were left in the books were stubs with dates, times, and callers' names.

I thought of Ken, the busy, russet-haired architect, showing up at work in the morning, picking up the right-hand sections of the message slips, making all these calls throughout the day, and still finding time to say hello to me on my breaks from class.

The tears came and stayed for a while. It wasn't a very good start. If I couldn't handle a box of old telephone message stubs without breaking down, how was I going to get through the rest of the material that surrounded me?

I needed a cup of tea. At this rate, it would be well past Halloween before I got through everything, but I needed to indulge myself nevertheless.

I stepped into my kitchen through the door between the house and the garage. From its spot on the counter, the answering machine showed a blinking light. I immediately remembered Beverly's call as Maddie and I were leaving this morning. Henry and I had entered the garage directly from the driveway and had had no reason to go into the house. I decided to let the message wait until I'd at least had my tea.

Besides the blinking light, something else attracted my attention as I made my way to the pantry. A white envelope was leaning against a wastebasket I kept near a small desk in the family room. It looked as though someone had aimed to throw the envelope away but missed by a bit. I couldn't remember doing any such thing. I picked up the envelope. It was empty, unmarked, from a box of stationery I recognized as one of my own.

I stepped back from the desk and looked it over. The top drawer wasn't fully closed. I pulled it open all the way and found the box of stationery the envelope belonged to, in the place where it always was. I wasn't the neatest person in Lincoln Point, but I never left my desk drawers partly open. I checked the slots on the desktop where I placed correspondence that needed attention and extracted a stack of letters and flyers. Nothing was missing as far as I could tell, but still the arrangement was curious. I usually left tidier edges on the stack.

I thought briefly of Maddie, but she never used the desk.

"Nuh-uh," she'd said when I'd told her she was welcome to do her homework there. "My dad told me not to touch that desk or I'd get yelled at if something got messed up."

Had I really made my son's life that miserable? I did remember warning Richard that the desk was mainly for his parents' use, since he had a perfectly good setup in his own room, and that if he did use the desk, he had to leave everything in it and on it the way he'd found it. No wonder he'd never touched it and passed a warning on to his daughter.

On the other hand, I'd invited Maddie to use the desk, with no restrictions. In fact, I hoped she would since she would then be nearby for chatting while I cooked or ironed. The desk issue was not the only one where I knew I was much more lenient with my granddaughter than I had been with my son.

I dropped the envelope into the wastebasket, though it wasn't damaged in any way, and felt a sudden chill. What if a stranger had been in my home? I stood stock-still and listened for a noise, but heard nothing other than the ticking of my living room clock and the humming noise from my refrigerator.

Thunk. Thunk.

I jumped. What a time for ice cubes to drop into the container on the freezer door.

I took out my cell phone and held it like a gun. I walked from room to room.

Nothing seemed disturbed in the crafts room, but how would I be able to tell? My crafts supplies and projects were organized in their own way, but I would never remember if I'd left a particular strand of polka-dot ribbon hanging from its slot in the multitiered ribbon holder. At any given time, I might lift the lids of several supply boxes, browsing among picture frames, mirrors, and baskets of different sizes, looking for an extra touch to a room box. More often than not, I'd leave the lids open so I'd know which of the identical blue plastic containers I'd already gone through.

It was hopeless to track whether anyone had been in my crafts room other than the wonderful women who treated it as their own. My crafters group had been here last night. Could one of them have needed a piece of paper and helped herself to my desk drawer? I doubted it.

I moved on to my bedroom, which seemed to be as I'd left it, as was the room Maddie used when she visited.

Was I imagining things? Had the envelope floated from the top of the desk when a breeze lifted it? I often left windows open. Had I written a quick note at my desk this morning and forgotten? I did leave in a hurry, and things had been slightly less than normal around here for the last couple of days.

Should I call Skip? And tell him what? That I'd found an envelope on the floor by the wastebasket and a drawer that wasn't closed tightly?

Put that way, it sounded silly.

I made myself the cup of tea I'd come in for in the first place and sat in my living room, facing away from the desk.

Half asleep on my soft living room chair, I decided I'd been thinking too much of *Macbeth* and his witches, and perhaps now the ghost of Banquo had also invaded my mind and my home. A worse suggestion came and went in a flash—that Ken was sending me a message: don't mess with my stuff.

Chapter 6

I woke up to loud footsteps entering my house from the garage. Before I was fully conscious, I grabbed the cell phone from the table next to me and tried to remember the emergency number. I was sure the steps belonged to the same intruder who'd gone through my desk. Then I remembered—I had no evidence that there had been an intruder.

I couldn't recall a time when I'd entertained so many strange fantasies and half dreams. Late-night visitors were taking their toll, especially those connected to homicide. I needed to get more sleep.

The very real footsteps got louder.

"Grandma, we got worried," Maddie said, tramping in with her heavy athletic shoes, which were nothing like the flimsy white sneakers I'd worn to gym class in the Bronx. Not content with simple white laces, both Taylor and Maddie owned shoes with colorful Velcro tabs, blinking red lights, and shiny wheels that surprised me every time Maddie rocked back on them and wheeled herself around me.

Henry was close behind Maddie. "Your garage door is still open," he said, sounding worried that someone might have walked in and stolen me away.

"What time is it?" I asked, craning my stiff neck to see the clock. Which must have been off by a couple of hours. "It can't be five o'clock."

It seemed it was. I'd slept more than three hours.

Maddie had made her way to my lap. Or at least some of Maddie was on my lap. Tall for her age, she no longer fit comfortably. Her legs dangled next to my still, stiff ones; her neck was bent to snuggle in mine.

"You didn't call," she said. "And you weren't answering your phone." She picked up my cell phone and frowned. "It's not even on. But we called your landline, too. You must have been really out." She held me as if she'd been worried that she'd never see or hear from me again.

"I'm sorry to make you worry, sweetheart, but I'm fine." I opened my eyes as wide as I could and smiled as broadly as I could, emphasizing my point.

I looked at Henry, standing by. "Sorry," I said.

"We're just glad you're okay," he said.

I remembered that my car was still in front of his house, from ten this morning. "I should go back with you and get my car," I said.

"Don't worry. I drove your car here, Grandma," Maddie said.

Even before she gave me her teasing grin, I tickled her all around her middle. Nice to know I wasn't that far gone.

Back from Henry's with my car, I thought it was time I retrieved my messages. Between my home answering machine and my cell phone voice mail, I had eight messages, not counting the many short ones from Maddie. The eight were from two people—four from Beverly and four from Susan. The gist of Beverly's sequence was "Can we have lunch today?" (the one I'd ignored as I left the house in the morning), followed by two versions of "It might be too late for lunch now," and finally, "Maybe I'll stop by for dinner."

Maddie curtailed her table-setting activities when she heard the last one and rushed to call her Aunt Beverly. (We had researched the question and found that one's grandfather's sister should be called a great-aunt, but Beverly refused any designation preceded by "great.")

"Aunt Beverly said she was coming over anyway," Maddie said, hanging up the phone. "She was worried when you didn't answer your phones. How could you sleep through all that ringing? I called the line in the kitchen a lot, even more than the times I left a message."

I doubted she was exaggerating. "I must have been really tired," I told her.

I supposed I should have been grateful and flattered that I was missed after only a long nap.

Susan's messages were also sequential. They began with, "Have you been to Oliver's place yet?" and ended with, "I'm anxious to hear what you found at Oliver's place." Susan spoke in a gravelly voice that was different from her usual lilting southern tones. I suspected she was also short on sleep these days.

I felt like a dud. With the whole day at my disposal, I'd opened only one of Ken's boxes, done nothing to help Susan, pawned my granddaughter off on other people, and was now barely scraping a dinner together. It was a good thing Beverly was family, or I would have had to rethink the platter of leftovers I was planning to serve.

My greatest wish was that I'd gone to Oliver's apartment

and picked up the miniature scene for Susan and found a suicide note the police may have overlooked. Cruel as that sounded, it would have brought a speedy close to Susan's questioning and started her on the road to proper grieving.

I had another wish. I wished I'd stayed awake, gone through every scrap of paper in every one of Ken's boxes and found only praiseworthy correspondence, perhaps one reading, *Dear Mr. Porter, we accept your high moral position and your exemplary decision not to join us in our shady dealings. Best wishes, signed, All the Other Potentials on Oliver Halbert's List.*

Yes, I had been a good creative writing teacher, I mused.

"You look a little out of it this evening. Is something wrong?" Beverly asked. She'd held her question until Maddie had left for the kitchen to fill three bowls with ice cream.

"Other than hosting a dinner of leftovers?" I asked, tensing.

She pointed to the nearly empty serving bowls on the table. "Chicken cutlets, potato salad, green beans with almonds, and homemade dilly bread. I'll take your leftovers any day."

"Me, too," Maddie said. "Except for mixing nuts with the vegetable." She made a disgusted face, which quickly brightened as she plunked a small tray on the table and handed out bowls of chocolate ice cream. By long-standing agreement, she deposited the bowl with the largest amount of ice cream at her place. I was glad to have her back, not for the dessert, but because it meant I didn't have to tell Beverly what was wrong with me: I was in essence investigating her brother.

* * *

This was a long holiday weekend for Maddie and she was mine until I delivered her to her Palo Alto school on Tuesday morning. Her parents were in San Francisco for a few much-needed days of relaxation, staying in a friend's oceanside condo. Though Richard cared deeply for his profession as a surgeon, the job was stressful. I was delighted that Mary Lou gently forced him into quarterly getaways and time-outs when he was required to leave his pager in a desk drawer.

I always loved extra time with Maddie; this weekend there was a bonus in that I could use her as an excuse to leave the boxes in my garage unopened and the foreign key in my purse unused. I had to babysit, after all.

On the other hand, our bedtime chat tonight was more like a conference Skip might have with his LPPD colleagues.

"Did you call Mrs. Giles back and give her a report on The Case?" Maddie asked. She was sitting up in bed, arms folded across her chest. The chief of police couldn't be more intimidating to his subordinates, the aroma of her strawberry bubble bath notwithstanding.

"Not yet."

"Didn't you find anything out today?" she asked.

Nothing I could share. (Where did she learn that stare?) I'd discovered that it was going to be harder than I thought to tear open cartons of material that had Ken's name all over it. I was no chemist, but I'd have bet I wasn't imagining things when I'd smelled my husband's slightly musky scent when I unsealed the box of telephone logs.

"No, I didn't find out anything."

"Then, what were you doing all day, Grandma?"

"It wasn't exactly all day. Just a couple of hours."

"It was from eleven twenty when you left for lunch with Mr. Baker to almost five o'clock. I wanted to come home sooner, but Mr. Baker said you needed some private time. I figured it was about The Case, right?"

"I took a nap, remember?"

"Well, I did," Maddie said.

That was a surprise. "You took a nap, too?"

"No, I found out something."

I'd lost the continuity and now saw that the "I did" referred to making good use of the day.

"You found out something about what?" This was one of those times when it would have been helpful to have a whiteboard and dry-erase markers in Maddie's room.

Maddie turned her head and gave me a sideways glance. "About The Case. I used Taylor's laptop to Google Oliver Halbert."

I wanted to ask if Taylor's parents were aware of the forensics investigation going on in their daughter's bedroom. There was no use discussing the bigger issue of sleuthing as a hobby for an eleven-year-old; Maddie won those debates hands down. I might as well reap the rewards.

"What did you learn?"

"He used to be in jail."

I grimaced. "I doubt it."

I should have learned by now not to question my granddaughter's research skills. She threw back the covers and went to her own laptop on her desk. This was not sleep inducing. What had happened to the days when I sat on her bed and read a soothing, happy-ending story with no more serious a crime than a trampled cabbage patch or a stolen coin? At an hour when she should have been nodding off with a sweet smile on her face, she was upright at her computer, clicking intently. I consoled myself with the fact that at least tomorrow, Sunday, was not a school day.

"Here it is," she said, beckoning me with a finger that seemed to have grown as long and crooked as that of *Macbeth*'s second witch, as I envisioned her. *By the pricking of my thumbs, something wicked this way comes.* Some things, once memorized, never left our consciousness.

On Maddie's monitor was a newspaper photo of a young Oliver Halbert. The caption read, "Local man arrested on DUI."

I studied the photo. The man, looking back over his shoulder at the camera (he couldn't have intended that), had the same high forehead, thick neck, and narrow eyes I'd seen briefly on Oliver where he was slumped on the Fergusons' porch and more recently in his sister's photographs of him. I doubted the arrestee was another Oliver Halbert from the small town of Bethelville, Tennessee. The newspaper was dated fifteen years ago, which would have put Oliver in his early thirties, well beyond the frat party phase.

Besides the pressing issue of Oliver Halbert's arrest record, there was the curious question of how Google got a photograph from a time when the Internet was barely developed and certainly not widely used. I pictured a room full of teenagers entering mountains of data and scanning photos from the past.

I wondered also how Oliver could have landed a government job in Lincoln Point when he had a record. Maybe this was a low-priority arrest. I'd have to ask Skip.

"See?" Maddie said.

I patted her head. "Good girl." A question formed in my mind: what were the chances that a person would be arrested once, as an isolated incident, in his thirties? I supposed he could have learned his lesson, but there was also a chance that this was a pattern. "Can you see if there are any more"—how to phrase it to my underage researcher—"things he might have been in jail for?"

"I already looked at all the hits and I couldn't find anything except one more that was part of a police thing. Something about bribing someone, but he didn't do it. They thought he did, but it turned out he didn't."

"Is that so?" I said, mostly to myself. "Can you show me that hit?" I asked Maddie, proud of my jargon.

"You mean 'open that link'?" my sassy granddaughter responded.

"Whatever."

The article, with no photo this time, was brief: Oliver Halbert was accused of offering a bribe to an insurance agent, to arrange for a larger settlement from the agent's company. The case seemed to be about mold in his home. According to the story, he'd been trying to convince the agent to backdate his policy so that it would cover more of the damaged area.

How could that be? Wasn't his latest crusade about bribery? Wasn't it bribery that got him murdered, according to Susan?

I remembered something Skip had told me a while ago—that the people who speak out the most loudly against a particular crime are often guilty of that crime themselves. He cited a few examples of people in the national spotlight.

"What makes a public person think they can get away with it?" I'd asked. Something I'd often wondered about.

Skip had gone on about people in power who not only think they're immune (even when their colleagues are caught) but also are great risk takers. I was glad I wasn't expected to understand that type of personality fully. Now, however, I wondered if Oliver Halbert had suffered from the same syndrome Skip had described and that I'd read about.

I didn't look forward to telling Susan what we'd discovered about her brother. Dismissed charges or not, there was a blot on the image I'd had of Oliver Halbert, the crusader for clean politics. Susan would be upset, unless she already knew of her brother's record, in which case, her worst nightmare would have come true—that I'd find out and not help her prove he was murdered.

I could almost hear her: "Just because my brother wasn't as white as the lilies all a-bloomin' in Nashville, it doesn't mean he wasn't murdered."

I agreed with her in advance. Strangely, I was now more inclined to use the key to her brother's apartment. The key that beckoned from my purse, three rooms and two baths away.

"Any more links you want me to open, Grandma?" Maddie asked, her words carrying that telltale slur that said she was fading.

"Not tonight, sweetheart," I said, leading her back to bed.

Maddie crawled under the covers, which I then lifted over her shoulders, tucking her favorite afghan under her chin. She still used the baseball afghan I'd made for her father in my extreme knitting phase. More than thirty years old, and washed at least once a week when Richard used it, the red, white, and blue strands were showing signs of wear. I wondered when my granddaughter would be ready for a more mature design. It had been a while since I'd knitted or crocheted anything larger than three inches, so I might have lost patience for crafting life-size bedcovers.

Maddie's final words of the day: "I told you, Grandma. I told you Mr. Halbert was a jailbird."

She was asleep before I could congratulate her as well as work on synonyms with her.

* * *

Eleven o'clock seemed too late to call Susan, though last night she hadn't considered it too late to just show up on my doorstep.

My three-hour afternoon nap killed any chance I had of getting in synch with a normal night's sleep. I wondered about going to Oliver Halbert's apartment, under the cover of darkness, but I still wasn't comfortable leaving Maddie alone in the house, especially at night.

One thing I could do in my own home was return to the project lying in wait in my garage. Maddie's room was separated from the garage by the fourth bedroom plus the entryway, so I didn't have the excuse that noise would wake her. Besides, Maddie was like her father in that very little could wake her from a sound sleep.

I put on a warmer sweater and sturdier shoes, ready to do battle with boxes. As I walked through my kitchen to get to the garage door, I had the thought of baking more ginger cookies instead of opening cartons. My snack supply was running low. What if Skip or someone else dropped by and my cupboard was bare?

It took only one full minute for me to come to my senses and enter the garage. Opening a box labeled *Bronx*, in bright red marker, seemed a safe enough venture. The box must have been on the shelf with the cartons from work and Henry took it down by mistake. I placed it on my workbench, pulled up a stool, and went to work on the sealing tape.

To my surprise, the contents of the box pertained not to our life-size apartment on the Grand Concourse in New York City, but to the wonderful dollhouse replica Ken built just before he became ill. Maddie and I were still working on furnishing the model. I smiled as I thought how the dollhouse version wouldn't have fit anywhere in the pocket-size (only six hundred and fifty square feet) apartment Ken and I lived in when we were first married.

Ken had piled all the plans for the miniature apartment, plus his notes and calculations, and scraps of extra material into the box when he'd finished. I'd been busy with a full teaching load at the time, as well as volunteer tutoring and, of course, my miniatures hobby, and hadn't paid a lot of attention to the day-to-day progress as Ken built the apartment replica. I'd been waiting for my turn—the thrill of decorating the interior. Now I realized what pains my husband had taken to get the details correct.

He'd collected a folio of photos of the real rooms as a reminder of the layout and structural specifications. The photos were candids he'd pulled from various albums and frames.

The Bronx apartment had been Richard's first home. I looked at a photograph of him as a toddler, his high chair wedged in a corner, his smiling, chubby face with probably more milk on it than he'd drunk. It was hard not to choke up.

Images flooded my mind—of my amazing granddaughter sleeping nearby, of my wonderful daughter-in-law, Mary Lou, of Beverly and Skip, and I felt a surge of gratitude for the family who were around me now, all stemming from Ken in one way or another.

I sniffed back any sad thoughts and reminded myself that I should be cheered by the lack of anything untoward in my first box of the night.

I pulled another box forward, this one with *Drawer, Bottom Right* in bold type on a label. I remembered when Ken's secretary, Esther, an older woman we were both fond of, called to tell me the boxes were ready and that she and Artie would be bringing them by the house. At the time, I was grateful that she'd labeled the boxes so carefully because that's what Ken would have liked. None of us could have known that I'd leave them alone while the tape dried and start to peel off, that it would take a crisis of giant proportions to get me to pay attention to the boxes again.

The contents of this box were predictable—bank records for the office account, calendars, memos to clients. I riffled through enough of the memos to be able to read the letterhead and rule out any correspondence with Patrick Lynch.

So far, so good.

At the bottom of the box was a large bulky envelope, marked *Personal*. I emptied the contents on my worktable and found myself facing an outfit for a child, from three to six months old, according to the brand's label on the pink-and-white onesie. I unfolded a white bib with pink trim, and a tiny hat and jacket, both in the same pattern as the onesie.

The lovely layette must have been put into the box in error. I imagined Esther mistakenly putting clothing that belonged to the baby of one of her friends or relatives in with Ken's records. The outfit seemed slightly worn, so it wasn't meant to be a gift. It had been in the envelope for a long time, as attested to by places where the creases had permanently faded the fabric. I wondered if Esther had ever missed the set.

I shook out the large manila envelope to be sure I'd seen everything. Out came a small white envelope containing photographs. I took out the three photos and peered at a Polaroid shot of a young Ken Porter holding a baby. I looked more closely. In the background was a sprawling institution of some kind. It was an east-coast kind of facility with a red brick façade and large maple trees lining a long driveway and a lush green lawn. A school or hospital, I guessed, but none I recognized.

The next photo was taken on the same property, it seemed, but close up to Ken and the little girl (judging from the plethora of pink on the child). From the child's size and the way Ken was holding it, I guessed it was not a newborn, but probably a few months old. Probably from three to six months, as the clothing label said.

Until he fell under the spell of leukemia, Ken had aged well. He'd never changed his hairstyle or gained or lost a noticeable amount of weight, so he'd looked the same (at least to me) over the course of decades. So, how old was he in these photos? It was hard to tell. I studied his clothing— casual pants and a windbreaker. Like his hair and his weight, his wardrobe was also a constant. He hadn't been one to follow the styles of the day. I tried to remember when Polaroid cameras were popular. It had been years since I'd seen one, but I assumed they were still available.

For now, without benefit of any other information, I had to say that in these photos, Ken was either a little younger or about the same age as when I met him.

The last picture was mostly an extreme close-up of the little girl, looking absently toward the camera; only Ken's arms and chest were showing.

I shuffled back through the three photographs. Ken had a serious expression on his face, neither happy nor displeased, but rather the straight-lipped expression he got when he was accepting something he wasn't quite thrilled about. Maybe he wasn't in the mood for a photo shoot that day. Maybe the baby was cranky, whoever she was.

My heart skipped. I didn't recognize the setting, but more to the point, I didn't recognize the baby, either.

How personal was this child?

Chapter 7

I must be very tired to get worked up about a photograph of Ken and a baby who isn't Richard.

The nagging thought that Ken might be the subject of an investigation by the late Lincoln Point city inspector didn't help. What else was there that I didn't know about my husband of more than thirty years?

I needed to think rationally. Wouldn't Ken have had friends with babies? Colleagues with children? His partner in the architectural firm was much older; the child could have been Artie's granddaughter. Indeed, the little girl in the photograph could have been anyone. His college roommate's young niece. A distant cousin twice removed.

Although the harmless possibilities were endless, the fact remained that photographs of this particular baby had been worth a special place among Ken's belongings, packed carefully among articles of clothing that it seemed would fit her, in an envelope marked *Personal*.

I had to take one more look at the clothing and the photographs and then I'd move on. I gathered the clothing on my lap and looked at it more closely. Besides the brand label, which I didn't recognize, I saw a number on each piece. A black laundry mark: four nine five. Did the child, the clothing, and the institution go together? Was I looking at an orphanage? Perhaps Ken donated money to them at one time and this was a publicity photo. Maybe it wasn't personal at all.

Did I really want to know?

Tap, tap, tap.

As light as the knocking was, it startled me. The clothing slipped off my lap. I bent to retrieve it and knocked over the pile of office correspondence and the Polaroids.

Someone was beckoning from the other side of the garage door. I moved toward it, gathering the fallen objects as I went.

"Aunt Gerry?" Skip's voice. "It's me. Are you okay in there?" More tapping. "The garage light is on. I figure you're working overtime on one of your architectural projects."

I smiled in spite of the discomfort I was feeling. The image of the large facility behind Ken and a strange child was burned in my brain.

Skip couldn't have known how right he was.

I thought of standing perfectly still, until Skip went away, or slipping back into my house and opening the front door to him. But it was hopeless pretending I hadn't been rummaging around in my garage. I acknowledged Skip's knocking, directed him to the side door of the house, and let him in through the narrow passage between my house and the next.

"What's up out here?" he asked, entering the garage.

"It's freezing. Aren't you cold?" He stamped his feet, presumably to warm them.

Ordinarily, I'd remind my California-native nephew of how distorted his ideas of "cold" and "winter" were. "If you'd ever lived in the Bronx," I'd tell him, "you'd know what real cold weather was like."

But tonight I didn't feel like reliving those days in any form.

I pulled my sweater closer. "As a matter of fact, I am cold," I said. "Let's go inside."

He looked at the papers I'd been going through, now spread over the concrete floor. I followed his gaze across the littered area, to the pages on the floor. In the short time I had before answering his knock, I'd dumped the pink clothes and the photos back into the box and put another box on top of it.

"What's all this?" he asked, his arms embracing the clutter.

"I'm just cleaning out some stuff."

He reached down to retrieve the pages on the floor. "Let me help you with these," Skip said.

"No need." I rushed to stop him, bumping into him. "Really, there's so much junk out here. It's about time I got rid of some of it. I need more storage space for my crafts. You know how much room I need when I'm building a dollhouse. I had a nap this afternoon so I'm not sleepy at all, and I thought I might as well do something useful."

While I rambled, Skip's gaze flitted from one box to another, some on the workbench, some on the dusty floor. I was acutely aware of the labels: *Consulting Jobs, Middle Desk Drawer, Files Credenza #1, Files Credenza #2,* and so on.

"This is Uncle Ken's stuff, isn't it?"

"As I said, I'm cleaning up."

"The stuff's been here for years." He pointed to the empty shelves above us. "I put it up there myself. There a reason you're choosing to go through it right now?"

My look must have been pitiful. Skip came over to me and put his arms around me.

For the first time in our lives, my nephew provided me a shoulder to cry on, instead of the other way around.

My cupboard wasn't bare, after all, and Skip availed himself of an assortment of snack food—slices of brie, crackers, an orange, and a handful of small ginger cookies—while I pulled myself together in the bathroom.

A few minutes later, we sat in the living room, the pale rug seeming to match my mood and, I believed, my complexion.

"I'm so sorry I did this to you, Aunt Gerry. It's my fault. I should never have told you about Oliver Halbert's stupid list." He sounded a lot like Maddie, calling things or events stupid when it was really people who were to blame.

"What if I'd heard about it another way, Skip? Imagine how much worse it would have been for me." What if I'd found out by emptying a box in the garage? I wanted to ask, but I had no intention of telling Skip the second cause of my distress, that I'd already discovered something unsettling in an innocently marked box.

He bit into the orange, then peeled away a section of its skin. The tangy aroma filled the air and made me thirsty. I made a motion to get up.

"What do you need?" he asked, holding his hand up.

"Just some water." Skip played waiter and brought me a bottle of cold, sparkling mineral water. He tried to foist a snack on me, but I didn't dare tax my digestive system. "How's June?" I asked, switching the topic to Skip's

Chicago-born almost-fiancée (his mother and I could only hope).

"I had a postcard from her of the Willis Tower. She wrote something like, 'Why don't you and Gerry build this in miniature?' It's not a bad idea, is it?"

"It's a great idea," I said, though I hardly meant it. My mental catalog of dollhouse styles did not include a skyscraper.

"If anyone could do it, it would be you and your group. Anyway, I talked to June today. She's enjoying her new baby niece," Skip said. He popped an orange section into his mouth.

"I'll bet she sent photos through her camera. Do you have them with you?"

"Yeah, as a matter of fact, she did send a couple of pictures." Skip gave me a serious look. "Do you really want to see photos of a baby you don't know?"

For the second time this evening, Skip had inadvertently hit the nail on its tiny head.

"No, not really," I said.

We settled into a short silence while Skip munched and I tried to relax enough to stop the pain in my jaw.

"I have some news on Oliver Halbert," he said, finally.

"I'm listening."

"He's not as clean as we thought."

"I already know that. He has a DUI."

"I suppose the little princess dug it up."

I nodded. "Which makes me wonder why whoever hired him for city inspector in Lincoln Point couldn't have dug it up."

"That's another story. It looks like he, uh, bribed his way into the job."

"Unbelievable."

"You know, some people think they're immune—"

"I remember the theory, Skip, but this seems like an extreme example."

"Agreed."

"Does this information give you more incentive to investigate his death as a homicide?"

The last slice of orange and the first sample of brie-on-cracker went into Skip's mouth, one after the other. "Somebody held up the paperwork on the ME's suicide filing, and now all this new information makes it suspect anyway. So, yeah, we're back to square one, and will look into the death as a possible homicide."

"It seemed very quick to me, anyway—the suicide ruling."

Skip looked around, as if for prying eyes or ears. "It did to me, too, so I asked around and dropped some hints. And, uh, that may have had something to do with the paperwork holdup I mentioned."

"You stopped the suicide filing?"

"Maybe."

It seemed too good to have hoped for, that Skip had actually investigated Oliver's death, whether because of my earlier insistence or not. My nephew had done what I hadn't had the energy to do and essentially kept my promise to Susan. I smiled at the thought—the cop was doing the investigating in this case, instead of his retired aunt who made miniature scenes. What a concept.

I allowed myself a flicker of cheer that I was now off the hook with Susan. I doubted she'd be too happy about the side effects of bringing up his sullied past, but not everything in this world was as rosy as we'd like it to be. A fact that was becoming entirely too clear to me and seemed to apply even to things I thought were rosy in my own life.

I remembered Susan's insistence that Oliver didn't own a gun and, in fact, hated them. "Whose gun was it, by the way?" I asked, not long after I considered myself off the hook. I had to admit that I was looking for ways to stay off a more delicate subject.

Skip shook his head. "Unmarked. Oliver never had a registered gun. It was a small factor in the decision to look further." He paused. "Can we go back to Uncle Ken for a minute?" Skip asked.

"I don't know."

Buzzz.

I jumped, then took a long breath and settled down. The doorbell ring was a single, short burst, leading me to the good guess that it was Beverly, who knew Maddie would be sleeping nearby and wouldn't want to disturb her.

Skip let his mother in. "Join the party," he said. Decidedly not the term I would have chosen.

Beverly's chatter, usually most welcome, started immediately. "I just dropped Nick off at the airport, and I drove by on the off chance that you were up, and what do you know, the lights were on, and you're up. Plus, even though I'm now without my boyfriend—what do I call him, anyway? The retired cop—I can still have the companionship of my son, the cop, besides that of my best friend." By now she had reached the living room and embraced me. "I think I told you Nick was going to Seattle for a family thing. I didn't go because I needed some quality time with my own family."

Beverly finished her entrance in the kitchen where she took a bottled water from the fridge. It was true that we hadn't spent as much time together as usual this fall since she and Nick had taken a couple of weeklong vacations to visit Nick's far-flung relatives, but on my better days I felt nothing but delight that she and Nick had found each other.

Tonight was the first time since I'd met Beverly, when

she was a teenager getting ready for college, that I felt awkward around her. I dreaded telling her (or not) about Ken. The two had doted on each other all their lives. Beverly was born with a heart defect, causing her big brother to be even more solicitous of her. Ken's prestige in his profession was a source of great pride for his sister; his death was a great loss to her. His good name was as important to her as it was to me.

The same was true for the other brother-sister pair who came to mind. Oliver Halbert and Susan Giles. I wondered if Susan had been told the status of her brother's case—and that of his good name.

I tuned in to my present-day living room in time to hear Beverly's question to Skip.

"Are you here on business?" she asked him.

He pointed to his plate, now a collection of cracker and cookie crumbs mixed with the peels from his orange and traces of its juice. "I came to eat."

For a dizzy moment, I saw the curvy orange peels as the face of a pumpkin, the scattered seeds located where eyes should be, the clear juice its blood. I shook my head and shuddered.

To my dismay, out of the corner of my eye, I saw that Beverly had caught the moment.

"Okay," she said, opening her palms in surrender. She heaved a loud sigh. "Am I missing something here? I know I didn't talk to you much this week, but how much could have happened in a couple of days?"

I knew Beverly was also aware that I'd never answered her question at dinner: was something wrong? I wasn't sure when I'd be able to respond, unless it was when I could say with certainty, "No, everything's fine."

That moment wasn't now, for sure.

Skip stood up, pushed his sleeve back, and tapped his

watch. "This is no time for a party, I guess. I'm out of here. Come on, Mom. I'll escort you to your car and even follow you home with lights and siren."

Beverly looked at me. "Gerry?"

"Skip's right. It's time for bed," I said. I yawned and hoped it looked real.

With a three-way standoff, there was nothing to do but say good night.

I'd been in bed only a few minutes when my phone rang. I picked it up quickly, since there would be an extension ringing also in Maddie's room.

"I've been trying to reach you all day, Gerry." Susan's normal voice was back, with its pleasant southern lilt. I appreciated it less at this hour. "Did you hear the news about Oliver? I'm so relieved."

It was a sad commentary on recent affairs—learning that Oliver had been murdered was what it had taken to give Susan some relief. I was sure her satisfaction had to do with her desire for justice for her brother. It also said a lot to me about how we viewed our loved ones and how we wanted others to view them. That Oliver was a victim was more acceptable to his sister than thinking he'd given up on life—on her.

"I'm glad the police came through for you, Susan."

"Me, too. And I'm sure you had something to do with it."

"Not really."

"I just wanted to be sure you know that I still want you on the case," she said, not acknowledging my confession.

Wasn't the term "on the case" reserved for sworn officers of the law? Susan and Maddie needed a lesson or two in the way the criminal justice system worked. Detective Skip Gowen would be happy to enlighten them.

"I don't think it's either necessary or wise for me to do anything about the investigation," I said, though I realized my half-asleep monotone couldn't be too convincing.

I had no intention of bringing up her brother's less noble pursuits, recently come to my attention, and was surprised when Susan introduced the subject herself.

"Is it because of what they're saying? My brother was not a criminal, Gerry."

Was Susan referring to Oliver's DUI, the insurance fraud charges against him that were dismissed, or the way he'd gained his city inspector job?

"Some of it seems to go back a long way, Susan."

"I know. I probably should have told you, but I figured if I did, you wouldn't bother with his case."

"It's hard to work without all the facts," I said. Susan didn't have to know that I hadn't spent as much as five minutes with the facts (and a key that would open doors) that I did have.

Before she let me try to sleep, Susan extracted a promise that I would at least go to Oliver's apartment, reclaim the room box, and look about, as she put it.

I turned over and wondered how long I'd be "looking about" at the clock on my nightstand.

Lying in bed early Sunday morning, I tried to come up with a plan to make the day constructive in some way.

I heard Maddie shuffling around in the kitchen. I pictured her in her mottled brown T. rex slippers with their large open-jawed heads, long tails, and short arms. They barely fit her anymore unless she crushed the back with the heels of her adult-size feet, but she'd rescued them from the trash more than once when Mary Lou tried to get rid of them. To keep them safe, she left them at my house, where she knew her grandmother would never do anything to make her unhappy.

Except for today, when I had to dispose of her in some way so that I could do my clandestine police work. I didn't feel I could impose on Henry two days in a row. Besides, Taylor had mentioned going to a birthday party today for someone in her class. Maddie, whose school life was ten miles away, not surprisingly hadn't been invited. I thought of calling my crafter friend, Linda Reed, but I knew Maddie would be bored since Linda was very fussy about who touched her miniature projects.

"Dollhouses are not for kids," she'd famously said at one of our meetings.

Rrring. Rrring.

I'd lost track of the number of times a phone call had come to my rescue this week. Here was one more to add to the total.

"I have an idea," Beverly said. I marveled at her generosity, that she didn't hold a grudge after last night's near snub. "I think what we all need is a day of fun. We could go to a museum or a dollhouse store."

Beverly wasn't that much into miniatures, notwithstanding the fact that she always oohed and aahed at the right times when Maddie and I showed her the fruits of our labor. I was touched that she was bending over backward to get things back to normal.

"Well—"

"Before you say no, let me remind you about the Rachel Whiteread show in San Francisco. Wouldn't that be great to see? Huh?"

My sister-in-law and best friend knew my weak spot, all right. I'd been talking about Whiteread, the British artist, ever since I'd read about her exhibit, Place, consisting of nearly two hundred handmade dollhouses arranged to replicate a hillside village. I'd heard from people who'd seen it, however, not to expect a sweet country scene. The doll-houses were empty and run down, lit with bare bulbs in some cases, red lamps in others, leaving the viewer with the experience of having visited a haunted, abandoned village.

It sounded perfect for my current mood.

Too bad I hadn't thought of doing something like that for Halloween, instead of building just one ordinary haunted house.

"I definitely want to see the exhibit before it goes on the road again, Beverly. But you know what would work better for me today?"

"What?" she asked, followed by a pause too short for me to answer. Then, "Say no more. What time shall I pick up the little princess?"

Clearly Beverly was open to doing anything for the sake of family unity. No wonder I loved her. No wonder it was tearing me up to keep things from her.

When I was finally brave enough to go into the kitchen to give Maddie the news about her day, she'd already poured out her cold cereal and had taken the orange juice out for me.

"I can make you some oatmeal, Grandma," she said, making me feel even more guilty about what I had to tell her.

I kissed her head, then pulled my robe tight around my body. "That would be nice, sweetheart. I love oatmeal on chilly mornings."

"I know."

She measured out two helpings of oats and water and went to work. I watched her movements, T. rex's jaw flop-

ping as she went from the counter to the stove. My granddaughter was grown-up enough to be trusted around a gas
flame, but still wore the slippers from her sixth birthday.

"Did you have a good sleep?" I asked her. Small talk
before the big announcement.

"Uh-huh. Uncle Skip was here last night, wasn't he?"

Her comment took me by surprise. I'd thought I was
home free. "What makes you think so?"

"I saw his car when I got up to go to the bathroom."

"Do you always look out the window when you get up
for the bathroom?"

"I do when I'm here." Point taken. "I wanted to come
out, but I was so tired I just flopped back into bed."

"That's good."

"Did he know about Mr. Halbert being a jailbird?"

"Yes, he did."

"Nuts." She ground the spatula into the pan and then
whipped the oatmeal into obedience. "I'll have to find out
something else. What are we doing today?"

"I need to talk to you about that."

Then I ducked.

Beverly came and whisked Maddie away. She'd been as
grumpy a little princess as I expected when she received
the news in my kitchen, but I knew she loved Beverly and
would never let on that she didn't want to go with her aunt
to San Francisco where she'd be entertained by sea lions
and street performers.

I noticed she took her laptop with her.

Chapter 8

Sundays were limited. Factories weren't open, so I couldn't visit the Ferguson twins' place of business; construction sites were abandoned, so talking to Patrick Lynch was out of the question. The key to the late Oliver Halbert's apartment rattled around in my head. Did I dare enter Oliver's home in broad daylight? He'd lived in an old complex on Hanks Road, only a few hundred yards from where he was found dead on the Fergusons' porch. I thought it better to wait until dark when I'd attract less attention. I didn't know his neighbors or how interested they were in the comings and goings in their building, even by someone with a key.

What was left? Where could I go on my day free of worry about Maddie?

An image flitted by. The crime scene. I'd meant to ask Skip if Oliver had indeed been killed on the stoop or placed there later. In any case, a visit to the Fergusons' home was the best idea I could come up with.

When I finally got back to thinking beyond what had been occupying my mind for the last two days—that my husband may have kept secrets from me—I realized I had no idea where the Fergusons had been during the murder, or what they knew about it. I hadn't asked Skip nor tracked it down in any way. I'd been selfishly turned inward, to what affected me most.

It was time to reach out.

I decided to take a gift to Lillian Ferguson. I'd make something special and also search my supply drawers and put together a collection of miniature accessories suitable for the Victorian-style dollhouse she'd bought at one of our crafts fairs.

Miniaturists always knew the style of dollhouse their friends and neighbors owned, just as Henry could tell me what kind of wood was used for the banisters in his friends' homes, and my nephew knew what kind of car everyone drove.

Taken as a group, my crafter friends and I would likely be able to rattle off all the dollhouses that populated Lincoln Point: Carolyn, the hairdresser, had a brown-and-cream Tudor, made from a kit she'd bought online; Isabelle, who worked in a supermarket one town over, had built a lovely Cape Cod from scratch; Patricia, a real estate agent in Gail's firm, was decorating a French peasant farmhouse handed down from her great aunt. We could go on.

My crafts table was a refuge in times of stress. During Ken's long struggle to stay alive, whenever I wasn't by his side at the hospital, I was here, making tiny things that gave me great pleasure. Focusing on the construction of miniature books and lamps gave me direction when I was at loose ends, searching for meaning in horrible life-size events.

I reached for a new Flower Soft kit I'd bought for making tiny stalks of flowers. I spread butcher paper on my table and laid out the materials: three plastic pots with colored foam bits, one yellow, one pink, and one lavender; strips of narrow, flexible wire; a container of high-tack glue. Fifteen minutes later, I had my special item for Lillian: a spray of variegated pink flowers wrapped in tissue and tied with a tiny pink bow.

I rummaged around and found a small box with varying lengths of trim and fringe that I'd torn off a swatch book. An interior design store on Springfield Boulevard had gone out of business and thrown away large books of samples for draperies, valances, cords, and other trimmings. It must have been a strange sight for anyone watching Maddie and me as we came upon the pile of books next to the store's trash bins and lunged for them.

I prepared a small (but not miniature) basket with the newly made flowers, plus trims, beads, and laces to take to Lillian. Just a friendly gesture from a concerned neighbor who heard about the terrible incident at their home. If further talk of Oliver Halbert's murder followed, so be it.

As I rounded the corner from Gettysburg Boulevard to Sangamon River Road, I half expected that Sangamon would be clear of Halloween decorations, in deference to the awful event of this weekend. I noticed that the Fergusons' home and environs were bare. The front lawn was clear—gone were the skulls, critters, and RIP headstones we'd seen on Friday. But on the rest of the street there seemed to be even more orange, black, and neon green paraphernalia than ever, perhaps inspired by the real-life spookiness that had visited them.

It was a little before ten o'clock in the morning when I

parked in front of the Fergusons' house. I sat in my car and gazed at the porch, now looking clean and safe in the bright October sun. The shadows cast on the lawn seemed light and nonthreatening; the breezes that lifted fallen leaves had a benign rhythm to them. It was hard to imagine that a lifeless Oliver Halbert had dominated the scene only two days ago, and that now his personal life and his secrets, and that of many others, would be exposed in all their nastiness for everyone to see and talk about.

I tried to remember why I'd thought it would be a good idea to come here. My recollection of the last time I was here brought on a chill and the sense of darkness on the street. How quickly my mood could change. Was I here only for Susan? So that I'd be able to give her some kind of report? Or did I have my own secret need to explore the mystery?

I'd seen official Lincoln Point police reports through the years since Skip had been a cop. In his early years, he'd ask me to look them over for grammar before he submitted them. I never asked if that practice was sanctioned, but I'd taken it upon myself to simply be sure his tenses were consistent and that he had no spelling or grammatical errors. I kept whatever I read confidential.

If I wrote up a report on my activities this morning, what would I say? *At ten hundred hours I was dispatched to Number Three-six-four-six Sangamon River Road in search of information regarding . . .*

I was reluctant to fill in the blank—that I was here as much for Ken and Beverly as for Susan and Oliver. The cases seemed to intersect at the Fergusons'—at Sam and Lillian's home and at Eliot and Emory's factory—making this visit as good a place to start as any.

End of narrative, as the police reports always said in closing.

I shook my head clear and got out of the car. I trudged up the walkway and climbed the porch steps, keeping as far as possible from the left-hand side, where Oliver's body had been perched.

Not that I was nervous or superstitious.

"Well, Geraldine Porter, what a nice surprise," Lillian Ferguson said. "Sam is out playing golf. He'll be sorry he missed you."

I followed the short, matronly Lillian into a comfortable living room decorated in an English country style. Floral designs covered the chairs, the wallpaper, the curtains, the scatter rugs, and even the lampshades. Her flowery house-dress blended in so well I wondered if she'd made every-thing herself, from the same enormous bolt of fabric. I wanted badly to see how she'd furnished her Victorian doll-house and where it was located. Whatever the circum-stances, it seemed, I was a miniaturist at heart.

I handed Lillian the gift basket. "I collected a few little trims that might work well in your Victorian," I said, imag-ining my forehead emblazoned with the word "busybody."

A model hostess, Lillian made tea and put out a plate (with a floral pattern) of sugar cookies. She sat down and picked up the basket. She lifted the floral spray, wrapped in light pink tissue, by its tip.

She adjusted her glasses and examined the flowers with her fingers. "The glue is still a bit wet," she said, looking up at me with a smile. "You made it this morning, especially for me?"

"Just for you, thinking of your dollhouse. It might need to sit in the sun for a few minutes to dry completely, but it won't fall apart."

"I'm touched," she said, placing the tiny spray on the

coffee table. She turned her attention back to the basket and hooked a short, chubby finger onto a four-inch-long section of loops of fringe in different shades of blue. "This is lovely, too. I know just where I'm going to use it. It will be perfect for the window at the end of the long hallway on the second floor."

I nodded, knowing exactly where in the dollhouse she meant. "I noticed you took down your Halloween decorations," I said, then thought I should have waited a little longer to move into an unpleasant topic.

"Yes, it did seem inappropriate to have anything festive or holiday-ish around the house. But we offered to be on the judging committee instead, and that way the Prebles can enter the contest this year. Not that anyone is really in a mood to celebrate, but it's for the children, you know—they look forward to it."

Maybe "for the children" explained the escalation of decorations in the neighborhood since Friday. I thought of Maddie's observation that there was one too many houses without decorations on Sangamon this year. "I noticed an extra house on the street that isn't competing," I said, in a gesture toward returning to small talk for a while.

Lillian stiffened. "Yes, the Pattersons have gone dark." She bowed her head. "Their son was the janitor who was killed in the fire that erupted in our factory last year."

I winced. I'd gone from bad to worse, reminding Lillian of a family who might be planning a lawsuit against her boys. "How awful. I read about that, but I didn't know they lived on this street." *And I didn't mean to bring it up.*

Lillian had her own way of dealing with awkward moments. She picked a five-square-inch carpet swatch from the basket I'd given her. "I think this will go nicely in the upstairs hallway, don't you? Not everything has to be a print."

I heartily agreed with her choice of placement for the swatch.

"You know, you didn't have to bring me anything, Geraldine," she continued. "I would have been glad to talk to you, anyway." She replaced the plain green carpet swatch. "I assume you're here about that boy's murder?"

"Was it a murder?" I asked, blushing at having been outed and at pretending ignorance of the nature of Oliver's demise, which I didn't know was common knowledge already.

"That's what my boys tell me. You remember Eliot and Emory?"

It made sense that to Lillian, who was close to either side of eighty, I guessed, men in their forties could still be considered "boys."

"Of course I remember the twins. They were among ALHS's star pupils." A slight exaggeration, which was called for, I felt. The boys were no more than about a B or B-minus each. "Did you or your boys know Oliver Halbert very well?"

Lillian put her cup down and folded her hands on her lap. She spoke softly. "We did have dealings with the man now and then since he had an oversight job and my boys are in business. I didn't pay much attention, but I think Mr. Halbert was going back and forth about my boys. First he said they were not to blame for that fire. The one that killed Andrew, the Pattersons' son, poor soul. But there was talk that he was opening up another grievance against E&E Parts. We didn't know what to think."

"It seems Mr. Halbert had called quite a few people under his scrutiny," I said. *Including my husband.*

"Yes, it makes you wonder," Lillian said, with a knowing roll of her eyes, just before she took a sip of tea.

"I was concerned that you might have been here, right in

the house when Oliver Halbert was killed. It's frightening
how close you might have come to being hurt yourselves."
I tsk-tsked.

I had had genuine concern for Lillian and Sam when I'd
been standing in front of the crime scene that was their
porch. But sitting with Lillian now, I was convinced the
murder had hardly touched her, physically or emotionally.
Had she hated Oliver Halbert so much for giving her boys
grief that she was glad he was dead? Had her boys done
anything to facilitate his death? It wasn't such a wild
thought.

Lillian tsked back, smoothing the cotton fabric of her
old-fashioned housedress. "Imagine our shock when the
police called us and we came home to that yellow tape."

"I'm sure it was horrible for you. I was here, out on the
sidewalk, as I'm sure you know, and I must apologize for
not attempting to see if you were home at the time. I had my
granddaughter with me, and there were teenagers who had
discovered Oliver's body. I was trying to keep everyone
safe and in tow. It was upsetting to all of us."

"I can imagine the state you were in. Not to worry about
it. We were all safe and sound at the factory."

"I must have been gone by the time you got home." I
sipped my tea. "And I suppose you have no idea why he
was killed—or at least left—on your porch?"

Lillian stiffened. "Of course not. We were all at the boys'
factory," she repeated. "Did you know that Sam and I still
work there a couple of days a week? I answer phones and
do the filing and the payroll. Sam"—she chuckled—"works
in the shop and thinks he's in charge of it, too. He's always
loved being around machines. It's nice to keep it all in the
family."

"It sounds like an ideal arrangement."

Clunking footsteps disturbed the otherwise quiet house.

A man in a blue windbreaker appeared, galloping down the steps that led to the front door. His gait indicated that he might have gotten a running start from an upstairs landing. Hanging over his left arm was a large amount of black fabric.

"Hi, Mrs. Porter," the man said, waving and moving at the same time. The black fabric swung over the banister and back. "'Bye, Mom. I'm late."

The man was traveling too quickly for me to determine whether he had a limp or not, but from the formal address to me, I assumed it was Eliot, my former student.

"Bye-bye, dear," Lillian said, offering no help in identifying her son.

"Was that—?" I began.

"My boys are always on the go," Lillian interrupted. "They don't mean to be rude. It takes a lot of hard work and dedication to run a small business these days." She gave me an indulgent smile. "Eliot is taking my Halloween costume to the factory. We're having our little party there as usual. For the children."

"Of course."

"It's not a very splashy event, especially this year. We invite our customers and a few friends. You're welcome to bring your little granddaughter."

"Thank you, Lillian, I just might do that."

Lillian's expression said that wasn't the answer she expected. "As I was saying, Sam and I were there at the factory with our boys the whole day on Friday." *Was this the third time she'd mentioned that?* "I think Eliot may have left for five minutes to pick up sandwiches, right around the corner in that new strip mall. You know we're way at the edge of town at the new Lynch Business Circle."

I knew the area. "Formerly the site of the defunct Lincoln Point airport," I said.

"That airport was a bad idea from the start. The county people thought it would ease the traffic in and out of the San Jose airport and bring Lincoln Point some revenue, but the plan didn't work. They didn't have sufficient parking, for one thing, nor enough commitments from airlines who'd agree to use the facility. And who wants to land in Lincoln Point anyway?"

I laughed. "That's a good question."

"But it's an ideal location for the factory, away from town, where noise and deliveries at all hours won't wake anyone up. And by the way, Emory didn't leave at all on Friday. He was doing repairs on some radar units the navy sent them."

If I didn't know better, I'd say Lillian was giving her family an alibi.

Once I'd had all the tea and talking in circles I could take, I left Lillian and walked to my car. To my disappointment, Sangamon River Road was still deserted. I'd been hoping to run into a neighbor or two and casually conduct interviews. Had anyone seen a stranger walking around on Friday? Or a resident walking a dog? Was someone carrying a gun? Any strange noises? (Other than the howling jack-o'-lanterns and screeching bedsheet witches scattered throughout the street.) Were any arguments or fights heard in the late afternoon?

I knew that the police would have canvassed the area already; I was going to have to be happy with their work. Skip would be pleased to know I appreciated him and his colleagues.

There was nothing more I could do, no one to question, not even a child on a bike or a homeowner mowing his lawn.

If only pumpkins had ears or witches could talk.

Double, double toil and trouble; Fire burn, and cauldron bubble.

I drove down Hanks Road, slowing as I passed the building complex Oliver had lived in. With nothing more brilliant coming to mind, I'd decided to risk a daylight entry into his apartment.

Oliver's building was as quiet this morning as the rest of this east-side neighborhood. I checked the numbers on the sign and saw that his apartment was in the back. All the better chance that my entering (not breaking, since I had his key, I reasoned) would go unnoticed even in daylight. Still, I thought I needed a little fortification first and kept driving farther down the road where there was a coffee shop. Seward's Folly, on the corner of Hanks Road and Springfield Boulevard, would offer a treat I felt I deserved.

Newcomers to Lincoln Point questioned the wisdom of naming a business establishment after a government purchase that was ridiculed at the time—the acquisition of Alaska from Russia by Abraham Lincoln's secretary of state, William Seward. All's well that ends well, however, and ultimately, with the discovery of gold, the deal was seen as a wise one. Though the purchase was made after Lincoln's death, when Seward was under President Andrew Johnson, Lincoln Point natives always gave Abe the credit for appointing Seward in the first place.

Seward's Folly (the shop, not the deal) had been a favorite of mine in the days before Maddie and her family moved up north from Los Angeles. Now I went more often to Sadie's Ice Cream Shop or Bagels by Willie, where there were more attractive choices for an eleven-year-old.

I walked into the shop and saw the reason for the deserted streets. Everyone was here. Milling around were dozens of people—some dressed as if for church, a couple of groups of sweatshirt-clad teens chattering loudly, and several uniformed workers, from EMTs to fast-food servers.

I stepped into the winding queue and eyed the case of pastries at the front. It seemed a long time since my granddaughter had served me that double portion of oatmeal for breakfast. I saw only one more bear claw in the case and hoped no one in front of me was after it.

"Did you see the pictures in the paper this morning?" a young woman in black jeans asked her companion. The two women were just ahead of me in line. "They showed the guy who was killed right over on Sangamon."

"Yeah, that was awful," the second woman said. "Someone shot him in the head."

"That was us," said one of the EMTs in front of them, a tall, fair-haired man who looked strong enough to take the entire rack of special coffees and aromatic teas in his arms and lift them off the floor.

The young women giggled.

"He means we took that call," said the other, smaller EMT. "Not that we shot the guy." The partners nudged each other playfully.

"Wow," said the first young woman. "I'm Amy and this is my friend, Savannah. Do you get calls like that all the time?"

I thought of joining the conversation (I had questions of my own) until it came to me, just before I embarrassed myself, that Amy and Savannah had deliberately opened the topic as an excuse to chat with the young male EMTs.

I was way out of practice for flirting or even spotting it when it was right before my eyes.

One of the coffee-shop employees, wrapped in an oversize brown apron with *Kayla* embroidered on a white patch, arrived to clean a side counter that held napkins, accoutrements to coffee, and four different kinds of milk products.

She'd clearly overheard the foursome and wanted to add her bit. "I hope you catch the guy who did it," she said to the EMTs. "We all liked Ollie."

The young men nodded and muttered something that made it sound as though they had the inside scoop, with phrases like "we're all over it" and "the dude that did it won't be on the street for long."

Since when did EMTs investigate crime? Since the LPPD began using retired English teacher/miniaturists?

"Ollie was in here all the time, you know," Kayla said. "He lived right down the street. It's awful what happened. When I heard they killed him right on the porch where his friends' 'rents live . . ." She stopped pouring chocolate powder into a shaker bottle and stared off in the distance. "He always got the coffee of the day, with room."

Thanks to my granddaughter, I knew that "'rents" had nothing to do with leasing homes but was special parlance for "parents"; and thanks to my own past history of frequenting coffee shops on both coasts, I knew a little café-speak: "with room" meant for the barista to leave room in the cup for the customer to add milk or cream.

More important, if I could believe Kayla, I'd just learned that the Ferguson twins and Oliver had been friends, not, as Lillian put it, someone with whom they had business dealings now and then. Was this a case of a parent not knowing who her sons' friends were, even when the children were middle-aged? I doubted it, since, according to Lillian herself, she was still active in their business.

I guessed instead that Lillian's sweet, flowery housedress was meant to mask her sharp mind and canniness.

"There wasn't too much blood this time," said one of the EMTs, in an attempt to bring the conversation and the women's attention back to themselves.

Amy (or Savannah) shuddered. "Eeew. I don't think I could do a job like yours," she said, looking up in admiration.

"He and those twins came in a lot," Kayla said. Her turn for attention. I wondered if I were witnessing a double date in the making, with the two EMTs and the knowledgeable Kayla acing out either Amy or Savannah.

I felt like a person from another planet listening in on a conversation among young earthlings.

Kayla wasn't finished. "Like, that same day, one of the twins was in here with him. I never can tell them apart unless I see them walking because one of them has this limp." Kayla gave a brief demonstration of a limp, taking two awkward steps to the other end of the counter.

I took my eyes off the bear claw, still safe in the case, on its doily, after three more customers' choices, and not worrying about the appropriateness, jumped in. "Excuse me, are you talking about one of the Ferguson twins?"

Kayla looked surprised to see me, but answered as if her tip depended on it. "Uh-huh. They're regulars, too. Their 'rents—uh, mom and dad—live around the corner."

I wanted to inform her that I was cool (wicked?), that I knew what 'rents were, but I had bigger issues to press. "So, Oliver and one of the twins were in here on Friday? Can you be sure it wasn't Thursday, for example?"

I studiously ignored the rest of the group, who seemed to be trying to identify that strange planet I'd come from.

"Uh-huh," Kayla said more forcefully. "I didn't work on Thursday, and I don't work on Saturdays. It was Friday. It's hard to tell them apart, but it was probably Eliot, the one who lives with his parents now. They were in here around lunchtime. We started having those premade sandwiches, you know, and they're very popular. Then, next thing you know I saw Oliver's picture in the paper."

Amy and Savannah had stepped to the counter, losing interest in Kayla, me, and even the EMTs, who were now checking their wallets and deciding whose turn it was to pay.

I hoped I wasn't responsible for nipping a romance or two in the bud.

I was lucky enough to nab the last bear claw and a free corner table. I needed to process not only the information I'd just gleaned, but also how reliable its source was. How much should I trust a young barista in the midst of a coed game of one-upmanship with her peers?

Lillian was too wise a lady to feed me a line that could be checked out this easily, even serendipitously by a casual observer.

It was interesting also that Lillian had failed to mention that one of her boys lived with her. Not an unusual situation these days with many people trying to economize, but I would have expected Lillian to bring it up while she was accounting for her twins' whereabouts. Did she think I might suspect Eliot of the murder, simply because he lived there?

I sipped my excellent "double decaf mocha extra whipped" and did a mental calculation. The Ferguson plant was at the south end of Lincoln Point, past the Nolin Creek Pines housing project, at least a couple of miles from the coffee shop. I stared down at two identical slices of almond atop my bear claw. Which twin had left the property to come into town for lunch with Oliver Halbert? Or to make a stop at the 'rents house? It didn't matter, since Lillian had said neither was gone from the factory for more than a few minutes to pick up sandwiches.

I ate the almonds with some delicacy and then took a large bite of the bear claw.

Was Lillian's memory going, or did one of her boys just lose his alibi?

Either way, Skip should know about my morning. I thought I might as well wait until after I'd done a quick tour in Oliver's apartment, picked up the room box, then I'd report to both Skip and Susan.

I wondered if Skip would believe that my motive for visiting Lillian was purely neighborly? Probably not. The irony was that I'd learned more when I was merely on a coffee break.

Was this why cops hung around coffee shops?

Chapter 9

I parked in front of Oliver Halbert's apartment building and dug out the key Susan had given me. I sat for a while, finishing off the rest of the mocha, getting the lay of the land. All around me was another deserted street.

My excursions today put me in mind of my years in New York. Ken and I would take the subway into Manhattan often and marveled that even the city that never slept was quiet once a week—only on Sunday morning, and only if you stayed away from St. Patrick's Cathedral. Maybe it had to do with the angle of the solar system.

I swallowed the last bit of mocha and went to work.

Oliver's one-bedroom apartment was sparsely furnished, as I imagined most bachelor domiciles to be. A nasty orange couch, two army green chairs, and a coffee table with a slightly slanted top dominated the living room and looked to have been purchased at a church rummage sale. Though freshly painted, the walls were a tired cream color with dull brown baseboards. An ugly paisley area rug was no more tasteful than the furniture. If I received this as a room box, I thought, I'd remodel and preserve only the strip of hardwood flooring around the perimeter of the living room.

I'd entered the apartment relatively easily, walking down a side alley, past several sets of rubbish containers and up an outside flight of concrete steps.

Before entering, I'd put on a pair of rubber crafts-work gloves—there was always a box of them in my car. (You never knew when a mini repair job would be necessary.) I had no idea why it mattered that I didn't leave fingerprints today, since I could rightly claim that this was a solicited visit from the deceased occupant's closest relative.

The most attractive feature in Oliver's living room was the small room box Susan had made for her brother in half-scale (one foot of real space represented by one-half inch in the room box). Susan had modeled the interior of a home construction site, to represent Oliver's profession. The whole box measured just eight inches long (as if it were sixteen feet in real life), five inches deep, and four inches high.

"If I make it too big, he might just toss it," she'd said at our crafts meeting, by way of explaining her choice of scale. Since she asked me to take it back to her now that Oliver had passed on, I assumed she knew that her brother had not discarded the gift. The box was the only decoration in the apartment other than a few photographs. The scene was in a prime spot on a scantily populated bookshelf, visible as soon as one entered the combination living room and dining room. I made a mental note to remember to tell Susan how prominently the box was displayed.

Susan had done some of the work on the room box with our group on crafts nights. I remembered how we'd all taken a turn at grating scraps of balsa wood to make sawdust, and at painting and laying miniature bricks (small pieces of foam board painted red) for the unfinished fireplace on the left wall of the box.

I admired the fine detail in the room box scene, from the planks of wood on a sawhorse to the scraps on the floor. A tiny surveying instrument stood on a tripod and various tools lay on the many surfaces. Maddie had been taken especially by the miniature hard hats and the tiny black lunch box, its sections spread open to display a one-third-inch-long thermos bottle.

There was one strange addition that I didn't remember seeing when the room box was at our meetings—an extra workbench against one wall. It seemed to be made from found objects—a plastic holder of some kind, painted (not very well) brown, served as the top of the table and a cork from a bottle of wine provided the base. The piece was less polished than the rest of the room, and I thought perhaps the cork had special meaning for Susan and her brother. Though I preferred a rich dessert, I knew Susan's favorite way to celebrate was to "pop a cork," in her words.

In any case, the structure of the table wasn't too surprising, since Susan was like me in that regard, using scraps found around the house to make furniture and accessories. We were both markedly unlike the others in the crafts group, especially Linda, the purist, who would never use a toothpaste tube cover or the cup that came with cough syrup for a lampshade, for example.

I hadn't come here to reminisce about our combined handiwork. Not for the first time, I asked myself—why *had* I come to Oliver Halbert's apartment? Why hadn't I insisted that Susan herself come to get her room box? Had I subconsciously wanted to see the victim's surroundings for myself?

I heard a noise outside and carried the tiny room box to the small window that overlooked the alleyway. There was still not much traffic, either foot or vehicular, except two young Asian women who might have been nannies pushing strollers with Caucasian babies along the sidewalk.

Directly below me, however, a black car pulled up near the gate leading into the alley. So as not to be conspicuous in Oliver's complex, I'd parked across the street, but this driver had taken the car as far as he possibly could to the bottom step without squeezing down the alley, crashing into the trash containers, and knocking off his side mirrors.

Two men, one tall and one short, exited the car. I had no reason to think they would head for this apartment, but I sincerely hoped not. What if they were friends of Oliver, come to visit, not knowing of his death? I didn't want to be the one to deliver the news. I had to admit that wasn't the only reason I willed the men to be connected to a different address in the complex—I didn't want to be found snooping, though I had every right to be here.

Something about the way the men walked caused an inexplicable wave of fear to come over me and I felt trapped in the small space, as if I wouldn't be able to leave without being seen and captured, and I wouldn't be able to stay without fainting from the bleak décor and the deadly silence.

He did the mash. He did the monster mash.

The music startled me. The sudden sound added to my stressful state and threw me so far off balance that I dropped the room box, which was partway back to its position on Oliver's bookshelf. I'd planned to take a brief look around the rest of the apartment, then come back for the room box and take it to my car.

The box hit the windowsill and landed on the hardwood floor. I cringed.

He did the mash. He did the monster mash.

The deep voice of Bobby "Boris" Pickett came from my cell phone. Maddie had programmed "Monster Mash" for my cell phone ring of the month of October. After thirty days of "School Days," the melody for September, I'd been ready for the classic Halloween song.

My hands were shaking so badly, it took both of them to open my phone and take the call. I distracted myself by questioning how eleven-year-olds knew about the hits of the sixties, when their grandparents had still been in high school.

"Hi, Grandma. It's me."

I steadied my breathing. "Hi, sweetheart. Are you having a good time in San Francisco?"

I picked up the broken room box as I talked. The end that had hit the wood floor first was slightly damaged. The side wall had splintered in one spot and several fireplace bricks had come unglued. A calendar with a picture of Rosie the Riveter had fallen from its spot on an unfinished wall. (This was Susan, sending a message to the imaginary construction workers.) The makeshift workbench was intact but loose in its moorings, the painted plastic top looking worse than ever. Susan must have been in a great hurry to have considered it finished.

"First we had breakfast at the Ferry Building." It was a struggle to remember who was on the phone and who might be climbing the outside steps toward me. "And then we shopped outside where there are arts and crafts. But not miniatures, just earrings and paintings and stuff. Nothing interesting." Maddie giggled. "Don't tell my mom I said that, okay?"

"You mean about the paintings not being worth your time, when they're your mom's passion and career?"

"Yeah, that. Now we're walking to Pier Thirty-nine.

Aunt Beverly says it's a long way around the Embarcadero from where we parked, but it's nice out and we didn't want to wait for the bus that takes you here."

"You're walking and talking?"

"Uh-huh. So is Aunt Beverly. She's on her phone with Uncle Nick."

Two people walking side by side, each on her own cell phone—one of the most common scenes on the streets from Lincoln Point to San Francisco. And who was I to talk about multitasking? I was planning the repair on the room box I'd damaged and searching the alley for the new arrivals while I spoke to Maddie.

"Thanks for giving me a report on your day," I said.

"What are you doing? And please don't tell me 'errands.'"

"I'm doing something for a friend. I'm going home soon and I'll be there to greet you when you get back. We'll do something fun." It was nice telling the truth.

"Did you go back to Mr. and Mrs. Ferguson's house?"

"I may have."

"Nuts. You have to save something for me to do, Grandma."

"There's a lot to do before Halloween. We still have to prepare all the witches and the ghosts for the room boxes and decorate the Bronx dollhouse." I thought how my real apartment on the Grand Concourse was about the same size as this one that Oliver had lived in.

"You know what I mean. Something to do on The Case."

Thump, scrape, thump, scrape.

My heart jumped. Footsteps on the outside stairway or walkway, sounding very close. I'd lost track of the men. If I remembered correctly the steps on this side of the building led only to this and one other apartment, with a shared concrete path one level up from the street. I hoped it was Oliver's neighbors who were having company.

No such luck. The footsteps stopped and I heard muffled voices and the rattle of the doorknob to this apartment. I held my breath and noted the sound of a key in the lock.

"Sorry, sweetheart. I have to go," I whispered to Maddie.

The last words I heard before pushing the power button off and clicking the phone shut were, "Are you somewhere you shouldn't be, Grandma?" Maddie was the master of the accusatory tone. It was a good thing I was still bigger than my granddaughter; I couldn't imagine how intimidated I'd have been otherwise.

I stuffed the room box into my tote lest its condition give away my presence. I tiptoed to the back where the bedroom and bath were.

It sounded like two men had entered the living room. I heard two voices and got a whiff of aftershave with an acidy edge to it. The odor, which probably wouldn't have been offensive any other time, caused my stomach to lurch. I had another unwanted taste or two of my mocha, then of my bear claw. I felt a chill in spite of my sweater and the comfortable temperature in the apartment.

When was I going to learn to keep out of Cases, with a capital C?

"What are we looking for, Boss?" one man asked. A somewhat weak voice.

"Anything that connects us," the other man said. A strong, deep voice.

"Like . . . ?"

"What do you think?" An annoyed voice. "Papers or notebooks or computer disks, stuff like that."

"Got it, Boss."

I had only moments to make a decision. To hide or not to hide? My prospects for staying hidden were looking dimmer and dimmer. The bed was a double futon that took up most of the room and sat on the floor with not so much as six inches to crawl under. I got down on my knees to inspect the area behind the bed, coming in direct contact with the dusty brown baseboards. I saw no space to hide even a pair of slippers.

I moved to inspect the bathroom—tiny, barely large enough for one person to move around in. If anyone opened the door, there I would be.

Oliver's apartment was even more like our tiny Grand Concourse residence than I'd thought at first. Like our former Bronx home, there was no closet here, but simply a narrow alcove, deep enough for a hanger, with no room to spare, covered by a thin curtain on a rod.

"Take the desk," the man in charge said. "Make sure you check under the drawers, too. I'm going to look for a computer."

"The police took it, remember?"

"Maybe there's another one."

I stood still but swallowed so hard, I thought the men might hear my gulp. I hadn't seen a computer in the living room. How did the man know that the police had already been here and taken it? Did he have a connection with the LPPD as I did? Probably not, I decided; he said it because it would be a matter of course these days. What were the chances one or both of the men would look here in the bedroom for a second computer or another desk where Oliver might have kept papers? Very good, I decided.

The door between the rooms was wide open, held there by a brick doorstop. There was no choice other than to make myself known, to act as though I belonged here. I could be part of the cleaning crew, or the landlady. I'd play it cool, as Maddie might have said before she switched to "wicked." I didn't want my appearance to be too much of a surprise to the men, so I deliberately made noise as I marched across the bedroom and reached the threshold between the bedroom and the living room.

So much of my attention went into that move that I tripped on the edge of the ugly paisley rug and fell into the living room, knocking my head on the brick doorstop.

The living room, as seen from the floor, spun full circle.

Then I tasted loose threads from Oliver's dingy rug and all was black.

I woke up lying on the ugly orange couch, with a splitting headache, and with what Skip would call "goons" sitting in the awful green chairs, which they'd pulled close together.

Where was Skip anyway? How long had I been here? I didn't want to know how I'd gotten to this position. The questions poured from my tired brain. Why hadn't anyone come looking for me? How come when I took a little nap in my own home, everyone missed me, but now that I was virtually kidnapped by two strange men in a strange apartment, no one noticed? The men were dressed as counter opposites: the taller man wore a beige sports coat and tie, the other man wore jeans and a denim jacket. Neither was especially large, but both frightened me.

And thinking of the police, why hadn't I called Skip before coming to Oliver's apartment? I could have had him meet me here. It wasn't as if I were planning an illegal entry. He'd have understood why Susan wanted me to come. My police detective nephew could have been pulling up at the curb right now. My own arrogance (stupidity?) had brought me to this end.

I looked across the room to the window. It was still light out, so perhaps I hadn't been here that long. When I tried to

sit up, the room traveled clockwise, stopped, and spun coun-
terclockwise. My head fell back down on the dirty, smelly
orange pillow. I'd fainted only two or three times in my life,
so I didn't have a good measure of when I could expect to
be back to normal.

Or if I could expect to leave Oliver's apartment alive.

I looked at the men, sitting in a relaxed position on the
chairs. The shorter one was so relaxed that his denim jacket
had fallen open to reveal the butt of a gun.

I felt another wave of nausea and tried to convince myself that if they'd wanted to kill me, they'd had their best
chance already. My instinct was to pretend I was still asleep.
For how long? Until they left? I knew that wouldn't work.

"Who are you?" I asked, when I could no longer stand
the silence and the fear that had built up in my mind. It
wasn't lost on me that these men could be Oliver's killers,
but someone had to start the conversation. I took it as a
good sign that the gun wasn't actually pointed at me. Maybe
it was something other than a gun. A tool of some kind. I
could only hope.

"Who are *you*?" the strong voice, from the taller man
asked.

I put together the pieces of what I'd seen and heard before my graceful entry. The strong voice belonged to the
man called "the boss." Good to know the pecking order in
a situation like this.

"I'm a friend of Susan's, Oliver Halbert's sister." My
throat was dry to the point of hurting. I wondered if I dared
ask for a glass of water.

"What are you doing here?" The strong voice again.

I could ask them the same question, but I didn't want to
trigger (so to speak) the appearance of a weapon.

"I came to get some personal items. His sister, my friend,
is not up to the task right now, and she wants to be sure the

landlord doesn't throw everything out before she can get here." I took a deep breath and complimented myself on coming up with a very reasonable story under extraordinary conditions.

"Items?" The boss said the word as if he were sounding it out, about to learn its meaning for the first time. "Like what items?" Again, he pronounced the word "i-tems."

Interrogation was apparently the boss's job, questioning a material witness to their break-in. Except, I recalled they had entered the apartment as I had, with a key. I'd heard it turn in the lock before I scuttled back to the bedroom. Did Susan provide their key, also? Did she lack confidence in me and hire others for the same job? I hoped they were getting paid more than I was.

My deteriorating mental state aside, I had to come up with an answer to the boss's "item" question. "I was in the bedroom looking for a watch and a medal his sister gave him." Not bad for on-the-spot fiction. All those years of reading and teaching composition were paying off. I didn't have a clear idea of why I hadn't owned up to taking the room box, except that I felt it might be too complicated to describe.

"What kind of medal? Like a war medal?" the subordinate asked.

"Nah, she means like a saint's medal," the boss said. "Right?" he asked, as though that had better be the correct answer. Were my captors practicing Catholics? Could I use the famous Catholic guilt to win my freedom? I tried to remember which shoulder came first in making the sign of the cross.

Too late I recalled Skip's advice about lying (make it as simple as possible) and my own when I taught creative writing (use what you know). I wracked my brain for the name of a Catholic saint. "A Saint Jude medal," I said, flashing on the name of the hospital to which I often donated money at the request of friends when their loved ones died. I wondered if that would count as points now.

"Ha, that's a good one. Patron of lost causes," said the shorter man, the nonboss, who laughed until the boss gave him a serious frown and a nudge that also looked serious.

I winced as if my own ribs had been slammed. I hoped I hadn't started a chain of violence. Weren't Catholic saints supposed to bring peace and love?

"Did you find them?"

"Who?" I asked.

"The i-tems. The watch and the medal," the boss said.

Ah, of course. "No, I just got here." I brought out the most sincere smile I could. "Is that what you came for, too? Did Susan send you?" I managed a hollow-sounding chuckle. "That would be just like her, wouldn't it? Wanting to double-check."

Make nice.

The nonboss started to say something, but the boss shot him that look again.

"Mr. Halbert is an associate and we are here looking for property of ours that was in his custody," the boss said.

Apparently real-life goons talked the way movie goons did. They even looked like movie goons, the boss with hardly any hair and a scar across his cheek, the underling with a rose tattoo on the back of his hand. The question was—were they the movie hit men who did the killing, or were they the good guys, ones dispatched to protect the innocent? I thought it best not to ask.

I took another shot at sitting up. The men reacted by putting their right hands on their hips. Were there two guns? Or did they both get an attack of arthritis pain at the same time? In other circumstances I would have been greatly amused. I stayed half up, half down, stuffed into the corner of the orange sofa, much the way Oliver had been sitting on the Fergusons' stoop.

"Did you find what you were looking for?" I asked, to fill the silence.

Another blunder. Had I learned nothing from my nephew? "Guilty people always chatter when there's silence," he'd told me. "My job is to wait them out."

Lucky for me, my captors chose to ignore my question. "Can we help you to your car?" the boss asked.

I nearly jumped from my half-sitting position. "I can go?"

Strike three for what not to do when armed men had the upper hand. A rule to live by: don't give them choices that could work out disastrously for you.

Although I knew I'd flunked the "interview" at every turn, the nonboss handed me my tote. Close up, I could see that the rose in the tattoo design had more thorns than petals.

"You don't mind that we looked in your bag? We had to be sure you didn't take any of our property by mistake," the boss said.

"No, no," I stammered. "That's all right. I just took a broken miniature scene."

"We know."

And you also know who I am if you looked through my bag, I thought. I considered that not good news.

"I'm going to fix the box," I stammered, as if it were his box I'd dropped.

Was there a game that had four strikes, the fourth pertaining to offering unnecessary information to captors who were about to emancipate you?

"We know." Now the boss seemed more anxious for me to leave than I was.

I stood and made a giant effort not to sway. I held my tote in front of me, chest high, wishing it were bulletproof, though it had been a while since I'd actually seen the handle of the gun, if that's what it was. I walked toward the door, slowly, at one point grabbing on to a floor lamp.

The nonboss rushed over to me and put his ugly hand under my elbow to steady me.

"I'm fine, thank you," I said, relieved when his beefy arm dropped to his side.

The men watched in silence as I tottered the rest of the way to the door. I wondered if they were going to shoot me in the back, too cowardly to kill me while looking me in the eyes. Oliver Halbert had been shot by someone facing him, I realized. How frightened he must have been. I shivered at the image.

Only a few more steps and I'd be out the door. Would I hear a gunshot aimed at my back? Or would I be dead before the sound traveled to my ear? What would they do with my body? Prop it up on Oliver's couch?

It was a bad time to remember something Skip told us about after a seminar he'd taken at the police academy. Legislation was being proposed to use a process called alkaline hydrolysis (or something chemical like that) to dispose of human bodies. Animal carcasses had been going this way for many years—burned in lye at a very high temperature and a great deal of pressure in a stainless-steel cylinder. Essentially, they were pressure-cooked, the remains being a syrupy residue that could be flushed down the drain.

I swallowed hard. My family would never find me. I continued walking, clutching my tote, listening for the gunshot.

The loudest noise I heard was the sound of the door closing behind me.

I stumbled into the driver's seat and immediately locked my car doors. I longed to lean back on the seat awhile to catch my breath and steady my nerves, but I also wanted to get out of gunshot range as soon as possible.

I dug in my tote for my keys and found them out of their usual inside pocket. The contents of my tote were all out of order. The coins that had been in my wallet were now loose at the bottom of the bag and the miniature construction site was a bit more banged up. I felt lucky that they were the only things that had been manhandled.

I had the crazy thought that I should have spent my own time in the apartment looking for papers, also, instead of examining a miniature scene that wasn't that different from a hundred others I saw at shows and in my crafts group. Perhaps I would have found more evidence of Oliver's interest in my husband—proof of Ken's absolute innocence of any wrongdoing would have been nice.

All in all, I was glad to be alive and happy that I hadn't been toting anything of interest to the goons.

Chapter 10

In the safety of my home, I curled up on my own handsome, cream-colored sofa with a steaming cup of chamomile
tea. I needed all the soothing I could get.

I toyed with the idea of calling Skip, but what a convo-
luted conversation that would be as I skirted around certain
aspects of my outing. At some point I'd have to tell him
what might simply have been fantasy from the barista at
Seward's Folly. I had nothing to report to Susan, except that
I'd found, broken, and nearly lost the little construction
scene she'd made for her brother. I'd wait until I'd had a
chance to repair the box before I called her.

I missed Maddie. What had I been doing out where I
didn't belong, putting myself in danger for no good reason,
when I should have been enjoying ice cream sundaes and
making orange-and-black garlands with my granddaughter?
If her parents knew how negligent I'd been, they'd probably
take away my visitation rights.

I dug out my cell phone, the closest phone to me, and

pushed speed dial for Maddie. I knew her ring comprised a few notes of a Madonna (the singer, not the Catholic saint) song that was popular when her parents were in junior high. I hummed the few notes in my mind as I waited for Maddie to pick up. Click on? Push talk? I feared I'd never catch up with the changes in common phrases brought about by technology.

"Wow, Grandma, you called me! Wow!" Maddie sounded so excited, I felt even worse about my neglect of her.

"How's your day in the big city?"

"It's okay. We're at Pier Thirty-nine now. It says on the Internet that the temperature here is sixty-three degrees, six degrees below the average high temperature for October in San Francisco."

Poor Maddie. How bored did an eleven-year-old have to be before she memorized weather statistics? Bored was better than "in danger" however. The thought that Maddie might have been with me in Oliver's apartment was too much to contemplate. Guns or no guns, the two men had been scary. I had a strong feeling that if I hadn't fallen and knocked myself out, they might have done it for me.

"How come you're using your computer to look up the weather with all there is to do at Pier Thirty-nine? Isn't there a lookout where you can see lots of sea lions?"

"Yeah, we did that."

"Aren't there jugglers and puppet shows? And the merry-go-round?"

"Please, Grandma. How old do you think I am?"

Apparently, ten years older than she was last year when she seemed to enjoy the entertainment. I pictured Maddie clicking away at her computer while tourists all around her took photos of the marine life and the beautiful hills of Marin County across the bay.

On the other hand, there was Maddie, with access to the Internet. An idea came to me. I tried to brush it away but gave in to it.

"Are you online now, sweetheart?"

"Yeah. It's kind of spotty, but we found this little restaurant with Wi-Fi. Aunt Beverly's in the restroom. But don't worry. There's a whole class of kids here with their teacher and she's keeping an eye on me. I mean, I don't need her eye, but Aunt Beverly made the deal."

"Can you look up a man named Patrick Lynch for me?"

"I already did."

She must not have understood me. "I'm talking about a man who's a businessman, a developer, in Lincoln Point." Not a rock star or a sports figure who may have the same name was what I meant.

"I know. I already found him. He has his own webpage so it makes it easier. I gave up researching Mrs. Giles's brother, because Uncle Skip already knows so much about him, so I switched to that other man you were talking about, Patrick Lynch."

"How did you remember his name?"

She sighed, sounding very tired of having to ask this question. "How old do you think I am?"

Never mind how old she was, my granddaughter was way ahead of every child in her age group. I was sure I was the only grandmother who felt that way. I wondered if there was a bumper sticker with that saying.

Now for the real question. "Was there a photograph of Mr. Lynch? Can you tell me what he looks like?"

"Yeah, there were lots of images. He's kind of gross-looking. He's bald and he has this scar on his cheek."

I swallowed, my suspicion confirmed. Should I feel better or worse that my temporary captor was a respected (by

some) businessman? Worse, I decided, since he was also a
murder suspect in at least two minds, Susan's and mine. I
felt a call to Skip coming on.

"Does that help with The Case, Grandma? Huh?"

"It's a big help, sweetheart. Thank you. You did so well
that now you can go back to enjoying the sea lions because
there's nothing more to do on the case."

"If I was sitting there next to you, you'd tickle me, right?
Because there's still a lot to do, right?"

I thought of asking her to look up Max Crowley also, but
I was fairly sure he was the second man in Oliver's apartment. If I needed to, I could try to find him on my own,
admittedly lame computer.

I glanced at Susan's sorry room box, now on my kitchen
counter, waiting to be moved to the crafts room for repair.
It was going to be hard to work on it without thinking of the
frightening men who'd handled it and of the chance that one
or both of them might be Oliver's murderer. I looked past
the room box toward the door leading to the garage and
pictured the piles of unopened cartons. I thought of Oliver's
list of "potentials for investigation," of his own sullied reputation, and Ken's name on the list. And the most command-
ing image of all, flashing before my eyes—the photographs
of Ken holding someone's baby.

"Right, Grandma?" Maddie repeated. "The investigation
isn't over."

"I mean it, sweetheart. There's nothing more to do," I
said.

Even if Maddie and Beverly left San Francisco immedi-
ately, they wouldn't be home for at least an hour. They'd be
traveling south on the 101 freeway, which was busy all day

long. At one in the afternoon, there was no telling how clogged up the lanes would be in both directions.

Beverly had taken the phone before I hung up with Maddie. "I give up," she said. "I think this was a bad idea. Maddie misses you."

"You mean she misses the action," I said.

"Uh-huh. We'll be home shortly."

I could get a lot done in an hour. The garage beckoned me. What other photographs or memorabilia lurked out there in the boxes that had sat on my shelves for more than five years? I could tear them all open right now and put the whole issue of Ken's other life to rest.

I could also call my nephew for an update. With one sentence he could end my agony—"We checked it all out," he could say, "and Uncle Ken's name was on that list only because he attended a meeting once."

"Whew," I'd say, and move on.

I decided to leave that fantasy alive and called Susan.

"There's nothing much to report," I told her. "Except that the wonderful room box you made for Oliver was in a very special place on his bookshelf. I'm sure you saw it there."

"I didn't visit him as often as I should have, Gerry," Susan said, her voice choking. "I loved my brother, and I didn't do enough for him."

"Nobody ever does, Susan."

I gave Susan a chance to pull herself together, then braced myself for two other things she needed to hear. I told her first how I'd dropped the precious box.

"But I know I can repair it very easily," I said quickly.

"Don't worry about that, Gerry. I can do it myself. I'm glad you took it away. I'd been worried that maybe the police took it or a cleaning person or something. I sure would like to have it. I don't know when I'm going to be able to go back to that apartment. Unless you come with me?"

"What about his daughters?" I asked, not willing to commit to a return visit to the orange couch. I could still taste the sticky fuzz from the carpet though I brushed my teeth and gargled three or four times when I got home.

"Jeanine and Casey were traveling around Europe with their mother and an aunt when all this happened. They're on their way back today. I hate to put the girls through the ordeal of going to their father's apartment."

"You don't need to decide anything right away, Susan. I know how many awful details you have to attend to, but can you take it easy for the rest of the day?"

"I suppose." The last syllable came out like a long sigh. "So there's nothing else?" she asked me. I wished I could have told her that Skip was putting handcuffs on Oliver's killer at this very moment. Images of possible suspects flashed through my mind. I startled at one of old Lillian Ferguson in a pink flowery housedress being carted off to jail. In the fantasy, she was followed quickly by a man with an enormous tattoo displayed on his naked upper torso.

I really needed to get back to the boring life of a retired schoolteacher.

"There is one question I have," I said to Susan, with a casual air. "Did you give the key to Oliver's place to anyone else?"

"No, of course not. Was someone there?"

"No, no. I just wondered. I wouldn't have wanted to walk in on anyone. You go and rest and I'll talk to you later."

I clicked off and let out a loud groan. I wasn't happy about the ease with which I was able to invent stories—lies—lately. I was angry with myself about lying to both Maddie and Susan. For their own good, I reasoned, but my stomach turned over and the chamomile tea seemed to have gone sour.

* * *

I pushed speed dial for Skip's cell phone. With his girlfriend in Chicago, he should be free to spend an hour with his aunt on a Sunday afternoon, preferably before his mother and Maddie returned from San Francisco. I'd have to take my chances on a scolding, but I hoped he'd be able to help me separate truth from fiction about the people involved in his investigation.

"Hey, Aunt Gerry," he said right away. Caller ID was one technological marvel I'd immediately embraced.

"Any news?" I asked.

"Do you have some kind of radar for these things?"

"What things?"

"We traced the gun in Halbert's hand to one that was used in a crime about five years ago."

"That's progress, isn't it?"

"In a manner of speaking, but you won't like what state the crime took place in."

It hardly took half a minute. "Tennessee," I said.

"There's that radar again."

"I'm sure there are a lot of guns in Tennessee, Skip, and that some of them end up in California." In Lincoln Point, in the hands of a Tennessee native? I hardly believed it myself. "It looks like whoever killed Oliver went to a lot of trouble to make it look like a suicide."

"Off the record, Aunt Gerry, who would kill himself on someone else's porch?"

"I'm glad you're coming around," I said.

"So, let's see if I can guess what you did all day," Skip said. "You got your newspaper, read it from cover to cover while you drank coffee and ate some toast, did the crossword puzzle . . ."

"I had coffee at Seward's Folly. You might want to stop in and talk to Kayla, who works there."

"Uh-huh. Shall I file this under 'anonymous tip'?"

"There's more. Can you stop by to hear the rest?"

"I can hardly wait, but I'm covering for Juan right now. And then I have to make a stop at Seward's Folly apparently. What's for dinner?"

"Whatever you like."

My habit was to use an address book until there were so many whiteouts, erasures, and marks that the pages were nearly worn away. I bought a new book every three or four years, but never threw out the old, out-of-date books, even though many entries were for friends now deceased or in another state with a different name and several different phone numbers.

I kept all the old books in a bottom drawer of the desk in my bedroom. Every now and then, for one reason or another, I needed to look at one of them. This afternoon, I had reason to look for the address book that might contain a home phone number for Ken's old partner in architecture, Artie Dodd.

I found the book I wanted, a small, black spiral-bound notebook with a tab for each letter of the alphabet. I rubbed my hands over the cover, though it wasn't dusty or crumpled. Anyone watching might have thought I was invoking the help of a genie, or casting a witch's spell over the contents. A good witch, I hoped.

A few minutes later I was entering a number I'd had several years ago for Artie Dodd. Not long after Ken died, Artie, who was at least fifteen years older than Ken, retired. He sold the consulting business, located a few miles to the south in Sunnyvale, to a couple of young architects. Ken and Artie's wonderful secretary, Esther, and I had promised to keep in touch. But as so often happens in such situations, we lost track of each other.

What were the chances that Artie still lived in Sunnyvale?

I took a few deep breaths, waiting for the results of my entry. I heard the familiar three-note signal, followed by a voice saying, "We're sorry, you have reached a number that is no longer in service." I wasn't surprised, but I was relieved.

Who tries to reach a number hoping there will be no answer?

I needed to focus. Did I really want to follow the trail from the children's clothing and photographs in the Bronx box back to Ken's past, no matter where it led?

I knew I wouldn't be at peace until I did.

Unlike Patrick Lynch, a professional with his own webpage, Artie Dodd was a mere retiree like myself, so I figured it would be nearly impossible to find him among probably thousands of other United States residents with the same name.

I tried to think back to times I'd been with Artie and his wife, usually at an opening ceremony for one of the firm's buildings or at a holiday gathering. Had they talked about where they might like to live in retirement? Many Bay Area professionals moved to Point Reyes or Inverness, about eighty miles northwest of Lincoln Point, on Tomales Bay, or to Lake Tahoe, or even to Phoenix, Arizona, as if California (even Sunnyvale) weren't sunny enough for them.

I tried directory assistance for a couple of likely destinations, but either Artie hadn't moved to the places I chose or his number was unlisted. I couldn't even come up with a recollection of what Artie's hobbies were. Was he a golfer headed for the attractions of Pebble Beach in Monterey? Was he a recreational gambler, headed for Reno? Did he sail?

I finally quit taxing my memory and decided to try to reach the people at the new firm tomorrow, Monday, to see if they had a forwarding number for the former owner of the company.

I imagined talking to Artie the following day. How would I phrase my burning questions? "Hi, Artie. Were you and your partner dirty?" I might inquire. "Oh, by the way, do you know if my husband had a child besides our son, Richard?"

I blew out a breath, keeping my cheeks puffed for a few seconds first.

Such simple questions I had.

"We're home. We're home," Maddie said, sounding as she did at the beginning of a long break from school. She ran down the entryway, through the atrium and gave me a hug that nearly knocked me over. I was glad she wasn't tall enough to reach the spot on my head that was still tender from its interaction with Oliver's brick doorstop.

"We had a great time," Beverly said, rolling her eyes. She dropped her purse and bundles on the chair in the family room, just off the atrium.

Maddie ran to her bedroom to change from San Francisco clothes (I'd convinced her to wear nice pants and a warm jacket) to her Lincoln Point fall uniform (jeans and a sweatshirt).

"I hope she didn't drive you crazy," I said to Beverly.

"Not at all. But I knew she'd rather have been here snooping around with you. She reminds me so much of Skip."

"Uh-oh," we said, almost in unison. Meaning, did we really want another cop in the family?

Thus began a series of reminiscences.

"Remember the time Skip staked out Mrs. Granzow's house to see if he could catch whoever was taking her newspapers and returning them later, obviously having been read?" Beverly had a broad smile on her face, as if she could see Skip at Maddie's age, standing in front of her.

I saw the image myself.

"Ah, yes. Poor old Mr. James, just trying to save a few pennies, never thinking anyone would be up early enough to catch him. And what about the time our little Skip wanted to interview all the shop owners on the street after his best friend's dad's car was towed?"

"He was looking for witnesses who might have seen the tow-truck driver dent the door. Maybe cops are born, not made, do you think?" Beverly asked.

We laughed, the way close friends do who have a long history together. It was beyond me why I hadn't felt that I could take my questions about Ken to Beverly. There was a good chance she'd know the context of the photographs and maybe even the pink layette. The only reason I could think of for keeping her in the dark was that I didn't want to be embarrassed at the answers. I was Ken's wife; I shouldn't have to ask anyone else about his life, not even his sister.

Yet, I was willing to talk to Artie? What was that about? It couldn't be sillier.

Beverly had selected a plastic bag from the bundles on the chair and had pulled out a T-shirt.

"I probably should wait for Maddie," she said. "She'll want to see your face. I'll just have this little present ready."

"Beverly, there's something I want to talk to you about."

Her face turned somber, as I supposed mine was. "Of course. What is it, Gerry? You know, I thought something was wrong, and I've just been hoping that eventually you'd—"

Clump, clump.

Maddie made her typical noisy arrival. "You didn't show it to her, did you?" she asked Beverly, her arms akimbo, her tiny brow scrunched in a frown.

"Of course not." Beverly swung the T-shirt behind her back and tossed it over to Maddie. I thought there might be a basketball term to describe the move. "She never saw it."

"Good," Maddie said, "'Cause I want to see her face."

Did we know our little girl or what?

Maddie unfurled the T-shirt and held it up to her scrawny chest, lettering facing out.

A red T-shirt with black letters: *Inch by Inch, It's a Cinch*, it read.

"Isn't that wicked, Grandma? Aunt Beverly says it means you can do anything at all if you do it in little pieces at a time."

Advice from a T-shirt. It seemed there was no end to the sources of wisdom in this world.

Chapter 11

The moment for talking to Beverly had passed, but we made a quick deal before she left, mostly nonverbally, to talk later.

"Taylor is back from her party and wants to go for ice cream," Maddie said.

"Didn't you have lunch with your aunt in San Francisco? Was she so mean to you that she let you starve?" I tickled the places where hunger might be felt.

When her giggles were over, Maddie explained. "Aunt Beverly wanted to take me to a nice restaurant, with cloth napkins and all. It was okay, but the portions weren't that big."

"I see. And Taylor didn't have enough cake and ice cream at the birthday party, so she's hungry, too?"

"She said the cake was from the supermarket and not very good."

I gave an understanding nod. "I see." It was hard to keep

track of this generation's taste: no fancy décor, but no low-end food, either.

"Not like the yummy ones you make."

Flattery never hurt a case.

"If you're really hungry, I have some spinach salad left over from last night."

I just wanted to see her screw up her nose. I wasn't disappointed.

On Sunday afternoon, Sadie's Ice Cream Shop was as crowded as Seward's Folly had been in the morning. I was glad Lincoln Point's independent businesses were thriving, even though it meant that we'd had to wait awhile at the doorway for a table for four.

We were seated now, decadent sundaes all around. Henry, who was very good at kid-friendly chatting, got us started on each girl's book report. Maddie had finished a biography of Benjamin Franklin; Taylor was in the middle of Louisa May Alcott's life.

"Mrs. Berry makes us use these lame forms," Taylor said. "We have to fill in 'paragraph one' and 'paragraph two' and say how many characters there are and describe them. And then write 'the rising action'"—she drew her third set of quotation marks in the air—"and the 'climax.' I'd rather just write what I learned, all by myself."

I was on Taylor's side this time, but held my tongue. Far be it for me to criticize a teacher managing thirty bright, strong-willed children like Taylor and Maddie.

"I'm so glad we're off school tomorrow," said Maddie, who usually liked her classes. I figured the idea of hanging around Lincoln Point where there was a case to solve was more appealing to her this week.

"I think they should give us a day off for everybody's birthday," Taylor said. She crowned her statement by sucking on an overflowing spoonful of chocolate ice cream and marshmallow topping.

"I thought you young ladies liked school," Henry said, digging into what I considered a strange combination of coffee ice cream and caramel sauce.

"Sometimes school's boring, Grandpa," Taylor said.

"Man, you got that right." A deep voice, not one of us. A tall, middle-aged man had pulled a chair up to the corner of our table between Maddie and me.

Emory Ferguson. Or was it Eliot? It had been Eliot whom I'd had in class, but that had been a long time ago and if I had a special way to discriminate between them, I'd forgotten what it was, unless they were walking, one with the limp, the other without.

"Hey, there, Eliot," Henry said, sounding sure of himself. Since Abraham Lincoln High School had only one shop teacher, Henry had had both twins in class. I'd have to ask him later what his secret was to tell the boys apart with such certainty when they were seated.

Henry introduced Eliot to Maddie and Taylor and made him feel more welcome than I was prepared to do. I had no doubt why Eliot had chosen this day to visit my table at Sadie's.

After one or two more gestures to the girls, telling them how lucky they were to be in school (though it hadn't been a priority for him, I recalled) and how good their sundaes looked, Eliot Ferguson got around to what I knew was his mission.

"So, I noticed you paid a call on my mom this morning, Geraldine. I just wanted to apologize for the way I ran out of the house. I was late for a meeting."

"It's still Mrs. Porter, to you," I wanted to say but didn't. And what kind of business meeting was held on Sunday?

I wasn't usually crotchety when someone invited himself to join my friends and me when we were in a public place. Lincoln Point was a small town and we all tried to keep everything on a friendly basis. I was annoyed today because I felt that Eliot was taking undue advantage of the fact that we were both at Sadie's.

"I was in the neighborhood," I said, with a smile.

"Mom and Dad are both great, you know, but they're getting up there."

I assumed he meant in age and not on a ladder. Why did Eliot think I cared, unless it was to make certain I didn't get the wrong (right?) idea about his alibi? I thought back to my tea with Lillian. I was fairly sure that Eliot was the twin Lillian mentioned as having left the factory for sandwiches on the day Oliver was murdered.

Tired of the game we were playing, I decided to take the lead. Irritated or not, I needed to take advantage of this conversation with Eliot to further my pseudo investigation.

"You live with your parents now, I understand."

"Yeah, it's a win-win, you know. They can use someone around the house for this and that, you know, and I'm just as happy not to be paying rent somewheres else."

More than one somewhere, I noted, and adjusted my mental grade for him from B-minus to C-plus. The free-rent arrangement was what Maddie or Skip would call "a no-brainer." I had to watch myself. If I weren't careful, the vocabulary and phraseology of the next generations would take over my verbal communication. Their speech patterns were already crowding my mind.

"How's your brother?" Henry asked.

A good question, and so much less intimidating when Henry asked it. I dipped my spoon deep into my sundae, scraping the side of the dish, foraging for hot fudge, and waited for Eliot's response.

"Great. Emory's great. Yeah, we all work at the factory, you know. Mom and Dad, too."

"And you were all there on Friday, I understand, except for your trip to get sandwiches," I said.

"That's right," Eliot said. His face took on a wary expression, as if he heard incredulity in my voice.

"And was it you or Emory who had lunch with Oliver that day, the day he was murdered?"

I hadn't planned to hear my voice echo throughout Sadie's. Nearly all of her customers had apparently chosen that moment to stop talking and sip their malts or chew on their waffle cones. Heads turned in the direction of our table. Maddie and Taylor took a moment from their intense bowl-scraping and giggled when they realized we'd attracted the attention of the masses. I hoped none of Taylor's classmates were present. I didn't want to be responsible for any embarrassing moments in school.

Henry gave me a look as if to ask, "Where's the real Geraldine Porter?"

Eliot looked taken back, as I'd intended. I'd had enough experience scoping out lies told to me by adolescents, but I'd lost my touch with the practice and had to rely on shock value.

"I don't know what you're talking about, Geraldine. As I said, we never left the neighborhood around the old airport grounds. I bought subs for lunch and took them back to my family."

Eliot, having had the advantage of knowing everyone was attentive to us, had kept his voice to a whisper. In other words, I was still the only loudmouth in the group.

A young waitress I didn't know came to the table and addressed Eliot.

"Can I get you anything?" she asked him, pad and pencil in hand.

Maybe she thought I'd made all the fuss just to get service for the latecomer to our party. Or perhaps she was sent to be sure there was no danger that a riot would break out.

"I'm good," Eliot said to her. He turned back to me, "You must be thinking about someone else, Geraldine."

"You're probably right," I said, waving my hand. "I'm sure the police will straighten it all out soon anyway."

Eliot got up from his metal chair and whipped it back to its original place at another table. The customer there flinched and thrust his arm out to protect his children. Fortunately, the chair never left the floor.

"Enjoy your ice cream," Eliot said to us, and was gone.

I mentally lost track of my companions for a moment while I tried to figure out what the encounter with Eliot meant. I could only conclude that Lillian had told him about the alibi she'd given him and his brother, and he'd felt the need to check out exactly what I'd taken away from the meeting.

I was glad I could give him even more to think about: the scoop from the lovely young Kayla, the Seward's Folly barista he probably wouldn't be able to pick out of a crowd.

When I finally checked in with my tablemates, I noticed questioning looks on all of them, as if they were waiting for an explanation. I had none, except to borrow another popular expression.

I took a long breath, and smiled. "That went well," I said.

Skip's first choice for dinner had been pot roast.

"Pot roast takes hours," I'd told him. "You'd have to give me more notice."

"Okay, then meatloaf, meatballs, cheeseburger. Anything like that."

"I think I get it. June is still in Chicago," I'd said, making a grocery list with the hand that wasn't holding the phone. Tenderloin strips. Mushrooms. Sour cream. Egg noodles. The makings of beef stroganoff.

"Yeah, you know what Lincoln's favorite dinner was?"

"I'm afraid I don't. Are we inviting him?"

"Rare steak. And he loved sweets. Bottom line: I'm in good company, and what my vegetarian girlfriend doesn't know won't hurt me."

Thus, at about four o'clock I found myself carrying a red plastic basket down the aisle of the supermarket, Henry at my side, swinging a basket for his own items. The girls were at the front of the store where there was Wi-Fi and a large bowl of free Halloween candy. I was beginning to worry that by the time Halloween night came around, Lincoln Point would be completely out of sweets.

"What a coincidence," Henry had said when I told him of my errand. "I need to pick up a few things, too."

Henry's car was parked closer to Sadie's, so the four of us rode in it to the supermarket.

The whole scene was a little too domestic for me: a gray-haired couple and their grandchildren climbing down from an SUV, shopping together, commenting on the price of cherry tomatoes and asparagus and the advantages of paper over plastic.

Ken and I went on this kind of outing often, except we'd have divided up our list. We'd go our separate ways through the aisles and then meet at the checkout stand, as if we'd been on a scavenger hunt. He'd have been responsible for the heavy goods, like five-pound bags of flour or rice, and items that came in large cans and glass bottles. I'd have picked up the fruit and vegetables, dairy, and condiments.

"You don't trust me to choose bananas," he might say.

"That's why you always get the produce." He was right. He ate bananas when they were greener than the felt carpeting in my dollhouse attic; I liked them soft, just this side of banana bread.

The supermarket was no place for tearing up, but I seemed to be worse than ever at dealing with my memories. I knew the great unknown that had reared itself through the cartons in the garage was partly responsible for this resurgence of melancholy and self-pity.

I hadn't told anyone about the photographs or the little girl's clothing I'd found in Ken's Bronx box. I'd all but promised Beverly I'd tell her what was "wrong." I knew Henry and Skip were standing by, ready to listen and to help. Henry had done me a great service, lending his back to the task of getting the boxes down from the shelves, with no expectations of satisfying his curiosity. I couldn't ask for better family and friends. Even the one begging me to solve her brother's murder.

No matter what, I was going to tear open the rest of the boxes as soon as possible, and then get to the bottom of the Bronx issue and anything else that surprised me. That was one thing I could take control of, even if I couldn't solve a murder single-handedly.

For now, I focused on selecting the freshest mushrooms in the bin and checking the expiration date on the tub of sour cream. There was nothing wrong with a little homey companionship around the little (if not miniature) things in life.

"Why don't you and Taylor join us for dinner?" I asked Henry. "Kay and Bill, too, if they're not busy."

Henry's smile was endearing, his eyes as wide as Maddie's when a new flavor of ice cream appeared in Sadie's freezer case. He whipped out his cell phone.

"Kay?" he said after a few seconds. "I've got some good news."

I took that as a "yes."

We picked up the girls at the front of the store. They were busy with their laptops, the area around them full of wrappers from chocolate candy rolls. In my day we were lucky if the store had a gumball machine or a stationary rocking horse for entertainment while our parents shopped. Free candy was out of the question and Wi-Fi hadn't been conceived.

"A party for dinner," Maddie said, as we left the store. She'd reverted to her old habit of waving her arms when she was excited. If she'd been seated, she'd have been kicking her legs, also.

From the backseat of Henry's SUV, Maddie called her parents and left a message that she missed them, but she was having the best day ever. She called Beverly and invited her, too. "We're having beef," she'd said, as if that were important to her. I knew what was important to my granddaughter was that our house would be filled with people she loved and that maybe her grandmother would return to her normal, cheery mood.

Maddie and Taylor were engaged in animated conversation over a movie that featured a futuristic cat. Henry was animated also, swinging by a couple of side streets (skipping Sangamon River Road) on the way back to Sadie's to collect my car, to see what was new by way of Halloween decorations.

Maddie cheered at an enormous fake snow globe containing a large, stiff ghost with a silly smile on its face. I suspected batteries were involved as white flakes fell from the top of the globe and then back up again in a never-ending snowstorm. Taylor counted the number of black cats she saw and announced the total every few minutes. Henry joined in when he spied one, and Maddie clapped every time.

I wondered at the extent of my crabbiness lately, if a simple dinner invitation could evoke this celebratory mood.

We turned down Gettysburg Boulevard, a wide street with tracts of homes on either side. The first house gave Taylor what she was waiting for.

"There's the fiftieth black cat," Taylor said, as her grandfather slowed down for a good look. Then she shrieked, "Gross!" and covered her eyes.

We followed her pointing finger to an olive green house that looked like many of the other houses on the street, except for the body hanging from it.

For a minute I thought the woman might be real. A lifesize mannequin dressed in a black evening gown hung from the tip of the A-frame roof. Her arms dangled; her dark hair fell to her shoulders. She swung freely, her fancy jeweled slippers catching the light from the setting sun. From the expression on her face she might have been happily waiting for her next dance partner. She seemed oblivious to the six or seven bats hanging around her shoulders.

I felt dizzy and glad I was seated as the image of the real, murdered Oliver Halbert came to my mind. Since our citizens were oblivious to good taste, I thought of asking the Lincoln Point city council to issue a directive to homeowners to remove all such so-called decorations from their lawns in deference to the recent murder. I didn't mind a jack-o'-lantern or two, but I found simulated murder scenes particularly offensive this year. My own newly generated party mood was now dissipating at a rapid pace.

If this mood lasted beyond the next traffic light, I'd call Councilwoman Gail Musgrave. As a member of our crafts group, Gail was subject to our requests now and then. We tried to limit our solicitations to matters of importance. In my present state, I though my complaint was justified.

Henry caught my expression and put his hand on my shoulder in a calming gesture.

It was a good feeling.

Chapter 12

I wondered what Skip would think when he saw that our meeting and the dinner I'd promised him had turned into a party. When we spoke on the phone and set up his visit for this evening, the implication was that we'd share information on Oliver Halbert's murder case.

By now he'd probably interviewed Kayla, but I hadn't told him about my visit with Lillian Ferguson or the goon incident at Oliver's apartment. I thought I might leave out the part with the gun. It hadn't been used, or even shown, after all; I'd tripped and gone unconscious all on my own.

Fortunately, I was pretty good at scheming and figured out a way to have the best of both worlds—a meeting with Skip plus the party everyone seemed to be dying for.

I had a plan.

Once we were home, I made a call to Skip from inside the walk-in closet in my bedroom, where not even Maddie would trespass.

"You want to meet where?" he asked, in a "have you lost it?" tone.

"See you in ten," I said.

In the supermarket, Henry had insisted on adding an-other package of beef tips and putting them in his own basket. Now he offered to help prepare the main dish, as I knew he would. Henry loved to cook and, in fact, I had a feeling the stroganoff would be much better in his hands.

I handed him an apron and made sure he was engrossed in browning the strips of beef. The girls had already trotted off to Maddie's room.

"I forgot something and have to run out for a minute. Will you be okay here for a short time?" I asked Henry.

"Sure," he said. "What are we missing?"

I paused. "Milk," I said, a beat too late.

Henry leaned over and whispered to me. "I'll toss out whatever that white stuff is in the fridge."

"Thanks." I patted him on the back. Our second physical gesture of the afternoon. (Just as well that I had no time to dwell on why that deserved to be noted.)

I could hear Taylor's squealing laughter through Maddie's slightly open window as I backed out of my garage and drove off down the street to not buy milk.

The unmarked LPPD sedan was parked in the front row of cars at the convenience store on Springfield Boulevard, just across from the high school. Skip exited his car as I pulled up and parked next to him. If either of us popped a trunk, the moment would have been perfect for the crucial drug-bust scene in a DEA movie.

Skip joined me in the Saturn. He sat on the passenger

seat of my car rolling a Styrofoam cup half filled with coffee slowly between his hands.

"This is a far cry from what Seward's Folly serves," he said.

"We have a lot of business to take care of, and a crowd is about to descend on my house," I said. I gave him a quick rundown of how the party got started and who would be there.

"Okay, you first," he said.

I began with the contradiction between Lillian's alibi for her twins and Kayla's statements this morning.

"You interviewed Mrs. Ferguson?" Skip asked.

I twisted my wrist in a "so-so" fashion. "I wouldn't call it an interview. More like a visit to check on her after the awful scene on her porch."

Skip shook his head. "Such a good neighbor."

"Did you talk to Kayla?" I asked.

Another shake of his russet head. "She split for the day shortly after her shift ended at noon. We're trying to locate her. No one else in the shop seems to remember the two men together."

"That's disappointing. Maybe Kayla is just bored with her job and was trying to impress her customers," I said. I'd already described the EMTs and what I thought was a singles party in the making.

"It happens. We'll catch up with her on Tuesday when she's back to work, if not before."

"I was in Oliver's apartment," I said. Funny how quickly I could get to a point with simple, declarative sentences when severely pressed for time.

"Okay," Skip said, drawing out the first syllable.

"Susan gave me a key," I added. "She wanted me to go in and look around."

"In case the dumb cops didn't do their job."

"No, no." I paused and smiled. "Well, yes. But she also wanted me to take back a room box she'd made for him, before the landlord went in and packed everything up."

"We're finished there. Why doesn't Susan pack it up?"

"Hard to explain," I said, thinking of how difficult it had been for me to clear our home of Ken's things. There was still a lot of Ken in our Eichler—I wore his pajamas and shirts on occasion and used many of his special desk accessories.

After a little teasing—"Did you find the crucial piece of evidence we missed?" Skip had asked—I told Skip about the other visitors to Oliver's bachelor pad, mentally cringing at what his response would be.

"I'm fairly sure one of them was Patrick Lynch."

Skip's grunt-like breath was louder than I expected. "Do you like putting yourself in danger, Aunt Gerry? Is there—?"

"Skip, we don't have time for this right now. Do you have an idea who the men were from my descriptions?"

He nodded. "Lynch, most likely. And the other one was probably Crowley. They're like Mutt and Jeff. One tall and one short, right?"

I wasn't completely convinced. "The shorter one behaved in a subservient manner. From what you've told me, I'd expect Lynch to treat Max Crowley as a peer."

"First, Lynch doesn't have any peers. He thinks he's above everyone and untouchable. And by taking Crowley on after the scandal, he's making him beholden."

"But they were both involved in the scandal."

"Private businessmen can get away with more than city officials can."

I thought of asking, "How come?" but there was only the slimmest of chances that I'd ever understand.

"They were looking for something. Seriously," I said,

thinking about the butt of the gun protruding from Max Crowley's belt.

"We went through the apartment. We took Oliver's computer and anything that looked relevant. So far we've found nothing except that list I told you about."

I took a troubled breath. "The list, yes." Ken's name flashed before me, somehow in larger font than the other names, and in bold print.

"Remember, it's just that. A list," Skip said, catching my expression. "There's no information about anyone on the list. We don't know why anyone's name is on it except Oliver thought it should be."

"Right. The list could mean anything."

"We were hoping his hard drive would have real data. We're still scouring it, but so far, there's nothing on it that helps us." Skip looked at his watch. "How long till your real company arrives at the house?"

"It's covered," I said, thinking of what a good host Henry would make for Beverly, Kay, and Bill. "I have something else." Skip watched intently as I took three photographs from my purse and handed them to him. "Have you ever seen these?"

He frowned and peered at the set.

"Polaroids? Who takes Polaroids anymore? These must be from the Elizabethan age." I gave him a curious look. He shrugged. "I'm taking a class in Shakespeare. You know, trying something different."

My nephew was full of surprises, but this one rattled me. "And you didn't tell me? Your aunt who spent twenty-seven years teaching Shakespeare, and you didn't tell me?"

"Now you know how I feel when you go off and do my job. "

"You have a point. For now."

"Sometimes I don't know what's worse, having you depressed, like about this thing with Uncle Ken, or having you in a great mood and interfering with a murder investigation."

"Luckily, you don't have to decide, do you?" I clicked the dome light on and pointed to the photos. "Do you recognize where these were taken? Or anything else in the picture?"

Skip held the photos to the light and squinted. "It looks like a young Uncle Ken. Can't make out the background. Some big institution."

I swallowed and wet my lips, which had gone dry in only the last few minutes. "And the child?"

"I don't know. Could it be Richard or me?"

"No. The background is completely unfamiliar to me. I know it's not either of you. I lived through your infancy and your cousin's, remember? And it's a girl."

"Oh, I guess you can tell from the pink."

"Correct." I didn't know why I wasn't disposed to tell him about the rest of the pink—the bib, the hat, the jacket, and the flowered onesie that had also been in the "personal" envelope.

Skip's face took on a serious thinking expression. He tapped the photos on his knee. "Do you mind if I take these? We have software that might help identify the site."

"You can tell where it is from software?"

"Don't get me wrong. We don't have those miracle computers you see on TV shows with those fictitious, high-tech multimedia crime labs that are cleaner than heaven. Ours are—"

I held up my hand. I'd heard this speech and sympathized with real-life law enforcement. "I know. Crime labs in the United States are understaffed, underequipped, and it's a wonder anything can be done for the cause of justice in this country." In spite of my light tone, I believed Skip's reports on the underfunded public forensic science agencies.

"Just so you understand. We do have a limited database that we can tap into with all the major institutions in the country. Schools, hospitals, government buildings, that kind of thing."

"I just want to make something clear, but I don't want any questions," I said.

"Shoot."

"These photographs are not related to Oliver Halbert's case."

"Glad to hear it."

"I mean, you may not want to use department resources—"

Skip interrupted my labored speech. "Don't worry about it, okay?"

I gave him the envelope I'd kept the photos in. "Thanks," I said.

I felt more excited than was warranted by Skip's caveats about the ability of the software to identify the building in the photos, but a long shot was better than no shot. If Skip was curious about who I thought the child in the photos was, he didn't let on. I was glad for that, and for the fact that he didn't seem to remember how I'd nearly jumped him when he'd tried to pick up papers from the floor of my garage earlier.

"By the way, did Mom tell you she and Nick are going on another trip? It's one of those 'if it's Tuesday, it's Belgium' tours through Europe," Skip said.

"She did tell me. It sounds wonderful."

"When are you and Henry going to take a little vacation together?"

It wasn't hard to translate—after many years as a widow,

Beverly, Skip's mom, had a new boyfriend, a retired police detective whom she'd met working as a civilian volunteer for the LPPD.

Wasn't it time I put myself out there, too? It wasn't the first time Skip or Beverly had hinted at that. I figured I could still count on my son to frown upon the idea, but probably not my daughter-in-law, and certainly not my granddaughter, who was desperate to BFF me with Henry.

"Let's go to dinner," I said.

Kay and Bill didn't seem to mind that their hostess had been missing. To my relief, no one queried me about milk. I'd have to ask Henry later what his cover story for me had been. It occurred to me that I was building a long list of things to ask Henry later. I looked forward to the session.

Beverly, always happy to meet new people (not just a boyfriend) had struck up a conversation with attorneys Kay and Bill about evidence laws and the one known as "fruit of the poisoned tree." As I walked by with a tray of cheese and crackers, I heard unanimity that the law should be revisited.

Henry, who anyone would nominate to play the role of Happy in a remake of *Snow White and the Seven Dwarfs*, hummed while he drained the noodles and prepared to serve the main course.

I thought the least I could do was hold the plates as he filled them. Maddie and Taylor delivered the steaming dishes to the table where special wine (from Kay and Bill) and a multi-ingredient salad (from Beverly) awaited.

Soon my dining room table was abuzz with compliments to the chef. I wasn't the least bit embarrassed to give Henry all the credit. The aroma of warm, friendly conversation filled the room and Maddie's smile was wider than I'd seen it all weekend.

There wasn't a whisper of murder.

Even dessert was accounted for. With a little more notice we would have enjoyed making it together, but instead Maddie and I had stopped at a bakery on the way home, after seeing the hanging lady from Henry's SUV. We'd chosen a lemon chiffon pie as a "light dessert" to go with the beef. Maddie was always happy to be in charge of the last course and offered to serve it as soon as the last tip of beef disappeared from Skip's plate.

Beverly had caught up with me in the kitchen between dinner and dessert and helped me rinse plates. "This is nice, Gerry. Just like old times," she'd said.

I assumed she meant three days ago.

Susan called just as my guests were leaving. She sounded so depressed, I wanted to give her a little hope.

"I'm working with Skip," I told her.

"I'd like to have the little construction scene I made for Oliver. Can I come and get it?"

"Why don't you let me fix it up first, Susan? I'll try to drop it by tomorrow."

"Okay, thanks, Gerry. Good night."

Susan's voice sounded melancholy and resigned. I guessed that her acquiescence on all counts was facilitated by medication.

Maybe I should look into that for myself.

I hoped Maddie would want to turn in early. I was in the mood to go out to the garage and tackle the rest of Ken's boxes.

"Who do you think killed Mrs. Giles's brother?" Maddie asked. The question seemed to come out of the blue as we were straightening chairs and pillows and filling the washing machine with the table linens.

"I don't know, sweetheart. You shouldn't be thinking about that, anyway. Let's talk about your Halloween costume. I'm still planning to go to your house that weekend so I can see you all dressed up and help Mom and Dad give out the candy."

Even with a big frown, her face was sweet. "I can't think of anything good to wear this year. Witches and ghosts are too boring. I'm too old to be an animal and, besides, I've done all the animals I like."

I had a whole album of Halloween photographs to back up Maddie's animal costume claim. Maddie as a tiger, a bear, an elephant, and three species of dinosaur, were the first six that came to mind.

"Did you get any ideas from our driving around today with Henry?"

Oops. As soon as I asked the question, I regretted it. The last thing I wanted Maddie to remember before bedtime was the swinging mannequin.

For once, Maddie didn't pick up on something that might lead to a "Case" discussion.

"A kid in my class is coming to the school party as a control freak. He's collecting all the remote controls he can and he's going to attach them to his body and frizz up his hair like a real geek." She laughed in anticipation of seeing him.

"That's very creative. Maybe we can think of something like that. Instead of trying to look like a person or a thing, you could go as a theme or even a word or a phrase."

Maddie's face brightened. "Like something from Shakespeare."

"That's an excellent idea," I said, wondering what was happening to my family. I thought of calling my son, to see what he was reading these days. One of the Richard plays? Maybe they'd all gone Elizabethan on me. Why hadn't this happened when I was trying to push it on them years ago? I guessed there was something to be said for not trying too hard to win people over.

Shakespeare always seemed to me the perfect source for Halloween material. One of my students at ALHS had written as much in an essay. I remembered the gist of his closing remark: "Witches, ghosts, and that awesome skull. What's not to like?"

"We can Google Shakespeare quotes. I'll bet we'll get, like, a gazillion of them," Maddie said.

"I'll bet you're right."

It had been tricky to make Shakespeare appealing to adolescents. I'd tried all sorts of gimmicks, one of the most successful being what I called Insult of the Week. My students picked up on the idea immediately. It gave me great pleasure to hear one teenager say to another, "If you spend word for word with me, I shall make your wit bankrupt," from *Two Gentlemen of Verona* or "Peace, good pint-pot, peace, good tickle-brain," from *Henry IV*.

Was it more civilized for one student to call another a "diffused infection of a man" or a "scurvy jack-a-nape priest" than to use the rude epithets they learned from television and movies? I liked to think so.

Maddie had found several possibilities for a costume, all the while expressing amazement at how many common expressions dated back to Shakespeare's plays and sonnets.

When she saw the expression, "Can one desire too much of a good thing?" on the list, her comment was, "Dad's always saying how you *can* have too much of a good thing."

I wasn't prepared to reveal the bawdy connotation of that and many other phrases in the Shakespearean lexicon.

She considered using the expression "wearing one's

heart on one's sleeve, for daws to peck away at it" until she learned that a daw was a kind of crow.

In the end, we decided we could have the most fun with the words of the second witch in *Macbeth*: "Eye of newt and toe of frog, wool of bat and tongue of dog, adder's fork and blind-worm's sting, lizard's leg and owlet's wing."

We'd make a sign for her back with the quote spelled out for those who didn't recognize the reference.

Shakespeare was back in my life. At one time it would have been all the joy I could have wished for.

When Maddie was finally tired enough to sleep, I was at loose ends. Should I return to searching Ken's files as I'd planned? Or work on the damaged room box for Susan? Should I work up a list to try to link Patrick Lynch, Max Crowley, or the Ferguson family to Oliver's murder? I could do any of those things. Or I could take out my worn copy of the *Complete Works of William Shakespeare* and treat myself to a comedy.

My work ethic triumphed and I headed for the garage. I'd get Maddie to help me tomorrow with the room box, and I could pay a visit to the Fergusons' factory on Tuesday, once I'd dropped Maddie off at school in Palo Alto.

As for revisiting *Comedy of Errors*, that would have to wait.

Now, why would I think of the play with two sets of twins as main characters?

The task seemed daunting as I surveyed the cartons piled on either side and in front of my car in the garage. I walked around my car, pulled a stool up to the workbench along the inside wall, plunked down the cup of tea I'd fixed, and prepared to dig into history.

Each time I cut the seal on a box, I held my breath. I

couldn't have been more nervous if I'd been told that one of the boxes contained anthrax or a poisonous snake. I didn't know which I dreaded more—finding another set of baffling photographs or uncovering evidence that would forever color my memory of my husband as a law-abiding, scrupulously honest businessman.

For about an hour, I sifted through routine material from Ken's office—drawings, proposals, impact statements, and telephone messages. I was never so happy to be bored.

I had on three layers of clothing—a turtleneck, a vest, and a jacket, plus heavy socks, but the cold had now caught up with me. One more box, I decided, then I'd call it a night.

This box, labeled *Memos*, was filled with neat packages of letters, clipped together by month. I couldn't possibly read every one of them. I was beginning to see the advantage of keeping correspondence on a computer where you could easily search for key words. Which words would I try to find, I wondered, if I had the choice? Would I search for "bribe"? "Graft"? "Hush money"? The whole activity was depressing.

I ruffled the pages of one or two packages, barely paying attention to the contents, until my crude searching came up with a grammatical error. The phrase "an arrangement which benefits many" caught my eye.

This needs a comma, I mused, or else it should read ". . . arrangement that . . ." The memo couldn't have been written or reviewed by Esther, who was more of a stickler for grammar and punctuation than I was.

It didn't surprise me that I noticed a small infraction while looking for something of great import. I was one who took comfort in rules. I liked to focus on the compactness of a tidy sentence, the perfect posture of capital letters used correctly, and the elegance of a well-placed exclamation point.

I slipped the memo from the stack to see what the context was.

The first bad news was in the "From" line. Patrick Lynch.

The memo was brief and somewhat vague:

With regard to our conversation of 2/1, I'm pleased that you are on board.

I'm confident this will be an arrangement which benefits many. I'm glad you'll be one of the EELFS.

At the bottom was written: *Enc.: Draft Contract*.

My head dropped to my chest, and not because of the misuse of "which." I supposed it was too much to hope that Ken was signing up to be "on board" for a cruise. Or to build a ship. And that the many who would benefit were the ordinary homeowners of Lincoln Point. And that the misspelled reference to elves meant that this was all about a holiday party. I had a tangential thought that I should write a book on the uses of "that" and which."

I plowed through at least a dozen more memos looking for similar language. Maybe "arrangement" was a word commonly used in memos between architects and builders. Before this weekend, I'd never have suspected anything nefarious about the term "arrangement" in a business deal. What made me think this was anything but a normal, above-board deal?

The goons-with-guns scenario, for one thing.

It didn't help that all of the other memos I sampled were of an entirely different, more specific character, with names, addresses, contract deadlines, and dollar amounts.

The prospects of finding the draft contract that had been enclosed with the memo were dim. There were entire boxes labeled *Contracts*. Having the date, without a year at that, would be of only minimal help.

I pulled my jacket closer around my body. When I finally stepped into my kitchen, I had no idea how long I'd sat in the cold garage.

Chapter 13

Still in my nightgown and robe, I went out to my atrium early on Monday morning. I needed to sit for a while with a mug of coffee before Maddie woke and confused me with her innocent, happy outlook.

I looked up through my skylight at the bright morning light, as if answers to my burning questions might stream down from outer space.

But nothing came easily; I was on my own.

It was time I constructed a concrete plan to solve the nagging issues that were keeping me from enjoying my granddaughter and all that was good in my life.

Oliver Halbert, whom I'd never met, had turned my world upside down. I was convinced that if it weren't for his "potentials" list, I never would have opened the cartons that had been gathering dust high on my garage shelves. One day, Richard or Maddie or Maddie's child would have had to deal with them, and I'd have gone to my rest oblivious of their contents.

Whether or not the list might have come to light eventually, Oliver's murder had precipitated my investigation. If he were alive and moving from potential to actual, I'd have had the chance to confront him and ask him just what complaint he had against Ken Porter.

Now I was left not only trying to humor his sister by pretending to work closely with the police but also dealing with the question of my husband's complicity in misconduct and—I could hardly think it—a "personal" secret he hadn't shared with me.

I tried to step back and take an objective look at how to confront the three ghosts that were haunting me more effectively than the scariest Halloween campfire story.

I breathed in the fresh air provided by my favorite plants and began to talk it out with myself.

First on my mind were the photographs and the accompanying child's clothing I'd found—had it been only two days ago? I seemed to have been worrying over the discovery for years. But this wasn't a worry session; it was an action session.

Actions: Call the people who took over Ken's firm and try to track down his partner, Artie Dodd. Check with Skip on whether he's been able to identify the institution in the background of the photos.

It was a mystery to me why I continued to leave Beverly out of the equation, though I'd shared (almost) everything with Skip. Beverly and I had been close since the day Ken introduced us; she was the one I'd turn to at a time like this. Admittedly, we'd seen less of each other since her relationship with Nick had begun in earnest, but I still considered my sister-in-law to be my confidante—up to now, when my strongest desire was to spare her needless pain. Especially if—when—it turned out that her older brother was completely innocent of business fraud and that the child in the photo was the son or daughter of a client.

I imagined a conversation with Artie where he laughs and tells me that Esther had mistakenly put the photos in a box with a present meant for a baby shower she'd been invited to.

Wouldn't that be nice? (So what if the layette was meant for a three-to-six-month old?)

I took a few sips of coffee, enjoying the warm liquid in the chilly atrium. I was glad I'd pulled on thick socks before coming out here. I couldn't imagine a less flattering outfit, but no one was around to criticize.

Back to work. The second, separate issue was Ken's dealings with Patrick Lynch, and/or Max Crowley, and/or Oliver Halbert. Whatever Lynch and Max Crowley were looking for in Oliver's apartment—I wanted to see it, too.

Action: make another visit to Oliver's apartment. Corollary action: have a better exit strategy in case the next visit was also interrupted by uninvited (by me) guests. Ideas for backup: take Skip? Take Susan? Take gun? (There was nothing wrong with a little outlandish humor on my to-do list.)

Third, who killed Oliver Halbert? Since I became aware of his "potentials" list, solving his murder took on more importance for me than just supporting my friend, Susan. I needed to know more about a man who considered my husband dishonest and subject to legal action.

I had a feeling that Eliot and/or Emory Ferguson and their factory were at the heart of the Halbert murder. For one thing, I had the statements of a barista who had no reason to tell a lie, other than its contribution to the flirty atmosphere at Seward's Folly yesterday morning. According to Kayla, the twins and Oliver were friends, and one of them had lunch with him the day he was murdered. Both assertions were in direct contradiction to what Lillian Ferguson had told me.

Another Ferguson link was that their prefire factory remodel was one of the last projects Ken ever worked on. There was a good chance that was the reason for Ken's name being on Oliver's list. Just a formality, where he included everyone who ever worked with Lynch during Crowley's tenure as city building inspector.

Another nice outcome.

I thought of the janitor who died in the factory fire. As far as I remembered from Skip's rundown of the case, the cause of the blaze was undetermined. A stairway next to the compressor had caught fire for one of three reasons: Eliot or Emory Ferguson forgot to turn off the compressor, leading to its overheating; or the developer decided to use inferior material for the electrical conduit near the stairway; or the architect's specifications were substandard, not requiring a conduit at all, to save everyone money and time. And, by the way, to get a piece of the money saved.

I shook my head at the thought of the last possibility. Of course, it was negligence in the way the specifications were carried out—that was the culprit, I told myself over and over, not the specs themselves. Ken would never have agreed to anything that was in violation of a safety code, no matter what the cost. No matter what the temptation.

I sounded insensitive even to myself, focusing on proving that Ken wasn't responsible for the fire. Either way, the poor janitor was dead and I felt terrible about that.

I put "who was responsible for the fire?" on the list, out of deference to the Patterson family, and hoped the experts would give them closure soon.

Why was every sorrow and every joy so complicated

once we passed Maddie's age? A question for another time. I was sure there was an answer in Shakespeare, if I could only get back to him.

Since Oliver's body had been found at the Ferguson home, I was sure the police had questioned the whole family. I needed to find out what they'd learned. It was hard to believe that a random killer, who had nothing to do with any of the family members, had decided to deposit a fresh corpse on a random Halloween porch on Sangamon River Road. Skip had slipped in a few more facts during our pre-dinner confab, and one of them was that Sam and Lillian's otherwise festive porch had been the murder scene as well as the crime scene.

Back to my determination to include action items in this ad hoc organization session, I added: visit the Fergusons' factory tomorrow once Maddie was safely at her school in Palo Alto.

Summary statement of important question to work on: was the fire in the Ferguson factory connected to Oliver Halbert's death? Summary of suspects: Patrick Lynch, Max Crowley, and all the Fergusons (why not?).

I had to laugh at myself and at my list, so compact and exclusive, ignoring countless other motives for murder and countless other suspects. With the luxury of someone not in law enforcement, I'd dismissed an ex-wife, for example, usually at the top of a suspect list. So what if she was in Europe? That's what hired guns were for.

Moreover, I knew nothing of Oliver's habits. He might have been a gambler, with a creditor hot on his tail, or he might have been trying to break off an adulterous affair.

I'd visited Skip's LPPD cubicle often and had seen the piles of paper connected to an investigation. He'd shown me a stack about four inches high that pertained to just one case. His homework that night had been to go through arrest reports, witness statements, warrants, police reports, property reports, medical records, transcripts, and faxes.

What made me think I could get anywhere working from the sidelines with a short to-do list?

Nothing. But since I'd generated the list, I might as well get started on it.

To-do lists, even when only mental, always gave me a false sense of accomplishment. It was my habit to congratulate myself on a job well done and treat myself to a break, as if I'd already started to carry out the action items.

That tendency was alive and well today. I gave myself a virtual pat on the back for straightening out all the threads of the past few days. Then I went to the kitchen, hoping Maddie was up and ready to distract me.

Maddie had started breakfast oatmeal for both of us. It didn't seem that long ago that I'd put her in her high chair and blow on her cereal to cool it before putting the bowl in front of her. She'd had a sweet tooth then and showed it now as she set out the brown sugar and raisins to make the oatmeal slightly less healthy.

Like her mother, Maddie woke up bright, chipper, and ready to go, with not much transition between waking and sleeping. Richard was more like me in that he found it hard to let go of worries about the past and the future, making it difficult to fall asleep in the present.

"What's the plan for today?" Maddie asked, collecting bowls from a shelf she couldn't reach just a couple of months ago.

"What would you like to do?"

"I get to pick?"

"Uh-huh."

"Really?" she asked, eyes wide, looking at me sideways as if she suspected a trick.

"What's the matter?" I asked. "Can't you think of anything?"

"Sure. But aren't you going to try to get rid of me?"

I was relieved to see the makings of a grin as she scooped oatmeal from the pan into two bowls.

"Sweetheart, how can you say such a thing?"

She set the pan down and hugged me as we both shook with laughter.

Sadly, it had crossed my mind that leaving Maddie for an hour or so would give me a window to visit the factory today. But her delight and surprise at not being pawned off, albeit to very friendly people who loved her, caused me to scratch that idea. What I needed more than anything was the delightful company of my granddaughter.

I'd told Maddie about the damage to Susan's room box, though I'd kept the circumstances of the accident to myself.

After breakfast, therefore, Maddie's choice was to head for the crafts room to work on the mini construction scene.

"I remember this," Maddie said. "Mrs. Giles made it a long time ago."

Here was another reminder of the different time perspective of children. Susan had constructed the box only about three months ago. But that represented a large percentage of an eleven-year-old's short life. It would tire me to do the math to calculate the percentage of my life three months or even a year came out to be, but it seemed like the blink of an eye.

"I love the hard hats and the little lunch box," she said,

as she did last summer. We assembled the materials we'd
need: wood glue, brown paint in various shades, tape to
repair the damage to the Rosie the Riveter poster. We considered adding a little something extra to the scene, like a
tiny half-peeled banana Maddie had bought at a crafts fair,
but decided the best thing would be to simply restore the
box to its original glory.

I looked at the makeshift workbench. It needed a little
glue to stabilize it. The less–than-perfect paint job wasn't
the result of the accident, but, apparently, Susan's haste as
she prepared it. I wondered if she'd notice if I touched it up
a bit—a further sign of my inability to stop intruding myself into other people's projects.

He did the mash. He did the monster mash.

A call on my cell phone sent Maddie into giggles. I realized that although she was the phone's official programmer,
she hadn't heard the ring as often as I had.

"I can't wait to hear the next tune you subject me to," I
told her, knowing she liked a challenge. I imagined a tune
with turkey lyrics for November, though I couldn't think
of any.

The caller ID told me Henry was on the line, if there
were indeed any physical lines involved in these days of
cyberspace.

We chatted about how nice the impromptu dinner party
had turned out and agreed to do it again at his house.

"So you can cook," he said.

I liked his humor.

"What are you doing today?" I asked.

"Do you need me to take Maddie?"

I was chagrined at the growing public perception of me.
"No, no. I really just wanted to know how you were going
to spend your day."

Maddie came up in front of me. "Is that Mr. Baker?"

I covered the mouthpiece, if it was still called a mouthpiece. "Yes, sweetheart."

"I wouldn't mind going over there."

Once my whole to-do list was complete, I was going to have to take stock of my merit as a friend and as a grandmother.

Not surprising, Taylor accompanied Henry when he came to pick up Maddie. He'd insisted that my time was more valuable. I doubted it.

"I can't believe I'm letting you do this again," I whispered to him as the girls buckled themselves into the backseat of his SUV. Maddie's backpack was laden with a tin of ginger cookies, a bag of crackers and peanut butter, and a six-pack of juice boxes. The least I could do.

"I know you have a lot going on," Henry said to me.

"Still . . ."

"I'm a very patient man, Gerry. I'm confident that one of these days we're going to leave Taylor and Maddie with someone else and go off by ourselves."

I felt my face flush but recovered in time to say thank you (or did I say okay?). I nodded my head in the direction of the girls and added, "I hope we don't wait until they have their own driver's licenses."

Who said that? I turned my back and walked away before Henry could see my red face.

I seldom had the occasion to visit the neighborhood at the southernmost edge of town, the site of a failed attempt to establish an airport in Lincoln Point. Now the area of about one square mile was the home of a number of industrial buildings, almost all of them one-story, gray stucco with blue or green trim. The last I heard, the twins' business was the production of small airplane parts. I saw from the signage that many more types of industries than those concerned with aviation were represented here. I passed by Valley Plumbing, Point Pest Control, and a slew of acronyms that were probably computer-related.

The streets in the district were named after personalities and events in aviation history. Amelia Earhart Parkway, Wright Brothers Boulevard, and Beryl Markham Thruway were among the main thoroughfares. Maybe they'd taken their cue from the founding fathers of Lincoln Point, who'd done a similar thing in the center of town, naming all the streets and landmarks after people and places in Abraham Lincoln's life.

I followed the map I'd printed out, turning from Apollo Court to Zeppelin Drive to Neil Armstrong Lane, ending at 3636 Hangar Way, the address of the Ferguson twins' factory. Their low-lying building was multiwinged (so to speak), surrounded by a neat lawn and an extensive parking lot.

The sprinkler keeping the grass green provided the only sound I heard.

I parked and walked toward the large glass double-door entrance, trying to remember why I'd thought it was so important that I come here. I hadn't even bothered to find out if any of the Fergusons would be working today. I'd noticed quite a few cars, trucks, and vans as I'd driven through the neighborhood, but I hadn't seen a single person once I'd arrived in the district. Although Maddie had the day off from school, this Monday wasn't a statewide vacation day. For all I knew, however, it was Chuck Yeager's birthday and all airplane-related industry was on holiday.

My to-do list came to mind. This trip was the action item

for number three—to make some headway in the murder investigation of Oliver Halbert. When I made the list this morning, I'd felt all would fall into place if I could simply get to the bottom of the relationships among the twins, the deceased Oliver Halbert, and the architect Ken Porter. I wished I'd thought out just how I was going to accomplish that.

I wondered which wing Ken had worked on during the first remodel of the plant. I looked for signs of a fire and a second remodel, but the outside of the building was as smooth as if it had been planned this way from the start.

There was still time to turn back. I could call Henry and have him take Maddie and Taylor and meet them at Rosie's Books for the children's reading program she held every Monday. Certainly that would be a better use of my time.

"Well, well, well. Look who made her way to the edge of town."

Too late.

Sam Ferguson stood on the threshold of the entryway to E&E Parts, the Ferguson twins' operation.

I nearly lost my balance though I was standing on a perfectly level walkway. I recovered in time to stammer, "Good morning, Sam. I heard you were out here some days." I thought how dumb I must have sounded.

"Oh, yes, we still keep it all in the family," Sam said, standing in front of me as if he'd also been caught off guard. The moment threw me back to my days at Abraham Lincoln High School when I'd approach a group of my students in the hallway and get the distinct impression that they'd been talking about me. I wondered if I'd caught Sam and the rest of the family talking about me. Maybe Eliot and Lillian had prepared everyone to be on the alert when I came around.

"I'd forgotten how windy it gets out here," I said, since he'd gone silent after that brief comment. I brushed my hair from my eyes but stopped short of telling him how I didn't usually wear my hair this long and was due for a cut.

"Something I can help you with?" Sam asked. Sam was wearing what I thought of as a scarecrow outfit—jeans belted high on his waist, a red plaid shirt, and work shoes. When he started to rock back and forth on his heels, the association with farmland was magnified. I remembered that Sam was originally from Georgia. Was that farm country? Not since fifth grade had I known all the states' capitals and major imports and exports.

Sam was missing only a straw hat to complete the image. And a bullet hole in the head, to be up to the minute with the news. I brushed away the memory.

Who killed Oliver Halbert and left him on your porch, Sam? I wanted to ask.

I settled on, "I'm cleaning out some of my husband's things, and I came across the paperwork for the remodel out here. It made me want to see his handiwork."

Sam smiled. He'd never seemed to me as wily as his wife. If he saw through me now, he wasn't going to let it bother him.

"Maybe you'd like a tour," he said.

I took a breath. "I'd love one."

Chapter 14

Sam couldn't help himself as we walked around E&E Parts. He was clearly proud of the operation, one of the last of the family-run factories in the county, he told me, chattering on about how respected his boys' business was in the industry. And was I aware that the boys were no longer renters in the complex but now owned the factory building.

"They must be very hard workers," I said, feeling that's what Sam was fishing for.

The work area behind the offices had the feel of an airplane hangar that had been partitioned off and stocked with machinery. I thought how Henry would have enjoyed the setting, an expanded version of his own workshop. (I thought about Henry a lot lately.)

The floor was littered with sawdust, wood chips, and metal filings, all of which left the place smelling strangely clean. I was glad I'd worn closed-toe shoes with nonslip soles as Sam led me around oversize shop equipment and pointed out lathes, grinders, and band saws, some of which had workers in overalls in front of them, and all of which looked ominous.

I was almost relieved to see a bag of golf clubs and an industrial-size bucket full of nonthreatening mops and brooms in one corner. A coat hanger on a nearby hook held a voluminous black dress and cape, which could well have been the costume Eliot carried down the stairs during my visit with his mother—Lillian's costume. I had the uncharitable thought that what seemed to be a witch's outfit was not inappropriate for her. The fact that the costume was hanging next to the brooms only added to the image. Bags and boxes around the cleaning supplies held what looked like crepe paper, pumpkins, and the makings of a straw man.

I pointed to the decorations. "I see you're getting ready for your Halloween party."

"Oh, yes. You should come and bring your adorable little granddaughter. The only requirement is that you bring a decoration."

"I think I can manage that," I said, though I had no intention of having Maddie deal with the Fergusons too soon. I didn't want to remind her of the crime scene that had begun our Halloween season, though it was on the opposite end of town from the factory.

"It's all in adapting," Sam said, back on track with the factory tour. "We started out strictly manufacturing, and we were going like gangbusters, but that first remodel was wishful thinking. We'd expected to grow a lot more, but then times got tough." Sam shook his head, remembering a low point, it seemed. "So we got creative and switched to brokering."

Brokering was a financial term to me. "Brokering airplane parts?" I asked.

Sam nodded and we paused for a lesson. "Say you live in San Jose and you want a special part because you're re-

building a Cessna in your backyard. Well, I've been all over
the country, going to shows and visiting dealers, and I know
a guy in Idaho who has the right engine for you, and another guy in Florida who has the cylinder stud assembly
you're looking for, and so and so on. I'll get you your parts,
take a little handling fee, and you're set to go."

"You're the middle man."

Sam didn't acknowledge the term but went on to the
next phase.

"The Internet changed all that. Now everyone can just
go online and find any part anywhere in the world, all by
hisself."

I smiled at the use of the possessive reflexive and Sam's
reversion to his native Georgia dialect. Over the years I'd
become convinced that no one ever really loses his child-
hood accent. I didn't need to be reminded of the times I
slipped into the Bronx dialect: "huh" for "her" and "Poo-
all" for "Paul," were among my most recent throwbacks.

"I guess the Internet has changed the way everyone does
business," I added, as if I had intimate knowledge of the
phenomenon.

"Yep, so we went back to manufacturing, but it just
wasn't working. There's not many able to make it that way
in this country right now."

"You seem pretty busy," I said, noting a pile of pallets at
a side door and boxes of unidentifiable (by me) parts every-
where. The assortment of gray shapes put me in mind of
robots, some with arms and legs, some without. I thought I
recognized one from an animated movie I once saw with
Maddie.

"We're busy all right. My boys are good. They rein-
vented themselves one more time, and now we're into repair and overhaul." He pointed to a high shelf over a large
workbench, about twice as long as Henry's. (There it was

again, a thought of Henry.) "We have radar equipment up there on the left, then brakes, airplane computer systems, landing gear, flight control panels." I followed his finger. "The bubble over the pilot, the windshield. A company will send us ten parts that failed. So we troubleshoot and test one, figuring they've all failed for the same reason. Usually we're right and then we fix all the rest."

Sam spread his hands as if to say, that's all there was to it. I waited for him to take me back to the navy radar systems on the left, the ones Eliot had allegedly worked on, on the day of Oliver's murder, half expecting him to repeat the alibi Lillian had provided for her son.

"What do you do here, Sam?" I asked.

Sam waved his hands. "This and that. All-purpose shop work. I love machines. I grew up with them but I never had my own factory. My boys have done very, very well."

Sam continued talking, possibly saying more about the radar systems. Or he may have been inviting me to lunch. I couldn't tell. I was too busy looking past him at a glassed-in conference room. At a large rectangular table sat the twins, Lillian Ferguson, and the two goons. Lillian, at the head of the table, faced us.

I gulped and shifted my large purse up from my shoulder to front and center on my chest. I did my best not to make eye contact, but as I turned away from the room, I sensed Lillian's eyes on my back.

I felt a bit shaky, encountering Lynch and Crowley again with only a glass wall between us, and I thought sure Lillian would bolt from the meeting any minute and rush out to shut Sam up. I needed to get a few questions in before that happened.

"What a shame about the fire," I said as Sam and I retraced our steps and walked back toward the front of the factory.

"Yup, it was a terrible setback for the boys. Terrible," Sam said, with a shake of his head.

I wondered if he'd ever given a thought to the janitor and his family. I had no reason to think otherwise. For all I knew he'd made a generous donation to the Pattersons.

I wracked my brain trying to come up with a way to turn the conversation to the cause of the fire. I hit upon something brilliant.

"I'm trying to remember what was determined to be the cause of the fire?" I asked.

Maybe not brilliant, but it got Sam talking.

Sam bent over and picked up a handful of metal filings. "These are magnesium filings. They're very combustible; they're used in bombs, in fact. You can have all the regulation sprinklers in the world, but this stuff"—he made an elaborate frown, moving his long chin sideways and knitting his brow—"it's deadly. If there's a spark from the grinder, it could ignite the filings on the floor or down in the cabinet where they pile up."

"I see what you mean," I said, not sure why I was getting this lesson. Did Sam think I had influence over an arson investigator?

"And look at that," Sam said, not finished. He pointed to a forklift near the delivery door of the factory. "That tank holds eight gallons of propane. Some idiot who was helping us one Saturday decided to put a space heater right near the lift because there was a cold wind coming in the door. Do you know what could have happened if one of us hadn't come along and whisked it away?

"I can imagine," I said, still wondering what my reaction was supposed to be.

"Do you know how many things could go wrong, every hour of every day in a shop like this?"

I didn't, and I was interested only in what went wrong on the night of the fire. I realized it was naïve of me to think that Sam would let anything incriminating slip from his tongue, especially since a lawsuit might still be pending, not to mention criminal charges.

"Sam!" Lillian's screechy voice rang through the plant. She used a high-pitched, scolding tone, apparently not as sure as I was that Sam would be prudent. "Sam," she yelled again.

Sam addressed me in a hurried tone. I wondered if he were always fighting against Lillian's authority. "See that electrical conduit up there?" he asked, pointing to a corner above a complicated machine. "Lots of times people cheat on the material, but not here. My boys follow the rules."

"Sam," Lillian said, catching up with us. "Emory needs you in the shop."

The last time I saw him, Emory had been seated at the conference table next to his twin. And since the entire shop was visible from almost every corner, I could see that he hadn't entered the area.

"Coming, Mother," Sam said, poking me in the arm as he left me. Lillian barely acknowledged my presence as she stalked off.

I certainly hadn't been a model parent and no right to criticize, but it seemed clear to me why neither of the Ferguson twins had ever married.

I made a dash for the door. Not that I was afraid of an old lady. Or a witch.

I shifted my tote in preparation for entering my car and fleeing E&E Parts. I dug out my keys and clicked the remote from a few feet away.

What had I learned from my visit to the outskirts of town? Only that Lillian was in charge. She'd been seated at the head of the conference table, the twins on one side, Lynch and Crowley on the other. Sam had been playful when she called out to him, but it was clear he meant to obey.

Crunch. Crunch.

Footsteps and a rustling of clothing on my left startled me.

"Let me get that for you." Lynch's deep voice. He came around me and put his hand on my car door.

My heart flipped. I couldn't imagine why. We were standing in broad daylight, and Lynch's voice had been pleasant, his hands free of weaponry. If I were one to participate in Halloween costume parties, this year it would be the cowardly lion for me, no doubt about it.

"Mr. Lynch," I said, embarrassed that he most likely knew he'd frightened me.

Over Lynch's shoulder, about twenty yards away, I saw Crowley and the twins hurrying toward three different vehicles. Emory, who supposedly needed Sam in the shop, must have changed his mind.

Crowley kept his head down. I peered at him to be sure he didn't have his hand in a bulging pocket. The twins took long strides toward their cars, one white and one blue pickup. Eliot, apparently unable to be completely rude to a former teacher, waved at me but turned his head away quickly.

I had the feeling they were all using Lynch to distract me so they wouldn't have to talk to me. Or had they sent Lynch to do their dirty work? I inched my body closer to my car, trying to put the open door between him and me.

"Geraldine. May I call you Geraldine?" Lynch asked. He

was taller than me by a couple of inches, maybe six feet tall, and he used every inch to appear to tower over me.

"Of course, Patrick." I was glad to hear, after the fact, that the intimidation I'd felt hadn't revealed itself in my voice.

It flashed through my mind that, all things considered, Patrick Lynch had done nothing bad to me; I'd tripped all on my own. He'd entered Oliver's house with a key, possibly given to him by Oliver. Who knew what complex relationships existed between a city inspector and his clientele? Lynch had simply been protecting himself against a possible intruder—me. That Lynch or Crowley had a gun in the first place was not surprising. Construction sites could be dangerous places. There were rats, for example. The nonhuman kind.

When I saw him at the apartment, Lynch had said that he was there to claim property that belonged to him. Maybe that was true but I doubted it. I figured he was more than likely there to claim property that might work against him, like a computer file. For now it helped me to consider all the benign possibilities that I could think of.

"We seem to meet in the most unusual places," he said, with a smile that relaxed me somewhat. "What brought you to E&E Parts on this beautiful day?"

I took a moment to gather my wits and think of my training from Skip (not that he intended to train me with his tidbits and anecdotes): when you're interviewing a witness or a suspect, you don't answer their questions; you try to get your own answered.

Now that we were on a first name basis, this might be the time to ask Patrick about the memo I'd found, from him to Ken, noting the "arrangement which benefits many," and a company or project called EELFS.

"I wasn't aware until recently that you had business dealings with my late husband."

Well, that wasn't a question, but I was a rookie.

Lynch's smile turned crooked, his long scar curving to the left side of his cheek. "Architects are an important part of my operation," he said. "We depend on their cooperation."

That was not what I wanted to hear. I felt a chill along my spine, though the sun couldn't have been warmer on my back. I didn't like having Ken considered part of the Lynch operation. I wished Skip were here. I'd ask him how to get information you didn't really want to know.

"I understand you worked together"—here I paused to clear my throat—"on the remodel of this factory."

Lynch's nod was slow and deliberate with a touch of a threat.

Why didn't I just ask him outright? Did Ken cheat for you? Did he take money to skirt regulations? Is that the arrangement you talked about in the memo? Is that why the fire broke out and Mr. Patterson died? Was that the EELFS project?

"We certainly did," he said.

I had a dizzy moment until I realized he wasn't answering yes to the questions in my mind, but simply acknowledging that Ken worked on the remodel.

"I'm sure it was a satisfying experience," I said. "My husband was a very respected and honorable businessman." Even to myself, I sounded like a doting wife—or indulgent mother, like Lillian.

"Now, see, that might be coming into question," he said. "That honorable part."

My throat tightened and my voice came out in a high-pitched whine, not as loud as Lillian's, but just as witchy. "Meaning what?"

"Meaning maybe we can help each other." He laughed. "Hey, you can be an elf."

"What exactly was the EELFS project, Patrick? Was it this remodel?"

He flinched, perhaps sorry he'd mentioned it. "I tell you what, Geraldine. You leave the past alone and so will I."

I hated the way he pronounced my name, emphasizing each syllable equally. "There's nothing in the past that I need to worry about," I said, my jaw so tight it ached.

Lynch touched his forehead, tipping an imaginary hat and turning to leave. "Wives don't always know everything, Geraldine."

"This one does," I said and got in my car.

Could he possibly know how unsure I was of those words?

I sat in my car, unable to move a muscle. I watched Lynch walk toward a white BMW. He had the air of one who had sealed a deal. What made him think he needed me to hide something in the past? And the reference to an elf, which, I felt sure, was related to the EELFS in the "arrangements" memo. I liked a good puzzle but not when the stakes of solving it were so high.

I pictured Lynch in a bright red costume for Halloween, horns and pitchfork jutting up and out.

I hated the thought that I might have just made a deal with him.

When I was finally able to take control of my body, I wound around Aviation Way, glad to be among very few vehicles on the road. The better to track someone following me, I reasoned. I imagined that I was leaving inhospitable foreign soil, where I hadn't understood the language and needed to leave word with my travel agent that I never wanted to return.

He did the mash. He did the monster mash.

Boris Pickett again. I flipped open my cell phone and saw Maddie's number on the screen. A welcome message from my homeland. I put the phone on my lap and pushed "speaker," obeying the letter, if not the spirit, of the "hands free" California cell phone law.

"Hi, Grandma. It's almost lunchtime."

"It's just a little past eleven," I said, a smile breaking out at the sound of the friendliest voice in the world.

"I didn't have much breakfast."

It felt good to laugh. "I'm hungry, too," I said, hoping I'd be able to keep something down by the time we got together.

"Here's Mr. Baker," Maddie said.

"Hi," Henry said. "Are you at a good point for a break?"

"More than you know."

"Fine, then. What shall we do for lunch?" he asked, as if we were a family.

"I'll meet you at Willie's," I said, ready for family.

I parked in front of Abe's Hardware, next door to Willie's, and took out my notepad. I'd written down the Sunnyvale number for the architectural firm that had taken over the business from Ken and Artie. It was time to tackle another item on my to-do list.

I punched in the digits and reached a voice mail telling me that all lines were busy but I was welcome to leave a message. I wished I'd written out a script for such an eventuality. I stumbled through a sentence about trying to reach

Arthur Dodd, former owner of the business with Ken Porter. I left my name and where to reach me, then flipped the phone closed.

There wasn't much more I could do except join my family for lunch.

Even more family than I expected had gathered at Bagels by Willie. I spotted Henry, Taylor, Maddie, and Skip in the back of the shop at Willie's largest table.

"Look, Grandma, we found Uncle Skip," Maddie said, as if Skip weren't a tall, stands-out-in-a-crowded-room redhead.

Henry half stood in greeting and smiled at me in a way that erased whatever had ruined my morning. He pulled out a chair and I sat next to him. Skip gave me a wink and a knowing look that reminded me of my days with adolescents in the ALHS cafeteria, and I gave him one back that said, "Don't you dare make a comment."

"Uncle Skip says knock-knock jokes are from Shakespeare," Taylor said, sounding very comfortable as another of Skip's admiring preteen "nieces," and as a member of the family.

I was thrilled about the latest scholarly outreach on the part of my nephew, now studying Shakespeare to round out his law enforcement training. I'd meant to give him some related literary criticism to augment his class material. I had file drawers full of articles that might now be of interest to him. It was probably just as well that I didn't push it on him.

I closed my eyes and tried to picture the relevant page in my well-worn text for *Macbeth*.

"'Knock, knock. Who's there, i' the name of Beelzebub? . . . Knock, knock. Who's there, in the other devil's name?'" I recited.

Henry started a round of (thankfully) subdued applause. "Wicked," Maddie said.

There was a time when I could have gone much farther in the scene. Then I might have deserved the kudos; now I blushed and held up my hand to stop them.

As far as I knew, there were only weak links connecting the porter's (not this Porter) passage in *Macbeth* to the current use of the phrase in endless jokes told by children of all ages. My students liked to think they were reading the jokes' origin, however, and whatever made Shakespeare seem like a regular guy, even a guy who invented jokes, was fine with me.

We placed our orders with a young waitress who was overly solicitous to Skip and continued our happy talk.

Maddie's report: Richard and Mary Lou had taken her last week to see a three-dimensional animated film, an experience that called for special glasses. I knew Mary Lou could relax enough to enjoy a kids' movie, but I wasn't so sure about Richard. Maddie's claim that "my dad even sat through it" made me proud of my son for sticking out what must have seemed like hours of sheer boredom.

Taylor's report: she'd seen the same movie with Kay and Bill and admitted how scared she'd been, ducking "even though I knew all those creatures weren't really coming at me."

"And sometimes they came from behind you," Maddie added, waving her arms to indicate many directions of attack.

Henry's report evoked more fear in me than flying creatures in living three dimensions: he'd read about a dollhouse castle, in one-inch-to-one-foot scale, formerly owned and built by a silent film star. The eight-by-eight-foot house was the dream project of the actress and her family. Its chandeliers contained real diamonds, emeralds, and pearls; its china was a set of Royal Doulton. In the chapel lay the smallest Bible in the world, printed with real type.

Those weren't the scary parts. What frightened me was Henry's closing suggestion.

"The castle is at the Chicago Museum of Science and Industry," he said. "I think we should all make a trip there to see it."

I cleared my throat and looked quickly at Skip. "And what have you been up to?" I asked, before he could comment on the trip proposal.

The idea didn't get by Maddie and Taylor, however.

They squealed in unison.

"Yes!"

The girls proceeded to complain to each other about how they'd never been to Chicago in their whole lives. They failed to mention how each had been treated to a cross-country tour before they started school, summer vacations up and down the West Coast, and countless weekend visits to theme parks.

I didn't repeat my own sad story, about seeing nothing west of the Bronx until I was almost thirty years old.

Maddie and Taylor didn't seem to notice that the adults at the table, including Henry, whom I couldn't bring myself to look at, had already dropped the subject. I knew I'd have to address it later with Henry, but not in public.

A strange feeling came over me as I felt my fear slip away and an image of my suitcase came to my mind. I would have been hard pressed to say for sure how I saw that talk with Henry going.

Skip declined to talk about his work. He treated us instead to a hint of what his Halloween costume would be. "It's from Shakespeare," he said.

"So's mine," said Maddie, delighted, while I made a mental note to get started on finding decent material for eye of newt, toe of frog, and so on.

The arrival of five bagel platters and drinks all around stifled chatter for a few minutes.

I took a bite of a cinnamon bagel with honeyed cream cheese. I was amazed to find that I'd regained my appetite.

Chapter 15

On the way home, Maddie and I decided to take a detour down another Lincoln Point street that was known for outstanding Halloween decorations. Appomattox Way didn't take competition as seriously as Sangamon River Road (which had been perhaps a little too serious this year), but its lawn and window decorations were quite extravagant.

One family had given over its entire front picture window to a life-size silhouette of an old woman sitting in a rocking chair, the scene unabashedly reminiscent of one in the movie *Psycho* that featured Norman Bates's mother. My one required course in college science was a dim memory, and now I wished I'd paid more attention. I wondered what kind of elaborate lighting system could produce a black silhouette on such a bright day.

We parked across from the immobile old woman and walked a couple of blocks, past a lawn that presented a man popping up and down from his casket bed, like a macabre jack-in-the-box, a trick that didn't seem as humorous as it might have without a real-life murder in Lincoln Point. Next door was a display of ghoulish black creatures—a vampire bat with a large wing spread, and three kinds of vulture.

"Wicked," Maddie said.

We were about to turn back to the car when we spotted our crafter friend, Karen Striker, disembarking from an SUV across the street. I'd forgotten that she lived on Appomattox. With her delivery date just around the corner, Karen had much needed help from her husband, who guided her to the sidewalk.

What a trick or treat, I thought, if Karen went into labor in the vicinity of the lawn decoration Maddie and I had just passed—a large black cradle marked *Rosemary's Baby*.

Karen spotted Maddie and me and waved us over.

Maddie was happy to cross the street where she could get a closer look at a family of pumpkins that served as candy bowls. It had already been a half hour since her last meal, so I could understand her need for food.

"We just got back from that big miniatures show in Mill Valley," Karen said, indicating several large tote bags being dragged from the backseat by her husband, Mark.

"You've been all the way to Marin County and back already?" I asked, discreetly pointing to her state of advanced pregnancy.

"I had to go," she said. "The next show isn't until after the baby is born. At the last minute, I decided on a Cape Cod for Baby Striker. I realized the Victorian I've been working on is never going to be finished before she arrives. I'm hardly finished sewing the dust ruffles for her bedroom. I had to get something I could decorate simply and quickly. So I bought a much simpler style and I already have enough furniture to set it up in just a few days."

Mark made a looping motion with his fingers, indicating

that his wife might be a little off balance. "I told her the baby isn't going to notice anything. She's going to be focused on breathing and eating. When she's even awake, that is."

"Can you imagine having the baby arrive home to a room without a finished dollhouse?" Karen asked. Her expression said that the idea was incomprehensible.

"Can we see the house?" Maddie asked, sparing me the need to respond. She'd just unwrapped her third piece of candy. I knew I should have been more solicitous of her eating habits, but what's a grandmother to do?

With the great patience he'd need to be a good father, Mark released the tailgate of the SUV and removed tape from a large trash bag. The green plastic fell away, unveiling a lovely prebuilt and painted Cape Cod with two floors and an attic.

With siding on the outside walls, sturdy shingles on the peaked roof, and shuttered, double-paned windows, the house might have been able to withstand the difficult weather of the New England coast as well as the real thing.

"I wouldn't usually get a ready-made, you know, Gerry, but timing is critical at the moment."

"I won't tell Linda," I offered, though I knew even our purist crafter Linda Reed would have excused a mother-to-be for not playing carpenter during her last month of pregnancy.

With Karen's permission, Maddie and I rummaged through the purchases that were accessible in her totes. Karen had some wonderful finds, like a miniature fireplace set and scatter rugs, as well as many accessories for each room. We came close to accepting her invitation to go inside for a full report on the dollhouse show she'd traveled more than fifty miles to attend, but the sight of miniatures reminded me of my promise to another crafter in our group, Susan Giles. If I couldn't

find her brother's killer lickety-split, I could at least repair her
room box in a timely fashion.

"I wish I'd been to the dollhouse show with Karen. I love
Bozo and Koko," Maddie said, as we settled ourselves on
stools in front of Oliver's room box.

I had fond memories of the two famous clowns, who,
under their bulbous red noses and oversized polka-dot outfits,
were Phyllis Hedman (Koko) and Barbara Jones (Bozo), the
tireless organizers of miniature shows.

We reminisced about shows we'd been to over the past
couple of years since Maddie had become involved with miniatures. I remembered an older couple who dressed in identical white suits and offered their beautiful inlaid wood furniture
for sale. Maddie tended to remember the accidents—the kids
on wheelies who knocked over a miniature book store; the
kitchenware vendor who complained about the neighboring
miniaturist with "a big butt" (a direct quote from the vendor)
who bumped into her table every time he got up and sent mini
silverware and tiny spatulas and strainers flying.

It was easy to laugh when we hadn't been the victims.

The mini construction scene room box of victim Oliver
Halbert beckoned and we set to work.

I reattached the Rosie the Riveter poster while Maddie
applied paint on a bashed-in corner of the box.

"While you have the brown paint on your brush, maybe
you can touch up that workbench top," I suggested.

Maddie picked up the loosened piece. "This must be new.
I don't remember the flash drive being here," she said.

Flash drive? Was that anything like flash fiction? Probably not, though I'd read that flash fiction, the designation
for stories as brief as fifty words, was undergoing a renais-

sance thanks to a rash of Internet sites that accepted and even paid writers for it.

I had heard the term "flash drive" as related to computers and had bought one for Richard's birthday a few years ago, from a catalog, at his request. I wasn't sure I'd recognize one in the flesh, however. "Where is it?" I asked Maddie.

She pointed to the makeshift finger-length bench top that I'd thought needed a better paint job, the one I assumed Susan had put together in a hurry.

"See, she used a flash drive as the top of the workbench. Wicked."

I took the item from her hand and looked at the piece of plastic, about three inches long, three quarters of an inch wide, one quarter of an inch thick. Its original red color showed through the sloppy brown brush strokes. I fingered a small metal hook on one end that I hadn't noticed when the piece was in place in the scene. I thought it might be for threading a key chain through it.

"What exactly is this used for?" I asked the resident specialist.

"It's just, like, another drive for your computer. You can transfer files with it. You put stuff on it and then you can take it away and plug it into another computer and work on the files, or you can give it to someone for their computer as long as they have a USB port. Are you getting this, Grandma?"

"Barely."

Maddie took the flash drive back from me and pulled on one end, removing a cover and revealing a rectangular metal protrusion. "Okay, see? You plug this end into any computer, just like you'd do with a keyboard or a mouse, and you can download whatever is on here, onto your computer."

"So, if there's information on that drive, I'd be able to

get to it from my computer?" I knew I sounded dense, but this was no time for pretense.

She handed the drive back as if it were nothing important, just another mini bench top that had been badly painted. "Uh-huh. Me and Taylor do it all the time."

Never mind my granddaughter's cavalier misuse of the objective pronoun, I had more important things to consider. I noticed that the shade of brown used to paint the flash drive was the same as that on the baseboard of Oliver's apartment as I remembered it, and I did have a good eye for color, if not for computer portals.

Had it been Oliver Halbert and not Susan who'd done the awful paint job? It seemed so. Oliver must have known he was in danger, or might be. It looked as though he'd tried to hide the flash drive containing incriminating information so it wouldn't fall into the wrong hands. He'd painted it quickly with what he had handy, then set it on top of a wine cork to make a crude table.

His information might have stayed hidden forever if I hadn't dropped the scene on the floor. And if I didn't have a very smart granddaughter.

The flash drive, or something like it, must have been what Lynch and Crowley were looking for.

Did they know I had it now? Probably not, or the threat I felt this morning would have been much more dire. Besides, they'd searched my tote while I was passed out in the apartment. If they'd known what they were looking for, they would have seen it.

Was Ken's name on the drive? Did I want to know?

I felt out of breath with the possibilities.

I thought back to the question Skip asked me after I'd visited Oliver's apartment: "Did you find the crucial piece of evidence we missed?" he'd asked, facetiously.

It seemed I might have.

* * *

I stood at my stove, waiting for water to boil. Maddie had left me to my reflections, having become caught up in fixing the strap on a miniature hard hat in Susan's room box. I'd slipped the flash drive in my pocket and left the crafts room to heat water for tea.

Should I try to find out what was on the drive, or should I call Skip immediately? Not an easy question. Why bother him with what might be nothing? I thought of Ken, of his "arrangement" with Patrick Lynch, of the photograph of him with a baby. There might be nothing on the drive; or there might be everything.

I took my cup of tea back to the crafts table. I handed Maddie the flash drive. "Can you use your computer or mine to tell me what's on here?" I asked, almost surprising myself.

My mind must have been made up somewhere between the whistling of the kettle and the pouring of the hot water.

"Sure. Probably mine is better; your computer is a little lame. I'm not even sure it has a USB one port, let alone USB two." She laughed as if everyone listening would get her joke.

I followed my granddaughter to her room and watched her plug the drive into her computer. In less than a minute a squarish white icon appeared on her desktop (the one that was a screen, not a shiny cherrywood). Beneath the icon was the phrase, *Potentials Data*.

Oliver had called his list of suspect businesspeople "Potentials." Ken's name had been on that list. What did "Potentials Data" mean? That, in a more detailed version of the list, Ken's name had been crossed out? Think positive, I told myself.

Its most obvious meaning was that Oliver had been more specific in this medium than he'd been on the handwritten list the police had found. I envisioned names, dates, and dollar amounts. I mentally ran a thick red marker through Ken's name, striking it from the list.

"Nuts," Maddie said, screwing up her face and banging on the edge of her keyboard.

"What's wrong? Do you need my computer?" I teased.

"It's password protected."

I felt a wave of relief. "Never mind, then. It's not important anyway." Putting off the inevitable had become a way of life for me.

"I can work on it. Sometimes I can figure them out, but only if they're short. Or, like, sometimes people just use defaults, like 'password'"—she typed it, and an *access denied* message appeared on the screen—"or, like, 'flashdrive'"—she typed it, with the same result.

"Try using 'like,'" I said, gently badgering her about her rampant use of the word, though I considered her better than most kids about good usage.

"Nuts." Maddie ignored my attempt at humor and blew a breath of defeat out the side of her mouth.

She tapped the drive, which was sticking out of her computer like some unnatural growth. "I'd have a better chance if I knew something about the person who owned this." She gave me a wide-eyed look that said a light had gone on in her head.

That could only mean trouble. "Don't worry about it, sweetheart. I told you, it's not important."

"It's about The Case, isn't it? I knew Mrs. Giles didn't have it in the room box when we all worked on it, so it must be her brother's drive, the man who died. That's where you found the mini scene. At his house, right? I'll bet the drive is his and he put it in the room box to hide it. Wicked."

She leapt from her chair and nearly danced around it. "I

should have known." She sat back down. "I have to crack this password. It will help Uncle Skip crack the case." She grinned. "That will be two cracks."

I put my hand on her shoulder. "I'm not sure whose it is or what it is or who put it in the box," I said, honestly. "But I think we should take it to Uncle Skip, just in case it's important to his investigation." I tried to emphasize *his* investigation.

While I was being so calm and logical, Maddie's fingers were flying across the keyboard, stopping every now and then to use the mouse.

"What in the world are you doing?"

"I'm trying things from Mr. Halbert's life. I just found his Facebook page. I should have thought of doing that before, instead of quitting after I Googled him."

Were my son and his wife raising the computer geek everyone in school made fun of? I had the feeling that schools were now full of Maddie's kind of geek.

"Shouldn't you be making mini ghosts for Halloween? Or working on your costume?"

"Our computer teacher says never to use anything obvious for a password, but most people do, so they can remember it. I'm trying his birthday and his daughters' names. Do you know if he had a pet?"

"How do you know his daughters' names?"

"Jeanine and Casey. It's in his Facebook profile. Probably if he had a pet, it would be in his profile. A lot of people use pictures of themselves with their pets or just their pets as their avatar."

Of course they did. What I knew of all the emerging networking sites didn't inspire trust. "Don't people lie on those profiles?"

"Yeah, they do, but you wouldn't lie about your children's names. It wouldn't make sense. You'd just say you didn't have kids."

"Do you have a Facebook page?" I asked.

She grinned up at me. "Duh."

At what point did I lose track of all the minutiae of my granddaughter's life? I knew that I had no private life until I went to college. My parents asked questions and I answered. Now I wouldn't even know the questions to ask.

"Am I on your Facebook page?" I asked.

"Uh-huh. Do you want to see it? I can set you up on Facebook and then we can be friends and write on each other's walls. That's what they call it when you send a message."

"Isn't that what text messaging is all about? And e-mail?"

"Yeah, but that's not really networking, like Facebook and MySpace and Twitter and—"

"Never mind."

I was just getting used to deciphering e-mail shortcuts such as CU for "see you" (used all the time by Maddie) and YTB for "you're the best" (from Mary Lou). Karen Striker had ended an e-mail to me last week, TTUL. "Talk to you later," she'd explained the next time we had an old-fashioned ear-to-ear phone conversation.

Did I want to extend my social networking skills and put myself on Facebook? Write on someone's wall?

"Do you want to be my Facebook friend?" Maddie asked, with a wide grin.

"Maybe some other time," I said.

Maddie had been typing while we talked. "I tried the hobbies Mr. Halbert listed, like rafting and chess. It's a good thing he didn't put a program on here to limit the times you can fail before they cut you off. I'd be in trouble."

I thought we might already be in trouble, withholding

evidence. "I think we should quit now and just give the drive to Uncle Skip."

"If I could go to Mr. Halbert's apartment, I could probably crack the password."

That wasn't going to happen, but I was curious. "How would that help?"

"Well, first, I'd look through his desk. Lots of people write down their passwords, which you're really not supposed to. Then, I'd look around his office. Like, if he has a poster of some rock group, I'd try the name of the group. Or if there's a rose bush outside his window, I'd try 'rosebush' or 'redroses.' That kind of stuff."

The things my granddaughter knew about human behavior astounded me.

"Ms. Anderson is teaching us better ways to crack passwords using special programs that you can install on your computer."

"Your computer teacher is showing you how to break into someone else's computer?"

Another charming grin. "You'd only do it in an emergency."

"I'm going to call Uncle Skip."

"Please, Grandma, just give me a little more time."

"You can work on it while I make the call," I said.

Skip arrived in record time, claiming he was in the neighborhood. I imagined he'd be anxious to take what might be pivotal evidence out of harm's way. I was sure he'd also want to protect Maddie and me, in case the drive was the known target of a search by people with a vested interest in its destruction.

Maddie had worked on figuring out the password right up to the minute the doorbell rang before she gave up.

Skip took the flash drive from her and bounced it in his hand, as if he were juggling the data itself in his mind. "This could be it," he said. I heard a capital I in his tone.

"I'm sorry I couldn't crack the password code," Maddie told Skip.

"But you found the drive, sweetheart. I've seen it lots of times and I thought it was just an old piece of plastic painted brown," I said.

"And my guys walked right by the thing when they searched Mr. Halbert's apartment and none of them recognized what it was, either," Skip said.

Maddie accepted the praise with a wide grin. "I wish I could have cracked it, though," she said, sounding too much like her perfectionist father.

"You know, I'll bet you could have if you had a bigger computer. Tell your dad to get you an upgrade."

Some things never changed—Skip always enjoyed hassling his cousin Richard, even remotely.

Skip lifted Maddie off the floor and swung her around—a far cry from what seemed only a short time ago, when he could pick her up and hoist her on his shoulders.

I had a brief moment alone with Skip while Maddie called her parents. We were asked to stand by in case either of her parents doubted the magnitude of her skills or her need for a new computer. I hoped Richard wouldn't stress out at the idea that she'd helped with police work. I trusted Mary Lou to calm him down if he did. After all, she was the one who told me that if Richard ever complained, I should invoke the universal rule: what happens at Grandma's stays at Grandma's. It worked for me.

"Any word on the building in that photograph I gave you?" I asked Skip.

"Actually, yeah. I was going to call you." Skip pulled the envelope with the photographs out of his pocket. "Did you ever hear of Sunaqua Estates? It's in upstate New York, in a town called Sunaqua Falls."

I shook my head. Upstate New York was about as far from the Bronx as California in some ways. Ken and I never owned a car in New York City and few of our friends did, so a trip to Peekskill, about an hour away, to visit former neighbors, was considered a major journey. So different from our lives on the West Coast, where we wouldn't think twice about driving forty-five minutes to meet friends for lunch.

"Do you even know what the term 'Estates' refers to? Could it be a housing development? A country club?" I asked Skip, keeping my voice low. Maddie had been busy enough with the flash drive; she didn't need to worry about another "case."

Skip had taken the photos from the envelope. He tapped his finger on an image of the building, most prominent in the long shot. "I think it's kind of a cross between an orphanage and a home for special-needs children."

"Special needs like learning disabilities? Is it a school?"

Skip shrugged. "It wasn't clear from the two-line caption in the database, but I got the impression it was more about sick kids. The database is not maintained very well, by the way, so there's no guarantee the place is still in operation or even that it hasn't burned down in the last few years. One of the techs said they don't have a website, and he didn't have time yet to Google it."

"Do you need Googling?" asked the returning heroine.

"Nuh-uh," Skip said, pulling Maddie into a hug while he stuffed the envelope in the pocket of my coat sweater. He kissed the top of her head. "Thanks, squirt, but the Lincoln Point cops have to do something to earn the big bucks they pay us." He released her and gave me a good-bye peck.

"Will you let me know how you crack the password?" Maddie asked.

"Sure will."

I guessed Maddie's fingers were itching to have the drive back.

My fingers were itching also. I needed to get to directory assistance for Sunaqua Falls, New York. If that failed, I'd have to Google.

With only one more depressed sigh and whine about not having been able to crack the flash drive password, Maddie was able to return to the crafts room with me.

We'd almost forgotten about the haunted dollhouse, the project we'd wanted to complete this weekend. The plan was to take the finished house to Maddie's school to use as a prop for their Halloween play. We still had one more weekend before it was due, but we decided it would be a good idea to get as much done as possible this afternoon.

"We should put furniture inside, in case some people look in the windows," Maddie said, helping me move the house to the center of the crafts table.

"I'll do that while you make the rest of the ghosts and witches."

"I think I'll add a couple of vampire bats like the ones we saw on Appomattox," she said.

"Good idea. I might have some filmy material around," I said, with a smile. In fact, as we both knew, there was a whole box marked *Material—Filmy* in my supply closet.

I supposed I shouldn't always give my granddaughter the fun parts of projects, but I figured she'd meet enough people in her life who would treat her the opposite way. Though anyone who treated her badly would have me to reckon with for a long time to come.

Her beaming "Thanks, Grandma" was enough to convince me I was taking the right approach.

Buzzz. Buzzz.

The doorbell rang as I was measuring the space for a bathroom mirror over the tiny sink in the dollhouse.

I'd phoned Susan and told her she could pick up her repaired room box anytime. She was overwhelmed with company, she told me. Oliver's daughters had arrived in town, as well as his ex-wife, plus her own ex-husband, who now lived in Florida. She didn't know when she could break away.

"I'm just so glad to know the room box is safe and sound," she'd said. "I can't thank you enough, Gerry."

Buzzz. Buzzz.

I was surprised she'd found the time to pick up the box so quickly. Perhaps she wanted to show the rest of the family the special gift.

I didn't plan to tell Susan about the flash drive. We'd added sawdust to the spot where the cork-based bench had stood and, to the best of our memories, restored the box to its original condition.

"I'll get it," Maddie said, zipping her lip as she ran to let Susan in. Her way of telling me that the existence of the flash drive was our little secret.

"Hello, there," I heard.

Not Susan's voice. A deep voice, and not one I recognized. I dropped the mirror, shattering it, and knocked over the stool as I hurried to the door.

The Ferguson twins stood in the doorway.

Chapter 16

The identical flat smiles on Eliot's and Emory's faces did nothing to put me at ease. I drew Maddie away so that she was mostly behind me, though the twins didn't look at all threatening, possibly because they had their mother's short, stocky physique, so I still had several inches on them.

"Mrs. Porter," said one of the brothers. Probably my former student, Eliot, now back thinking of me as his teacher.

I was tempted to ask them to stroll back down the walkway so I could tell which one had the limp.

"I hope we're not catching you at a bad time," said the other brother.

The twins were dressed as opposite images of each other—one wore denim pants and a khaki shirt; the other wore khaki pants and a denim shirt. I thought I saw grease spots on both shirts in the same place, but that was likely my agitated imagination.

I wondered if they'd chosen their outfits deliberately to be complementary. I remembered identical twin girls in our Bronx apartment building. As teenagers they never wanted to be dressed alike, but inevitably, if they shopped separately, they'd come back with the same items and be annoyed at the fact. Their parents claimed the girls' personalities were as identical as their looks. Research on twins bore that out, leaving me to wonder about "the evil twin" stories. Wouldn't they both be evil?

The thought was no comfort as I stood in front of the Ferguson twins.

I was aware that the evening had turned cold, and I was leaving guests standing in my doorway while I reflected on twin lore. If I'd been alone, I wouldn't have hesitated to invite them in and pick their identical brains.

"Maddie, sweetheart, would you be a dear and go call your Uncle Skip for me? He left something behind and he needs to stop by for it." In a small town like Lincoln Point, I didn't have to mention that said Uncle Skip was with the LPPD; the twins would be aware of the fact.

Maddie ran off without a word. She couldn't have missed the tension in my body. Sometimes we communicated as if we were twins, and I was glad this was one of those times.

I turned to Eliot and Emory. "Please come in," I said.

I took them as far as the atrium. If Maddie caught my cues, she would have locked the glass doors closest to the bedrooms. "Would you like coffee? A soda?" I asked.

Was it just me, or did all women think they had to offer refreshments to everyone who entered their homes, suspected murderers included?

The twins declined, shaking their heads in unison. Now in their late forties, the Ferguson twins wore their thinning hair the same way, with a side part, and sported glasses with identical gold wire frames.

I wondered what it would be like to go through life with another person who was essentially me. Same DNA, same responses and personality. Only their fingerprints were different, I'd read. I thought one of me was plenty.

On the way to our taking seats in the atrium, I'd studied the twins' legs and made up a mnemonic: denim pants equals limp equals Eliot.

"It's been a long time since we've had a chat," Emory said.

I tried to keep from wringing my hands in my nervousness. My guests seemed calm, not worried that an officer in the LPPD might show up at any minute. It was up for grabs whether Maddie had actually phoned Skip or had decided that I simply needed to let the men know that we had personal protection at our beck and call.

"We won't keep you, Mrs. Porter, we just wanted to set the record straight about recent events," denim-pants Eliot added, putting quote marks in the air around "recent events." "Our whole family is upset about Oliver Halbert's death. We know you're tight with his sister and we hope you'll give her that message."

"She's easy to reach, Eliot," I said, flaunting my keen powers of observation. "You might want to tell her yourselves." I realized too late that it wasn't a good idea to sic the twins on Susan, and I hoped they wouldn't ask for her address. I wondered if there was a class I could take for chatting under duress.

"It's awkward," Emory said. "There are some unresolved issues that might be clouding things." This time the air quotes went around "unresolved issues."

Another characteristic the twins shared: inappropriate use of quotation marks. At least one of them didn't have me to blame.

Moreover, the only thing cloudy was this conversation. I needed to clear things up.

"Are you referring to the fact that Oliver Halbert was investigating the cause of the fire in your factory, and that his findings might have cost you a lot of money, not to mention the possibility of criminal charges?"

More long-winded than I'd intended, but certainly direct. I'd stirred things up enough for the twins' facial expressions to stiffen and for them to uncross their legs and lean toward me, elbows on their knees.

Eliot began, "We're not the only ones who were on Halbert's list, you know. There are certain others—"

"And it could get very embarrassing for you," Emory finished.

Now I wasn't afraid, but annoyed. Maddie was safe in her bedroom; Skip might be on the way; and they were shorter than I was. I wondered if I could change Eliot's grade after the fact so he'd lose his high school diploma.

"What are you implying?" I asked. "That you'll smear the name of my husband unless . . . unless what?"

Eliot's turn again. "We saw you at the factory, and we have reason to believe you've had access to a damaging fl—"

"Paperwork," Emory interrupted.

I paused a beat and repeated the lines in my head. I was convinced that Eliot had been about to say, "flash drive," but how would they know I'd found the drive? I'd only known myself for an hour or so.

All I could think of was the deal Lynch wanted to make with me. Somehow all of these men knew, or thought they knew, that, in spite of Halbert's being out of the way, evidence of widespread business fraud was about to come to light. I would have bet also that among the deals buried on the drive was the one that caused a fire that claimed a life.

Where did Ken and I fit into this picture? Was it widely

known that he was among those who would be exposed? Were all the others in collusion to hide the evidence, needing only my cooperation? I couldn't think of any other explanation for the sudden interest in me on the part of Lincoln Point's business community.

Buzzz. Buzzz. Buzzz.

The twins and I all jumped when the doorbell rang, seeming louder and more insistent than usual to me. Skip, I thought, but I'd been wrong the last time.

I noticed Eliot and Emory stretch their necks and straighten their collars as I got up to answer the door. I used the peephole, just in case it was Lynch and Crowley, which would put me at a distinct four-against-one disadvantage, and even worse if there were guns involved.

I couldn't remember being happier to see Henry Baker on the other side of my door.

The action in my atrium took on that of a clumsily choreographed dance. As Henry entered, Eliot and Emory rose from their chairs, Maddie came from her room, and I let the twins out the door.

In between, the dialogue was sparse. "We were just leaving," from Eliot; "We'll get back to you," from Emory to me, and, "Bye, now," from Henry to the Fergusons.

I didn't know why Henry appeared so intimidating to my guests. He was taller, certainly, but had a very gentle demeanor and certainly not a hint of a weapon.

My guess was that the twins were unwilling to share the purpose of their visit with anyone not involved in the drama of their current lives.

Whatever the reason, I was grateful to Henry and showed it by a quick hug. But not so quick that I didn't get a comforting whiff of sawdust and paint.

*   *   *

Henry and I sat at the same table the twins had rested their arms on not fifteen minutes earlier. I'd wiped it down first.

"I couldn't reach Uncle Skip on any of his numbers," Maddie had told us. "So I called Mr. Baker."

Good choice.

Maddie was now finishing her ghosts, witches, and vampires back in the crafts room, probably talking to Taylor at the same time. Or else she'd figured out a way to make minis with one hand and TM with the other.

"Thank you very much for coming," I told Henry for perhaps the third time. "I doubt that I was in any danger, but with Maddie in the house—"

"I'm glad she thought of me."

It didn't take long to update Henry on our finding the flash drive and on the gist of the Ferguson boys' message to me. He did extract a promise that I'd tell Skip every word of the latter, unless I wanted him to set up camp in front of my house indefinitely.

The suggestion had a strange appeal, but I chose not to share that feeling with him.

"Any resolution to that matter of Halbert's list?" Henry asked. He held up his hands. "If you feel like sharing, that is."

I knew the only name on Halbert's list that Henry cared about was the same one I cared about—that of Ken Porter. I thought a minute and knew it was time to bring Henry in through the wall I'd built around myself in this crisis and share my second concern regarding the late Ken Porter. I took the small white envelope from my sweater pocket, removed the photos, and laid them on the table.

I felt sure Henry would accuse me, gently but rightly, of overreacting as I explained my fears of Ken's deception.

He heard me out, then drew a long breath. "I can see

why you've been upset lately, Gerry. I don't know how I'd keep it together if I found something like this."

"Then you think Ken—"

"Not at all. From all you've told me about Ken, I'm sure there's an innocent explanation, just as surely as he didn't take any bribes or otherwise dishonor his profession. I'm just saying that until we find out the circumstances of these photos, you won't be able to let it go."

I couldn't have said it better. "It seems I'm always needing to thank you, Henry."

"That's not a bad thing." He offered a disarming smile. "Have you had a chance to look up what this Sunaqua Estates is all about?"

"Not a minute."

"Then let's do it."

I gave him what I hoped he interpreted as my most appreciative look.

"Maddie has the best computer in the house," I said, at the same time thinking how Henry wasn't much better than I was as far as facility with the Internet. "And she's not one to do things blindly. She has to have her curiosity completely satisfied if she's going to help."

"I have one of those myself," Henry said. "Let's start the old-fashioned way." He pulled out his cell phone and asked for directory assistance for Sunaqua Falls, New York.

I took a deep breath, feeling as though I were about to enroll in a class I didn't want to take but needed in order to graduate.

I grabbed a notepad and pen when I heard Henry take the next step and ask for Sunaqua Estates. A shiver ran through my body as Henry recited the phone number. There really was a Sunaqua Estates in Sunaqua Falls, and it had a working telephone.

I looked at my watch. A little before five p.m. on the West Coast, eight o'clock in New York. I could only hope that all estates were closed for the day.

"It's too late to call," I said.

"Not if it's a hospital or some other kind of medical facility," Henry said. I frowned at the reasonableness of his argument. "Unless you don't want to know?" he added.

Buzzz. Buzzz.

Ah, another reprieve. A nonthreatening one, I hoped.

Henry rose quickly and put his hand on my arm. "I'll get it," he said.

He looked through the peephole and opened the door to Susan, who probably wondered at the enthusiastic welcome we both gave her.

"I hope I'm not interrupting something?" she said. Along with other giveaway forms of dialect, her habit of ending sentences with a question mark had returned, after she'd spent years trying to get rid of it.

Yes, you are interrupting, I thought, *and I thank you for that.*

My breathing was erratic as I carried the (almost) restored room box from the crafts room to the atrium for Susan's examination. Would she notice a little disturbance on the floor against the far wall? Maddie and I had used fake sawdust and wood shavings in an attempt to cover up the residual glue where the bottom of the wine cork had rested.

I had my answer as soon as I saw Susan's troubled expression. Seated next to Henry, she held the box at eye level.

"Is something wrong?" I asked. "I was worried about the

match to the original shade of brown on the outside. I didn't have natural light when I was mixing the acrylics, so the color might be a little off."

Covering for Maddie came naturally to me, but I regretted having had my granddaughter work on the box with me. I'd thought she was ready to glue splinters together and mix paint, but she should have had more experience before tackling the tasks. There was a lot of skill required in choosing the right glue for each job, and color matching required a trained eye.

I'd failed my friend in a simple task of patching a miniature scene, something I did on at least a weekly basis for one project or another.

"The color is fine," Susan said. On closer inspection I interpreted her frown lines as concern rather than disappointment. "Is this how you found the box in Oliver's apartment?"

I hesitated. I looked at Henry, who knew the whole story. "Is something wrong?" I repeated my question to Susan.

Her lips were almost completely folded back into her mouth; her face had gone white. She looked at the spot where Maddie and I had removed the flash drive–cum-worktable. "Wasn't there a"—Susan squeezed her eyes shut, then opened them—"something else here? Where's the brown worktable?"

Now it seemed it was Susan herself who'd painted and hidden the flash drive.

My head was dizzy with my back-and-forth theories of the camouflaged drive.

First, I was sure Susan had done a poor, hurried job of painting what I thought was an unimportant piece of plastic, to add an extra element to her little scene. Then I assumed it was Oliver who'd used his leftover house paint to disguise what was actually a flash drive. Now I was back to the notion of Susan's rushed, uneven painting, but this time to hide the fact of the drive.

I tried to think of a reason she'd have for wanting to keep the existence of the drive from the police. And from me. The drive's most obvious import was that its contents could show just how many people had a good motive to kill her brother. Something Susan should have welcomed.

Besides, Susan used computers every day in her job as a market analyst. And she was about ten years younger than me. (I had a slightly jaundiced view of the computer literacy curve, matching the age curve exactly.) Susan would know how to retrieve information from the drive and offer it as proof of murder, or destroy it if it made her brother appear less than pure as he'd carried out his inspection responsibilities.

Unless she also had trouble getting through the password protection.

Susan placed the scene on the table and lowered her head until it touched the top frame of the room box. At the first sound of sobs, Henry put his hand out and rubbed her shoulder.

"You built the extra workbench? Using the flash drive?" I asked.

Susan nodded without lifting her head. She whispered a weak "Yes."

I had a hopeful thought. Maybe Susan thought the drive was old, with nothing on it, or that it was an extra one, like the dozens of discs and other pieces of plastic that were scattered around computer areas these days, ready to be scooped up by a miniaturist needing a structural element in a dollhouse or room box. The title of the drive had come up *Potentials Data*, but perhaps Susan didn't know that and saw what she considered a useful found object for a last-minute addition to her present for her brother.

Her continued distress—she'd sat up straighter now and tried to control her breathing—said she'd known exactly what she was doing. Hiding information. Hiding evidence.

"Do you know what's on the drive?" I asked.

"No, I couldn't find the password in Oliver's files and I couldn't hack it in the short time I had. I just wanted the drive to be out of harm's way until I had access to better software. It was stupid, but I was trying to protect my brother, in case . . . just in case."

I thought back to Susan's withholding the small facts of her brother's DUI and the bribery charges lodged, if not filed, against him during his tenure in Tennessee. She might even know of the bribe it took to get him his Lincoln Point job. Susan had handicapped me from the beginning, and as much as I felt sorry for her loss, a wave of annoyance came over me. She'd used me, sending me to Oliver's apartment, hoping I'd find the room box before the police or Lynch and company did. She counted on my not noticing the flash drive.

"I don't understand," I said. "The flash drive probably has the proof you need that Oliver was about to bring down a lot of people. Isn't that why you wanted the police to comb through his list of potentials? Isn't that why you pressed me into service—to spur them on."

"I knew what was on the hard copy list the police picked up right after he . . . died. I hoped that would be enough to find his killer. I didn't know for sure what was on the flash drive. I found it in my desk drawer after Oliver had just left my house a couple of weeks ago. There was no way to tell if he'd done it intentionally or not. Maybe he was trying to hide it, or maybe he wanted me to have it in case something happened to him." The tears began again, streaming down her face. "I just couldn't take a chance until I saw what was on it."

"You thought the drive might have something on it that incriminated your brother." I saw only the slightest of nods. "And if there was, you'd have destroyed it?"

"I don't know," she said, and I believed her.

As short a time as a week ago, I might have judged Susan harshly for considering doing something illegal, like hiding evidence of a crime. Tonight I understood.

Henry, who'd left the atrium, now returned with a cup of tea and handed it to my guest. "Take this, Susan, and try to relax. You know if you don't tell Gerry everything, there's no way for her to help you, and she's already wasted a lot of time."

"I know. I'm sorry."

"Why didn't you go to Oliver's apartment and retrieve the room box yourself, Susan?" I asked as more confusion washed over me. "In fact, why did you give the drive back to him after you found it in your desk?"

"I know it sounds crazy, Gerry. I made the workbench with the flash drive and the cork and took the assembly over there shortly after I found it. Things were starting to really heat up with Lynch and Crowley. I slipped it onto the floor of the workroom scene, thinking that disguising it was the best thing. And then if Oliver asked for it, I'd be able to tell him where it was. But then he . . ." She choked up and stopped. "I never even got to ask him about it."

Though I felt I had a handle on who did what to the flash drive when, I knew it would take a notepad and pen and a lot of doodling for me to track its journey. I saw an image of a small piece of plastic, first red, then brown, traveling from Oliver to Susan, back to Oliver, and now back to Susan.

"And you sent me to get it because . . . ?"

"I was afraid to be caught there with it. What if the police came back while I was there and confiscated what I had—it would look awful if I had evidence on me."

"But it would be okay if they found me there with evidence?"

"Uh-huh." I gave her a strange, frowning look. "You know, with your nephew and all, I didn't see it as a problem. Or what if Patrick Lynch or Max Crowley came?"

I started to tell her who exactly did show up, with at least one gun, but decided she wouldn't be able to handle that right now. "What if?" I said.

"I figured you could act perfectly innocent because you wouldn't know what a flash drive was, Gerry." She paused. "No offense."

"None taken. You didn't count on Maddie." I felt a certain pride, as if my granddaughter were making up for my shortcomings. Wasn't that the principal mission of the next generations?

Susan gulped down the tea, prompting Henry to remove the empty cup and take it to the kitchen for a refill. We were silent until he returned, both using the time to draw deep breaths.

"Susan, is there anything else you're holding back?" I asked.

Henry said, "If you'd like me to leave, so you can be more open—"

"Henry knows everything," I said, wondering what I meant, other than the fact that I didn't want Henry to leave.

"It doesn't matter now, anyway." Susan looked at me. "You already gave the drive to the police, didn't you?" I could see that she hoped she was wrong.

"It's really the best thing," Henry said. "We'll just have to wait and see what's on the drive. I'm sure the police have more resources for getting into these things."

If they don't, they should, I thought.

I had a silly question. "Susan, was it really you who painted that drive and glued it to the wine cork?"

"Awful, wasn't it?" she said. I saw the first sign of a smile. "I was in a big hurry."

"I won't tell Linda," I promised.

I was happy to see my friend's smile widen.

Susan began to relax. I hated to take advantage of her vulnerable state, but I hoped she'd be able to offer pieces to a puzzle in my mind: what was the relationship among all the players in the city inspector's office?

"Once Oliver was accused of bribery years ago, it made him very sensitive to the crime and he went looking for trouble, sometimes in dangerous places," she said.

"Crowley being one of those places," Henry said.

Susan had nodded. "Except Crowley didn't even wait for trouble to come his way. He preempted it. Crowley paid off the powers that be to look the other way about Oliver's DUI, without Oliver knowing about it. Oliver just figured his past troubles were overlooked because they were so long ago and so minor."

"And Crowley then had something to hold over Oliver's head," Henry said.

"So if he turned out to be the kind of inspector who didn't want to cooperate with Lynch and the others, they could always blackmail him," I said, proud that I'd kept up with all the cross-references.

"Uh-huh. They could threaten to go public that Oliver got his job under false pretenses," Susan said. "Unless Oliver could gather enough evidence against them."

"Kind of like nuclear deterrence," Henry said.

I trusted that the analogy was apt, though I knew little of the strategy for either blackmail or war.

One mystery solved, however. Oliver wasn't as much of a cad as Skip and I had thought. The revelation brought me relief, as if somehow a course of good "brother" karma had begun and my own husband, Beverly's brother, would be exonerated as well.

The labyrinthine reasoning didn't bother me as much as it should have.

"So you think the flash drive has evidence against Lynch and Crowley?" Henry asked Susan.

"I surely do," she said.

We all fell silent. I figured we shared the same thought in one form or another—the flash drive was a dangerous item to be caught with.

I was relieved that it was now out of my hands and my house.

I wondered what was keeping Maddie busy all the while we were talking, especially since it was getting toward dinnertime. Susan had said, "No, thank you," to my offer of food. She'd excused herself to fix her face, as she'd put it, and gone home with her room box, swearing there would be no more holding back information. I promised to tell her as soon as I heard anything from Skip.

I'd decided to honor Maddie's plea (more like a whine) for pizza—"I haven't had it all weekend, and it's a holiday"— and placed a phone order for home delivery. It was the least reward I could give her for her excellent detective work. If it weren't for my granddaughter, the police would not be decoding the flash drive—and clearing my husband's name, I dared think—as we spoke.

"You must have been pretty busy back there," I said, as Maddie, Henry, and I set the table and listened for the pizza delivery. "How many vampire bats did you make?"

"I wasn't making decorations," Maddie said.

I'd thought, optimistically, that she'd been in the crafts room, happily making miniatures. I wanted her to learn that spending time alone with a hobby could be entertaining and rewarding. Until now, Maddie would work on dollhouses or miniature scenes only with me or with others. I wanted her to experience the pleasure of going into a different world, by herself, and feeling exhilarated by the creative process, and calm at the same time.

Some other day, I hoped.

"Last-minute homework?" Henry asked.

"Nuh-uh."

"TMing Taylor?" I suggested.

"Nuh-uh."

"Devyn?" I asked, continuing the game. I knew she still kept in touch with her best Los Angeles friend. The stock for postcard-rate stamps had surely gone up since they'd been separated. As I saw Maddie write out the greetings, I'd been glad to see that e-mailing and TMing hadn't completely ruled out the joy of receiving a colorful, physical card.

"Nuh-uh."

"Taking a nap?" Henry offered, followed by laughter from all of us.

Finally, she threw up her hands at the useless guesses from the old folks. "I'm still trying to crack the password for the flash drive."

"It's gone," I said. "What do you mean?" Had she slipped her uncle a different drive? Had Skip, in collusion with Maddie, left it with her on purpose?

"I cloned it."

"You what?" I asked, in utter confusion. Did Maddie have a biology lab under her bed? A sheep?

"I cloned the flash drive. You know, copied it and put it on my hard drive before I gave it to Uncle Skip."

I wondered if I should be grateful that there was one hobby Maddie worked on by herself and seemed to derive pleasure from.

What was foremost in my mind, however, was that I hadn't gotten rid of the crucial flash drive after all.

Chapter 17

I couldn't bring myself to scold Maddie for holding on to the flash drive, by whatever means she could. I should have known it would take more than confiscation of property by the police for her to give up a challenge. That spirit was what got her father through medical school and beyond and her mother a place in a major San Francisco art gallery, not the easiest field to turn into a career.

Our talk while eating a delicious pizza—one side with cheese only, for Maddie, the other side with mushrooms and olives for Henry and me—was free of conflict, ours or anyone else's. We talked more about three-dimensional animation, which Maddie was expecting to learn at her next session of technology camp; we discussed which store had the best Halloween candy for the best price; I promised to get a supply of Maddie's ghosts and witches to the Ferguson factory party; and we made plans for another dinner with Taylor and her parents.

I enjoyed our version of a normal family dinner, with only a few ghosts and goblins flitting around my mind.

It was seven o'clock before we finished bowls of ice cream. I could tell that Henry wasn't eager to leave, but Maddie and I had a project to complete. And not on the cloned flash drive.

We needed to get to work on the haunted dollhouse.

I walked Henry to the door.

"Do you want me to pursue contacting Sunaqua Estates?" he asked me.

I thought about it. Maybe all the interruptions were telling me something. Let the past be, it might be saying. "I'm not sure," I said. "But thanks for the offer. And thanks for coming. You can see where I'd be if I'd had to wait for Skip to rescue me from the Ferguson brothers."

"My pleasure. Skip hasn't called all evening. Are you concerned about him?"

"No more than usual. It's always hard to picture him out there with scary people."

"I hear you. But he looks like a man who can take care of himself."

"That he is."

Henry started down the path toward his car. I had the door half closed when he turned back. "What are you doing tomorrow?" he asked, catching me off guard.

"I'll be driving to Palo Alto, taking Maddie back to school in the morning."

"Want some company?"

I found I did. "Can you be here by seven?"

Henry gave me a salute, which I took as a yes.

What had I been thinking, agreeing to have Henry ac-company me on the drive to Palo Alto? I didn't know how I was going to break the news to Maddie.

Ever since her family moved to northern California from Los Angeles, and we set up a schedule for regular visits, our commute time had always been special. I learned as many things about my granddaughter while we were buckled into my car, looking straight ahead, as when we sat face-to-face. My red Saturn Ion served as a therapy office as we talked out everything from how to deal with losing a soccer game to the homesickness Maddie felt when her family moved here from Los Angeles to whether there really was a heaven.

I couldn't define it, but there was something about the extra generation that separated grandparents and grandchildren that fostered a unique bond.

Would Maddie see Henry as an intruder on our time together? I knew she liked him a lot, but would this be too much togetherness? More important—had I always been such a worrywart, stressing even over who would sit in the front seat?

I decided to put off telling Maddie the arrangement until her bedtime, when there was a chance she'd be more mellow.

For now, I had to try to extricate her from her computer and plunk her down in front of the dollhouse.

"I have to crack this password," she said.

"I know you do, sweetheart, but sometimes it's better to leave this kind of challenge for a while, let it stew in your brain. Then when you go back to it, something will snap into place. It happens to me all the time."

"Like when?"

"Well, I might be trying to think of a new way to make a mini table or decoration, or maybe I need just one more word to finish a crossword puzzle. If I concentrate too hard for too long, my brain gets overloaded and I have to step back. Then, when I'm cooking or watering my plants, not thinking about it at all"—I snapped my fingers—"it comes to me."

"Okay."

Really? That had been easier than I thought. I'd been ready with more examples, like trying to remember the name of a song or a movie and having it come to me hours or days later when I'd forgotten about it and didn't care anymore. Maybe it was only my brain that worked that way, but the pep talk got Maddie away from the computer, and that's what I wanted.

We headed for the crafts room discussing how to attach a miniature ghost to the haunted dollhouse so it would look as though it were flying out of an upstairs window. I hoped immersion in miniatures would take both our minds off the elusive contents of the flash drive.

"It didn't work, Grandma." Maddie held up a set of com-pleted ghosts. "I worked on something different, but I didn't get any answers yet."

"Sometimes it takes longer than a couple of hours."

"How long?"

I checked for evidence that she was teasing. I was happy to see a barely contained grin.

Maddie was in bed and we were having our last chat of the day. There was no more stalling. I had to tell her the plans for Tuesday.

"It's back to school tomorrow," I said.

She frowned. "I'd rather stay and work on you-know-what."

The cryptic naming of the flash drive was Maddie's way of following my advice not to think about it. I had to work on being more clear about the process.

"You know that once you're in the classroom with Mr. Ramsey and all your friends, you'll be very happy to be back."

"I know."

"We'll leave about seven as usual, but there's one change."

"Mr. Baker's coming." Maddie's tone was casual, I was glad to hear, as if he accompanied us every week and I'd simply forgotten.

"How did you know that?"

"I just figured."

"Do you mind having someone else join us on our trip?" I asked, tucking her father's baseball afghan, which she now considered hers, around her shoulders.

She rolled her head on her pillow. "Nuh-uh. I like Mr. Baker. Are you going steady with him?"

I cleared my throat. Twice. And took a breath.

What did "going steady" mean to an eleven-year-old? Maddie had told me how her classmates chose "partners" of the opposite sex in school, sometimes without ever talking to them alone or going off together at lunchtime (that was a relief). They would simply designate a boy or a girl in their class and spread the word that they liked that person. Friends would be dispatched through a chain of questions to determine if the feeling was mutual. If it was, they'd be declared boyfriend and girlfriend. Then, at some point, they'd "break up" and another pairing would be announced.

Was I going steady? Not in the fifth-grade sense. Henry and I had certainly spent a lot of time together lately. I liked being with him in a way that I never thought I would with anyone again. We took for granted that we'd check in with each other on a regular basis. Not every day, but not more than two or three days passed without a word, either.

Henry Baker was certainly what I needed at the moment, someone steady and trustworthy. What was he getting from me? Surely going steady meant reciprocal support.

I wished I could answer Maddie's question.

"You don't have to tell me, Grandma," Maddie said.

"I'll tell you when I know," I said, grateful to see her eyes close.

I put the light out in Maddie's room, left the door open three inches, as required, and wondered if I had a boyfriend.

He did the mash. He did the monster mash.

The caller ID on my cell phone showed Beverly's number. It wasn't unusual for one of us to call the other this late, not until recently anyway. When had I ever dreaded talking to or reconnecting with my sister-in-law? I felt as though we'd been estranged; the last few days seemed like months, as if we'd had a falling out, and it was all my doing.

Beverly had been making valiant efforts to be patient with me while I sorted out my feelings and my fears, though she most likely didn't have the slightest idea that's what I was doing. Pretty soon I'd have to have a heart-to-heart with her.

"Gerry" was all she said when I picked up, and I knew this wasn't a "Let's chat" call. Something was wrong.

I thought my heart was beating in my throat. "What is it?"

"I'm at the hospital."

That was enough to cause me to drop the phone. It banged on the counter next to the stove, where I'd been brewing late-night tea.

Beverly had heart disease from rheumatic fever, which had struck her when she was a child. Now, for the most

part, she could be as active as the next person, but sometimes had to withdraw for long periods of rest. She was so
good at hiding the distress her condition caused her that
even those close to her sometimes forgot about it. Her weak
heart had sent her to the hospital more than a few times
since I'd known her.

It came to me while I fumbled to get my phone to my ear
that Beverly was not seriously ill herself or she wouldn't be
on the other end of this call. That was the good news.

"Skip?" I asked, my hand struggling to keep steady.

"He's okay, but what a scare, Gerry."

"What happened?"

"He was attacked not long after leaving your house. He'd
gone to the convenience store on Springfield Boulevard. I
mean, he was within shouting distance of his office. Who
mugs a cop?"

"How is he? Is anything broken, or . . . ?" I couldn't ar-
ticulate "irreversible damage." I thought I'd need my tea
more than ever and did a one-handed pour from the teapot
to a cup.

"Right now they think the worst of it is a couple of broken ribs. The doctor said he never lost consciousness." I
allowed myself to feel hopeful. "TJ, the clerk at the store,
knows all the cops and he called it in right away. It's a good
thing Skip is fit and has had all that training, since it was
two guys who ganged up on him."

I thought immediately of the most recent pairs of men
I'd had contact with—Lynch and Crowley, and the Ferguson twins. I couldn't see Skip being victim to either pair.
But who knew how many other hoodlums they had in their
employ? I had no trouble picturing money changing hands
with a photo of Skip as part of the package.

One possibility for why Skip was attacked hit too close

to home. What if Oliver's killer somehow knew that, thanks to me, Skip was in possession of the flash drive? I swallowed the thought.

Beverly continued, repeating the obvious, disbelief mounting. "Who in the world attacks a strong, young cop in broad daylight a few yards from the police station?"

Beverly's voice sounded more angry than troubled now, talking as much to herself as to me. I hoped her worry was fading because she could see that her son was not seriously injured. I wanted that opportunity as soon as possible.

"It's very strange," I said, wanting to calm her down now that I'd heard the worst. "How long will Skip be there?"

"They're just keeping him overnight. Skip says he doesn't need to stay, et cetera, et cetera, that he's not feeling that bad. But he'd never admit it, anyway. He didn't even want to come to the hospital, but I'm glad TJ forced him to. You never know. He might have hurt his head." Beverly blew out a loud breath. I felt her distress. "I think he's more embarrassed than anything that the guys got the drop on him."

"The drop?" Beverly's training as civilian volunteer for the LPPD, plus her close relationship with retired officer Nick Marcus was showing.

"Yeah, it means they surprised him, took the upper hand, that kind of thing. I thought you were an English teacher." She laughed, as if anticipating a joke. "Oh, right, it was actually English that you taught, not slang."

Beverly's nervous rambling sounded better than ever to my ears. I knew it meant that she wasn't upset with me for keeping her out of things, and her lightening tone confirmed my guess—Skip wasn't so badly off that she couldn't clown around.

"I'm just so glad to hear that he's okay. Are you going to stay at the hospital for a while?"

"I haven't been here that long. Nick and I were out and we had our cells off, which now I will never do again, so they couldn't reach me all evening, and he wasn't awake enough to give them your name."

I finally put together the timeline. Skip had been assaulted in broad daylight, Beverly had said, but she was calling me at eleven o'clock at night. She'd just found out herself.

"Maddie's still here," I said. "Or I'd come right over."

"I know, and Skip wants to talk to you, so here's what I thought. I'll go to your house and stay with Maddie and you can come to the hospital. Are you alone?"

I laughed, getting her point immediately. "Yes, I'm alone."

"Too bad." She chuckled. "I'll be right over and we'll switch places."

I tried not to assess whether it was indeed too bad that I was alone.

Beverly had already started to forage in my refrigerator when I zipped past her to the garage. I'd rattled off a list of snack possibilities—leftover pizza, a pot roast sandwich, and no end of desserts, including Sadie's hand-packed ice cream.

We'd both noted how it was a good thing Maddie was asleep. It would have been hard to explain to her that her adored uncle Skip had been hurt, but she couldn't visit him.

Now I wound my way up Lincoln Point's only hilly street where its hospital was spread out at the top. I'd finally been able to visit friends here without having my eyes tear up at the memory of the long months Ken had spent in its depressing rooms. Lately, at least, the images came and went more quickly and became dimmer in my mind as long as I didn't dwell on them.

I parked in a familiar spot, entered the main building, and followed blue stenciled footprints on the linoleum, marking the path to the main desk. Not that I needed directions; I could have made the trip blindfolded.

A few minutes later, I sat next to Skip. I wasn't surprised to see a flurry of young female nurses hovering over him. I almost hated to interrupt, but I knew the bag full of magazines and ginger cookies that I'd brought would be a suitable substitute, given that he was spoken for, as we used to say.

"I'll bet the guys who jumped you look a lot worse than you do," one of the nurses said, with a wink as she was leaving. "We'll be watching the ER for two banged-up dudes."

I was glad June wasn't with me to see the level of attention they gave their cute, good-natured patient who also carried a badge and a gun.

"I just got off the phone with June," Skip said. "She wants to jump right on a plane and come home, so will you please call her and tell her I'm perfectly fine?"

"Certainly. Is that what you wanted to see me about? To ask me to call your fiancée in Chicago?"

"Not exactly," he said, meaning, I knew, that June wasn't exactly his fiancée and also that wasn't the reason for his summoning me.

"I didn't think so. What happened to you?"

"You mean how could I let two guys get the jump on me? I should never let my guard down like that."

"Skip, you're only human, and only one person."

"Yeah, well. Anyway, one guy held me down while the other fished in all my pockets. They ended up taking my jacket, Aunt Gerry." Skip shook his head and gritted his teeth, seeming to relive the moment. "That's where I'd put the flash drive. I'm sure that's what they were after, and they got it. My guys found the jacket later, with empty pockets, of course, in the bushes right outside the station. Can you believe the gall?"

"How would they know you had the drive in the first place?"

"They may not have known exactly what they were looking for. They were probably told that I had evidence on me and to take whatever was likely—papers, disks, whatever they found—and they were smart enough to recognize a flash drive."

Unlike me, I thought. "So they knew or they suspected that you picked up something at my house?"

Skip nodded. "I'm guessing they followed me after I left you and Maddie and planned to jump me when I got out of my car, wherever that would be."

I shifted in the uncomfortable seat, as orange as the couch in Oliver Halbert's apartment. Who thought orange was a soothing color for sick people? The hospital sounds from outside Skip's room, which I'd gotten used to when I practically lived here with Ken, now rattled me. It stung my ears to hear the clanging of one metal tray on another, the call bell, the humming machines reading out vital statistics. I wished I could take Skip home with me immediately.

"How would they know the drive, or any evidence, was in my house?" I asked, with increasing concern, my worst fears realized. "Only Maddie and you and I knew about it."

Skip put on a sober expression. "I've been trying to figure that out." He swung his arm, which was attached to a drip bag. "It hasn't helped that they pumped me full of stuff when I got here. My head still feels like mush."

He sounded a lot like his uncle Ken. "You should be grateful for modern medicine. Can you imagine the pain you'd be in?"

"At least I'd have half a shot at thinking clearly. When

you contacted me about what Maddie found, I called in to
the station to say where I was going, and that I'd be bringing
in evidence. I wanted to alert the technicians to be standing
by." Skip scratched his head. "Standard procedure."

"That would mean someone at the station slipped up
and the word got out to the wrong people. Is that what you
think?"

"I wish. I know I was vague enough about the evidence,
not saying what it was exactly or what case it was connected to or anything like that. Someone had to be on me
from the start and this was what they needed to hear. They
knew you were sniffing around, and they knew I took something from your house."

My mind was reeling. "Are you saying that a police officer set you up to be mugged?"

Skip closed his eyes. I saw a wince that might have been
due to physical pain or the idea of a reprobate colleague, or
both. "That's the way it's shaping up. There's no other explanation for how they seem to know what's happening as
soon as I do."

"Unless it's just random," I said, hardly believing it.

"A couple of guys looking for trouble saw me get out of
my car and said, 'Oh, there's an easy mark.'" Skip's chuckle
brought on another wince, but he continued to imitate the
random guys. "'Let's not bother taking his wallet; let's just
see if he has a computer accessory on him.' Right, Aunt
Gerry."

"Skip, you're accusing your department of . . . what? . . .
Being corrupt? Having a mole working for Patrick Lynch
or someone like him?" On second thought, I realized that
term was probably restricted to spy matters, but Skip knew
what I meant.

"I hate to admit this, but Lynch is a very powerful man.

If he or some pol in the city has a cop or two in his pocket, I wouldn't be shocked."

I folded my arms across my chest, shutting out Skip and the entire LPPD. I noted the enormous stand-up "Get Well" card on his side table, obviously quick-action greetings from his buddies. I knew many of his fellow and lady officers by name. Now I was being asked to believe that one of them had sent thugs to hurt him.

"Well, I am shocked."

"I know you'd like to believe the world is full of only good, honest people, Aunt Gerry. But even law enforcement has its share of bad apples, and that includes one or two in Lincoln Point."

"It doesn't mean I have to accept it."

"No, it doesn't." Skip sat up, as much as he could, wrapped as he was in hospital swaddling. He blinked his eyes, rolled his head around his neck. "Boy, these meds have fried my brain something wicked."

It was painful to watch him try to shift his body around the narrow bed.

"Let me help," I said. I stood and fluffed his pillow. I wished I could make the pain go away as I sometimes could when he was a toddler.

"Okay, here's the thing," Skip said. "These guys have what they want now, so I don't think they'll be after anyone else, but we have to keep you and Maddie safe. I sent Nick over to your place."

"Nick is there, too?"

"And there's a car out front. Plus, you might not have noticed, but you had an escort following you at a discreet distance on your way over here."

If Skip was trying to scare me, it worked.

I wanted to ask how he would know whom to trust? I felt

a shiver, as if a cold wind had blown through the room. I thought of Maddie in her comfy bed under her red-white-and-blue baseball afghan. I was suddenly very glad she'd be going back to Palo Alto in the morning.

And shouldn't I be home with her now?

"Why exactly am I here?" I asked him.

"I thought it might be more effective to tell you this in person." I knew what was coming. "It's time to back off, now, okay? No more snooping around playing cop, unless you sign up for the academy."

"I'm not playing cop. What do you think I'm going to do? Buy a gun?"

"No, that would make sense. I wish you would. I know you promised to help Susan Giles, but that's not your job. Give her back her little box thing—"

"Box thing? Ouch. Have you learned nothing from hearing me talk for years about room boxes and mini scenes?"

He smiled in spite of the serious tone he had taken with me. "You've already done a huge amount. Eventually, we'll figure out what was going on with Halbert's investigations and get other evidence against whoever is responsible for his death."

"I should tell you—"

"It's my fault that we don't have the drive anymore, not yours."

"But—"

"No buts. I can't keep someone on you twenty-four-seven until the case is solved." He pointed to his bandaged chest, his water bottle, the blue-and-white curtain around his bed. "If they did this to me, what do you think they're prepared to do if they decide you're in their way?"

"Who are *they*?"

"I don't really know. Even though I said Lynch probably

has a guy on the force, it doesn't mean I'm sure or that I have any proof. And he's not the only one with connections, as I told you. What we can say is that, in all likelihood, whoever is behind the assault on me today was likely also on Halbert's list and is probably his killer."

I took a long breath. "I get it."

"So, I'm making myself clear?"

"Crystal."

"Sweet. Now, before you officially retire, is there anything you need to tell me?"

"About what?"

"Oh, I don't know. Other evidence you dug up. Or a confession maybe? I know you've been out there."

"Out where?" Oh, dear, I was beginning to sound like Maddie, prolonging an argument, being annoyingly literal, unbecoming an adult. "There's just one more thing," I said, and told him about the visit from the Ferguson twins, Maddie's trying to reach him, and Henry's appearance.

Skip slapped his head as best he could with his restraints. "While I was sprawled in the convenience store's parking lot."

"I'm sure we weren't in any danger, but I didn't want to take a chance, with Maddie there. They just wanted to make their point."

"You know the worst thing about all of this?"

"Your broken ribs are going to keep you out of the softball league for a while."

"That, too."

"What, then?"

"Without even realizing it, you managed to obtain what was probably our best evidence in this case, and poor Maddie spent all that time trying to crack the flash drive password, and then I go and lose it. We're back to square one."

"Not exactly."

Skip gave me his suspicious, sideways look. "What do you mean?"

I smiled, a proud grandmother's smile. "Maddie cloned it."

I said it as if I'd known what that meant before a couple of hours ago.

Skip leaned back. I saw a proud cousin-once-removed smile. "The little squirt." He shook his head and his smile broadened. "The little squirt. We may crack this case yet."

I certainly hoped so.

Chapter 18

Skip made arrangements for a trustworthy officer and technician to escort me home. Charlie, a young officer I didn't know, insisted on driving my car while I rode with Gene, the LPPD computer technician, also very young, in an unmarked beige sedan. Gene threatened to use the lights and siren as we drove up Springfield Boulevard toward my Eichler neighborhood. I knew that would have pleased Maddie, waking up to such excitement, but we were beyond mischief like that at just past midnight.

Beverly opened the door to us. I assumed she'd checked the peephole and probably even recognized the vehicle as belonging to LPPD's fleet. Nick, looking like backup, was by her side.

"A suitably grand entrance," Nick said, greeting my escorts by name. He and Beverly had already moved Maddie's computer to the dining room for easier access by Gene. Being laid up in a hospital bed didn't seem to be cramping Skip's networking style.

Gene worked at Maddie's computer while Charlie looked on and Beverly, Nick, and I talked about the day's events. It didn't seem possible that this was part of the day that began with my touring the Ferguson twins' factory.

I was glad for Nick's presence, not because I thought I was in any immediate danger, but because I didn't look forward to being alone with Beverly and two secrets about her brother. I doubted that I could stand her scrutiny, face-to-face, at this vulnerable hour.

It was difficult for me to keep up my end of the conversation, not knowing how much Skip had told his mother and Nick about why the information on the drive was important. I waited them out and determined that they knew only that the drive had files pertinent to the Oliver Halbert case. Since Beverly seemed happy and unconcerned, I figured Skip hadn't told her what it might say about Ken's past business dealings.

One question kept us going for a time: what would Maddie's reaction be in the morning when she noticed what had been going on at her computer while she slept? Guesses ranged from delight that her skills had been useful to annoyance that we hadn't wakened her. And further annoyance that Gene removed the drive from her computer, or at least I think that's what happened to get it out of our custody.

"Are we going to have a chain-of-custody problem with this evidence?" Beverly asked Nick.

"That problem started long before tonight. We don't know who put the information on the drive in the first place, let alone all the back-and-forth there seems to have been. But it's the DA's job to introduce the contents in the proper light, and it should be okay. You'd be amazed at the kinds of messy evidence the lawyers get sometimes."

Whatever that meant, I didn't think I wanted to know. I pictured Maddie's having to testify that she had indeed cloned the drive and not added or subtracted from it. She'd be thrilled.

I hoped it didn't come to that.

Charlie and Gene left in about a half hour.

Gene had waved a shiny blue (did they come in all colors?) flash drive at me. "Got it," he'd said. He mentioned the number of gigabytes he'd downloaded and the rate of transfer, but I wasn't knowledgeable enough to be impressed.

I hoped I was correct that both Charlie and Gene were too young to have been corrupted, and thus that the drive would get to the police station and in the right hands soon.

"We'd be glad to stay with you tonight," Nick said.

"Absolutely not," I said. "I really think all the drama is over for the day, and besides, there's an LPPD car out there."

"You could always call Henry and have him come over," Beverly said, holding back a grin.

"What a ridiculous idea," I said. I ushered them out the door before there could be any more discussion.

I waved to whoever was in the unmarked on the sidewalk and locked my front door. I leaned against it and asked myself why it would be so ridiculous to call Henry.

Because we're not going steady, I answered myself. Yet, I added.

An early morning round of e-mails circulated among the adult Porters, plus Nick, and Henry (to whom I sent a special note at one in the morning). We collectively decided that since Skip was due to be discharged from the hospital before noon today, there was no reason to tell Maddie anything about the attack on him. There were some things an eleven-year-old, even one going on twenty-five, shouldn't have to deal with.

As far as her computer went, we'd tried to return it to its exact location on her desk. When she realized after the fact that it had been tampered with, we'd deal with it. She didn't usually access her computer on mornings when she was packing to go home, so we might be safe for a while.

I was ready to leave Oliver's murder investigation in the hands of the police technicians who would work on cracking the flash drive password. In their hands also would be the answer to another question, but Ken's name was either there or not, no matter how much I tried to worry it off.

Even with those two items mentally crossed off, I had an important mission for Tuesday. I needed to track down either Artie Dodd or Sunaqua Estates, or both, and organize all the Halloween projects I'd committed to.

While Maddie was getting dressed for school and packing her things, I made a call to the number Henry had written down for Sunaqua Estates. Six thirty in the morning in Lincoln Point, nine thirty in New York. A reasonable hour; I had no excuse.

I punched in the number and waited through four long rings, almost hanging up after each one.

"You have reached Sunaqua Estates, home for special-needs children," a voice said. No one—"

"Want some oatmeal, Grandma?" Maddie asked.

I clicked off.

What was wrong with me, choosing this time to make a call? It was as if I wanted to be interrupted, as if I could handle only one small bit of information at a time. I took a breath. I had my bit for the morning—"a home for special-needs children."

"Grandma? I'm making some oatmeal. Do you want some?"

"No, thanks, sweetheart. I'll eat when I get back."

If ever again.

I'd awakened several times during the night, worried about Maddie's safety, and gone into her bedroom. A couple of times I kissed her forehead, feeling her warmth, relieved she was alive. If my able-bodied homicide detective nephew was at risk for assault, what could happen to my little granddaughter? Maddie seemed to get smaller and more fragile every time I looked in on her.

Each time I got up, I checked to be sure the unmarked was still outside and considered going out to make sure he was awake. I wondered if it would have been insulting to offer a thermos of coffee.

I'd never been so pleased to be dropping Maddie off at her Palo Alto school.

As I predicted, once Maddie saw her friends spilling out of SUVs and sedans in front of Angelican Hills School, she seemed happy to enter another world, far from murder and mayhem.

I'd seen the phenomenon often through the years, where children like Maddie, who could act very intelligent and grown-up around adults, switched to kid talk and a healthy silliness once they were among their peers and (they thought) unobserved.

Maddie unbuckled herself from Henry's SUV, gave me a quick kiss, and said, "'Bye, Grandma. 'Bye, Mr. Baker. See you tomorrow afternoon, Grandma."

I'd almost forgotten. Tomorrow was Wednesday already and Maddie would be back for our usual crafts night.

I hoped Lincoln Pont would be safe again by then.

* * *

Henry waited until I phoned Richard and Mary Lou at home to let them know Maddie was back to school. Then he got down to business.

"Have you gone through all the cartons in the garage?" he asked. He pulled away from the curb, waved to the crossing guard, and maneuvered around SUVs of every color, each with some form of proud parent bumper sticker.

"I've done as much as I need to. I couldn't look at every single document, but I've sifted through a great deal of correspondence, contracts, and meeting reports. I sampled just about every package. I'm satisfied that I found the only suspicious memo."

"The one suggesting that Ken had an arrangement with Patrick Lynch?"

"That's the one."

"Good. Then as soon as we get home, I'll put the boxes back up on the shelves."

I noted the ease with which Henry talked about going "home." I relished the comfort that gave me.

At first I thought how nice that he'd get the cartons out of my way again. Then . . . "No," I said. "I'm going to burn them." Henry turned to me briefly, a question in his eyes. "I know now that there's nothing I need from those boxes. I already have the personal things that matter." I thought of the scrapbooks we'd kept of our trips, of happy memories on both coasts, of our son and grandchild, of my thirtieth-anniversary pearls, the last piece of jewelry Ken bought me. "What was out there was none of my business in the first place."

Henry gave his steering wheel a purposeful tap. "All right, then. I'll come around sometime with my truck and load them up and take care of that for you."

"Thanks," I said, aware of how inadequate that sounded.

"The next thing is to go home and finish that call to Sunaqua Estates."

I gulped. "I don't even know what to say when they answer the phone. Whom do I ask for? All I have is some pink clothing and three faded Polaroid photographs with no names or dates. I don't even know the child's name."

"You know Ken's name."

Another gulp and a loud breath. My pleasant ride with Henry had taken a disquieting turn. "You're not going to let me off easily, are you?"

"You'll thank me later," he said.

"Where have I heard that before?"

"From your own lips."

"Can we stop at Seward's Folly for coffee first?" I asked, sounding like Maddie, the best negotiator in the family.

"Coffee afterward," he said, and took the exit nearest my house.

Henry could be tough when he had to be.

I liked that.

Henry honored my request that I be alone when I made the call to Sunaqua Falls.

"Of course," he'd said. "I'll be back with my truck within the hour, but if you need me before that, give a call."

I couldn't ask for better conditions as I sat in my atrium and picked up the phone. It was just before lunchtime in Sunaqua Falls, New York. I punched in the number that I already knew by heart.

"Sunaqua Estates. How may I direct your call?"

If I only knew, I thought, collecting myself. "I'm trying to track down a child who was in your institution—"

"Home." The voice was perfunctory.

"Pardon me?"

"Sunaqua Estates is a home with a hospital wing. It's not an institution. What's the child's name?"

"I'm sorry. I'm a little nervous. I'm looking for information on a child—"

"Who are you with?"

"Pardon me?"

"Are you social services? Hospice? Police? Who are you with?"

I wondered if I could get away with "police." Should I add masquerading as a police officer to my résumé?

"I'm a private citizen," I admitted, "and I'm writing a family history." I paused to clear my throat. I might write it someday, I mused. "I found some photographs of one of my ancestors holding a child in front of your insti—in front of Sunaqua Estates."

"Hold on, please, I'll transfer you."

I could easily have hung up then and there. I'd gotten one more piece of the puzzle—that Sunaqua Estates was a kind of placement for children needing social services or hospitalization. Or were in the custody of the police.

I stayed on the line.

"How can I help you?" A softer voice this time, one belonging to an older woman.

I repeated my genealogy pitch. "The only thing I know about the little girl is that she was related to Kenneth Porter"—I nearly choked, never having admitted that out loud until now—"and this would have been some time before 1972."

I'd given voice also to my greatest wish, that whatever had happened had taken place before Ken and I met.

"Kenneth Porter? Who is this, please?"

"You know, I realize now that's a very long time ago, and I'm sure your records don't go back that far."

"We have records from our founding in 1937. Are you a relative of Kenneth Porter?"

I'd always been so proud when people asked me that, at a ribbon-cutting ceremony or an awards banquet. "I'm his wife," I'd say, thrilled that he was so well known.

It was a different story now. I was disappointed that he was known at Sunaqua Estates and wary as I said, "Yes, my name is Geraldine Porter."

"Is this about the Porter endowment?"

Endowment? Was Sunaqua Estates a charity Ken supported? That would explain everything. He'd given money to an institution—a home and hospital, rather—and had had his photograph taken with one of the little patients. All that worry for nothing.

"Yes," I said. "It's about the endowment from Kenneth Porter."

"Thank you so much for calling, Ms. Porter. We've been trying to reach him, but his firm seems to have gone out of business, at least at the location we have for him."

"He . . . passed away."

She drew in her breath. "I'm so sorry. He couldn't have been very old."

"You knew him?"

"Oh, yes. It was so sad, when his little girl died. Those of us who were here at the time remember the case so well. He loved her very much. And the fact that he's been so generous in her name all these years—it was 1970, I remember, the year my own daughter was born—well, it's such a tribute to little Angela. She really was an angel." A pause. "May I ask, will you be renewing the—"

I hung up.

My breath caught; I felt light-headed and dizzy. If I hadn't been sitting down, I'd have crashed to the floor.

I'd hung up in the middle of the woman's sentence. Would she have my phone number from caller ID and try to reach me? Why had I given her my real name? I had a lot to learn about detective work. Why had I called in the first place?

Why has any of this happened?

I addressed the last comment to Kenneth Porter.

Chapter 19

I wasn't one for heading to bed during daylight hours. I might fall asleep in my chair now and then, or in a darkened theater watching a kid's movie with Richard or Maddie, but it wasn't my practice to fall on my bed and try to sleep, or to shut out the world.

When I got off the phone with Sunaqua Estates, I needed to escape and the only place I'd been able to think of was my own bedroom.

I buried my head in my pillow, at first facedown, until I could hardly breathe. Then on my left side, where I stared at my dresser and mentally traced the outline of the knobs on the drawers. Then flat on my back, staring up at the fan and the swirls in the ceiling. Then on my right side where I could have seen my outdoor plants through my patio door if I hadn't drawn the drapes closed. Then . . . it was useless to think of resting.

My phone rang several times while I tossed and turned, fully clothed. I knew Henry would be trying to reach me, but I couldn't bear to talk to anyone right now, especially one who'd be expecting a report on my attempt to get in touch with Ken's past.

How could my husband have kept something like this from me? It wasn't something, I realized. It was someone. Angela.

Did this erase more than thirty years of a wonderful, loving marriage? A question I wasn't prepared to answer and probably wouldn't be for a while.

There was one thread I could hold on to—according to the woman at the home, someone with no reason to lie to me, the child had been born in 1970. Two years before Ken and I met. Surely that mattered. It wasn't as if Ken had cheated on me in any way. He'd simply had a life before we met and had chosen not to share it with me. Wasn't that allowed?

I wished I knew.

When I left my bedroom, I was surprised to see that only an hour had passed. It seemed an eternity since I'd been talking long distance, both literally and figuratively. I walked by my answering machine, which was blinking madly, to the front door, curious to see if the LPPD still considered me at risk.

I shuffled down to Maddie's room, breathed in the smell of her strawberry-scented bedding, and looked out the window. There wasn't a police car, but there was a beige pickup. In it was Henry, reading a newspaper.

It felt good to smile.

Straightening my clothes as I walked, I went to the front door and opened it.

Henry folded his paper and got out of his truck. Seeing

him brought the tears I hadn't been able to summon during my bedroom retreat.

As he put his arms around me, I let go of my pain.

"Her name is Angela," I said.

I insisted on helping Henry pile the boxes onto the bed of his truck. I needed to do something physical, otherwise all my energy would be directed toward keeping my jaw clenched. I'd resealed the cartons, though loosely, just enough to keep the streets of Lincoln Point clear of reams of old paperwork.

As Henry pulled away from the curb with the first load of boxes, the LPPD arrived, but only in the form of my nephew. The two men waved at each other.

"What are you doing up and about?" I asked Skip. "Did the doctors clear you?"

"Close enough," Skip said. "I've got things to do, people to see"

"Does your mother know?"

"What am I? Twelve?"

"Sometimes you act it."

I took comfort in our usual banter, always lighthearted (though I really did think he should have been in bed), always motivated by a great affection.

"I left you a message," Skip said.

"I've been busy," I said, leading him into the atrium.

He gave me a curious look—I read: how busy were you that you didn't have time to press "play" on your answering machine?—but he didn't pursue the issue.

We sat at the table in the atrium. I was glad to feel the sun pouring in through the skylight. I'd been chilly all morning, outside and inside.

Skip plunked a folder of papers down in front of him.

"This looks serious," I said.

"It's all good news."

"I could use some."

"Bottom line—Uncle Ken was as clean as we knew he was."

Not exactly. "I'm glad to hear it." I fingered the edges of the folder. "And the proof is in here?"

"Yeah. We got through the password on the flash drive. Well, I didn't, but Gene did."

"That was faster than I expected."

"We're not finished reading everything, but breaking the password went pretty well. There's this software called COGGWARE that sniffs the network and uncovers weaknesses in password protocols."

"Oh."

Skip laughed. "Don't I sound like I know what I'm talking about? I've been practicing, in case I ever need a new pickup line."

I laughed. It was hard to stay gloomy very long with Skip joking around, even though he was the one most recently in the hospital. "If that line works, times have really changed."

"I couldn't wait to show you this, Aunt Gerry. It'll be a while before we go through every project Oliver had been investigating, but I whizzed through the names to find Uncle Ken."

I was glad Skip had told me the bottom line—Ken was "clean." I didn't need more suspense today. He took a few pieces of paper from the folder. On top was a familiar memo, the one from Patrick Lynch to Ken.

"I've seen that," I said. "I didn't like the implication. 'On board' and 'arrangement' and so on."

"Right, but look at this." Skip removed a paper clip and showed me the second page of the set. Another memo. "Read this. Oh, by the way, that EELFS name? It's just a cute form of Eliot and Emory and Lillian Ferguson with S for Sam tacked on at the end. Get it?"

I got it. I pulled the memo closer and read the correspondence from Ken Porter to Patrick Lynch.

> I apologize if I didn't make myself clear: I have no inter-est in the EELFS project. I'm returning the contract folio unopened. Please remove my name from your list of potential collaborators. My lawyers will be happy to talk to you if there is any further misunderstanding.

Clear enough, and clean enough to suit me. I gave Ken one point on the plus side. I was surprised I didn't feel more satisfaction. After all, I'd just heard that my husband had not acted in consort with what might have been widespread corruption in Lincoln Point's business community, that he had, in fact, explicitly refused to do business with the ring-leader.

Yesterday I would have cheered, I knew. Today it was just one more fact of Ken's life that I hadn't been part of, albeit an honorable one.

It was a good thing I'd spared Beverly any whiff of my fears in this regard. She need never know about the EELFS, and certainly she didn't need to hear about Angela.

I was aware that Skip expected more of a reaction from me. I tried to sound upbeat and grateful. "This is a huge relief, Skip," I said.

"Then why doesn't it seem that way?" he asked.

"I'm a little tired," I said, "but I really am very relieved and thankful to you."

"I hope you're not upset that I brought it up in the first place. I guess eventually I'd have seen both these memos together and you'd never have had that anxiety."

I leaned forward and took Skip's hands. "Don't worry about it, dear." I couldn't explain how his alerting me about Oliver's list was what had spurred me to dig into Ken's boxes and ultimately brought me to Angela. "If you hadn't told me, I would never have cleaned out the garage," I said.

"That reminds me. Did you get anywhere with Sunaqua Falls?"

"Not yet," I said. "I might just drop the whole project."

"Are you sure you don't want me to dig a little more?"

"Positive."

"Well, moving right along. The stuff on the flash drive gives us, like, a gazillion more motives and suspects. Lynch and Crowley are at the top of the list still, since they had a half a gazillion suspect projects themselves."

"Did you arrest them?"

"Warrants are being prepared. It'll be on the news soon. I just couldn't wait to tell you." He sat back, the smile of victory on his face. "When they realize their attempt to ambush the info on the flash drive has failed, they are going to be so pi-p-put out."

"Don't let me cramp your language style."

Skip usually watched his tongue in front of Maddie. I didn't need to be protected from a vulgar word or two, but I loved him for being so considerate.

He did the mash. He did the monster mash.

I checked my cell phone. "It's Henry," I said.

"Ah."

I tried not to interpret Skip's smile.

I clicked the phone on.

"Okay to come back?" Henry asked.

"Why wouldn't it be?"

"Okay, then."

A man of few words. No long discourse on how I might want more time alone or whether I was discussing something family-only with Skip. Just, "Okay."

I added that to the list of things I liked about Henry Baker.

While I was between gentlemen callers, my landline rang.

"Geraldine, this is Artie Dodd."

Too late, I thought. "Hello, Artie. It's been a long time."

"I hear you're trying to reach me."

I took the phone to the chair in my living room that faced my patio doors and my garden beyond. If I were going to stay in the relatively good mood brought on by Skip and Henry, I'd need something cheery to look at. "That's right. How did you find out?"

"I still have a friend in our old building, and after you left that message, the new people asked around and it got back to me. I was surprised the old number I have for you works. You're still in the Eichler in Lincoln Point?"

"You make it sound like a bad thing," I said, half teasing.

"We couldn't get away from all that Bay Area hustle and bustle fast enough. We're way up here in Sea Ranch. Came up where we get our mail a week after everyone else. Ruth and I love it."

"I'm glad to hear it."

"Sorry I haven't been in touch. It's the old story about being busier in retirement, you know, golf on all the days that end in a 'y'." He laughed.

I'd been to Sea Ranch a couple of times with Ken on

drives along the Sonoma-Mendocino coast. Ken loved the award-winning architecture in that area: timber-frame structures that were meant to blend in with the natural environment. We'd both agreed that we'd never want to live there, however.

"It's too far from the Bronx," Ken would say, and I'd know he meant not just in miles but on many levels.

"Artie, I had a specific reason for calling you."

"I figured."

I let my gaze fall on my beautiful orange zinnias and reminded myself to breathe. "I was going through the boxes of material from Ken's old office and I came upon some things I wanted to talk to you about."

"I wondered when you'd get around to it. I did my best to get to Esther before she boxed everything up. I was hoping eventually you'd just toss everything without looking at it."

"I almost did. Anyway, I found out what I need to know, so I'm all set."

That was one way to put it.

Artie took a few seconds to respond. "He felt awful keeping it from you, Geraldine. I found out only by accident when I opened a bank statement that came to the office. I know he wanted to tell you, but a promise was a promise, and you know Ken."

I thought I did. "Yes, well . . ."

"Did the Estates contact you?"

"No." I tried not to sound rude, but I wasn't eager to share any more with Artie.

"Good. I sent a note to them shortly after Ken died, saying that the last payment would be on such-and-such a month, so that should have been it."

"Well, thanks, Artie. It was nice of you to call."

"Come and visit sometime. Ruth would love to see you."

I took down Artie and Ruth's new numbers and promised to check my calendar for a time to drive up the coast.

I couldn't put my finger on the reason, but I knew I'd never visit Artie. And I had a feeling he knew it, too.

Henry seemed happier than I was that the files on the flash drive cleared Ken's name.

"Isn't that terrific news," he said. Not a question, so I didn't feel I needed to answer. He paused and I saw that he was studying my face.

"I should let Maddie know in general terms what a great help she was." I checked my watch. "It will be a while before she's home from school."

"You shouldn't expect to be able to rejoice right away, Gerry," Henry said. "You've had a lot to process today."

How transparent was I that everyone could tell my mood?

"I'm very relieved," I said. "I thought it would be obvious."

"Okay." I wouldn't have blamed Henry if he yelled, "Grouch," and left, but he didn't, for which I was very grateful. "Does all this mean that Lynch or Crowley killed Oliver?" he asked.

"I'm not sure. Skip didn't mention that, just that they're all suspects now."

"And the fire?"

"I don't know about that, either."

A little selfish, I thought, just because my two big questions had been answered, I seemed to be tuning out of the investigation. I hadn't been in contact with Susan at a time when I could have given her some comfort. And there was still a killer loose in Lincoln Point.

"What are your plans for today?" Henry asked.

I hadn't looked much further than getting through the day. Now I decided I'd spent enough time being glum.

"Halloween," I said. "I'm way behind. I need to make Maddie's costume and finish a haunted house."

"Can I help?"

"Do you know where I can get eye of newt?"

I couldn't have asked for a better distraction—spending the afternoon doing crafts with Henry in his workshop. He'd convinced me that he had better supplies for the projects we needed to finish.

As if we were two mates in preschool, Henry and I made costumes for our granddaughters. Taylor had decided she could have the same costume as Maddie, since they attended different schools. Thus, their grandparents were busy making newts out of pieces of rubber and forming eyes (of frog) out of resin.

If Maddie hadn't been playing police computer tech all weekend, she might have been able to finish her costume herself. But Taylor had sewn her own pinafore and helped Maddie with hers, so they'd at least participated.

"Do you think the girls would get as much of a kick out of this as we are?" Henry asked, attaching an amazing orange light over the outside door of my haunted dollhouse.

"Impossible," I said.

Henry had prepared a resin mold for tongue of dog and blindworms. My job was to add the appropriate colors and cut wiggly shapes. I'd trade that for expert wiring any day.

Henry peered over my shoulder as I stirred a sickly pink color meant for the slippery tongues of dog I was creating. "Do you think this is what Shakespeare had in mind when he wrote the witches' speeches?" Henry asked.

"No, but he'd be delighted," I said. "I wish I'd thought of getting my students involved this way."

"You could have sent them to my shop."

He did the mash. He did the monster mash.

I saw Skip's caller ID, usually one of my favorite sights, either because I was expecting an update on an investigation or just because I loved him. But at the moment, seeing his phone number meant I had to leave the sphere of springy miniatures of "adder's fork and blind-worm's sting, lizard's leg and owlet's wing" and pay attention to the often nasty life-size world.

"It's a great day for criminal justice," Skip said.

I was glad the men in my life had a positive outlook while I was in my moody phase. "You figured out who killed Oliver Halbert?"

"Not quite that, but we finally have closure on the fire at the E&E Parts factory. Would you believe that all the sprinklers in the work area of the factory were fake? Now Lynch and the twins are duking it out over whose idea it was to pull that trick. They just stuck the little gizmos on the ceiling, but they weren't hooked up."

"Why would anyone do that? Weren't the Fergusons putting their own property at risk?"

"Greedy people can be shortsighted."

I was dumbfounded. "You're saying that if the sprinklers had been working, it wouldn't have mattered how the fire got started. It might have been drowned out quickly."

"Exactly. All they cared about was money and time, just getting the building past inspection. Maybe they planned to go back and put in real ones later, but with Crowley at the desk, they could get approval with the fake ones."

"And it cost a man's life."

"That's the awful part."

"Was the whole family involved?" I pictured foxy old Lillian signing off on orders and never mailing them.

"Hard to say. One thing for sure, Lillian did everything to protect her boys from suspicion, including giving them false alibis for the day of the murder."

"Did Oliver know all this, by the way? About the sprinklers?"

"Uh-huh. The files are on his flash drive. Memos back and forth, work orders, you name it. The guy was one sharp investigator. We could have used him on the LPPD."

"The LPPD has you."

"Thanks, Aunt Gerry. I'm glad you're feeling better."

I was embarrassed that my distress over personal issues had caused my loved ones to be concerned about me and had blinded me temporarily to the real problems my friends and neighbors were facing.

I resolved to spend not another minute in resentment over the past.

"I need to bake some cookies," I told Henry when I clicked off. "I should take a package over to Susan."

He smiled. "And some for me?" he asked, now hunched over an electrical gadget that was going to revolutionize the lighting in my dollhouse, he'd boasted.

"For you, a double batch."

Then, to my utter amazement, I leaned over and kissed his cheek.

Chapter 20

My kitchen smelled of warm ginger. All my Halloween decorations and projects were complete. Three of the four major puzzles that had consumed the last few days had been solved, with reasonably acceptable results. Ken's reputation was intact and some or all of the consortium of Lynch, Crowley, Ferguson, and Ferguson would pay for the fatal fire that resulted from their greed.

The rogue cop who was Lynch's inside man—no one I knew, I was happy to hear—had been suspended, pending investigation.

To top it all, Henry and I had plans for dinner later this evening. Things were looking up.

To add to the sunny mood, my ringing landline showed that I had a call from Maddie from Palo Alto.

"Are you home from school already?"

"I'm in the car. Mom picked me up. She says I can't go to Lincoln Point tomorrow afternoon because I might be getting a cold. Nuts."

"I'm sorry to hear that. Are you feeling bad?"

"I'm just stuffy and my throat itches a little, but it might be better by tomorrow."

"I think you should stay there, sweetheart, and get some extra rest. You don't want to be sick for the Halloween party. Mr. Baker and I finished your costume today."

"Taylor's, too?"

"Taylor's, too, plus the haunted dollhouse."

"Can we go to the party at the Fergusons' factory this year, too?"

"We'll see." I was sure Maddie had a good idea this meant "no," as it usually did for generations of parents and grandparents. "But definitely I'll be there for your school party."

"I made enough witches and ghosts for the factory party, too. Can you take them over?"

"I can do that. Now, I have some good news for you."

I told Maddie how her magic computer skills helped the LPPD find out about a lot of dishonesty that was going around in Lincoln Point. I kept it as general as I could.

"They cracked the password? How? How? Did they use that special software my teacher talks about? Will they show me how to do it?" I pictured her kicking her feet in the front seat of the Porters' SUV.

"We'll have to ask Uncle Skip, but I'll bet he can arrange a tutorial for you."

"Really? Wicked. Grandma, wait till you see this one street in Palo Alto. Everyone must have worked on the weekend because it's all decorated, but not as good as Sangamon River Road. One house has a scarecrow that jumps around, though. You know, like the one Mr. and Mrs. Ferguson used to have?"

I remembered; I was sorry Maddie did. But I heard only good spirits in my granddaughter's voice.

"You take care of yourself, sweetheart. I'll miss you."

I didn't dare mention that I was glad she wouldn't be back to Lincoln Point until Friday at the earliest, thus giving her uncle Skip another few days to discover who killed Oliver Halbert.

"I'll miss you, too. Mom wants to talk to you."

Mary Lou had been tuned in through a contraption on the visor of her car and now took over.

"Nice that all that stuff about the corrupt city inspections has been settled."

If you only knew, I thought.

Mary Lou and I made plans for my trip to Palo Alto for the Angelican Hills Halloween party, where Maddie would appear as "eye of newt" and so on.

My daughter-in-law offered to cook dinner for all of us.

"That would be wonderful."

"Henry, too, of course," she said.

"I'll see if he's free that day."

Mary Lou howled. I couldn't imagine why.

Was I back in junior year of high school? I had a big problem with what to wear to dinner on Tuesday night. It would be the first time Henry and I would be meeting without an excuse. We'd be getting together not because our granddaughters wanted to play, or because we had a woodworking or miniatures project to complete, or because I needed some brawn to help me in the garage. It would be just us, adults having dinner, "at a restaurant with cloth napkins" was all Henry would say.

I looked through the section of my closet that did not consist of clothing I could wear to do my gardening. There were beige slacks, cream-colored tops, an off-white sweater set, a brown tweed jacket, and more of the same. Was I re-

ally this colorless? Apparently I'd been putting all my color
energy into dollhouses and room boxes.

I kept clothes I hardly wore at the back of an antique
armoire. I opened a side drawer in the giant piece of furniture and found a royal blue silk shell. It was a start.

Henry had seen me in layers of mismatched sweaters
and socks; he'd heard me cry and witnessed my worst
moods. I didn't need to worry about what I wore tonight.
Henry had invited a colorless grandmother and crafter to
dinner.

It still took me a half hour to decide.

Later, in an elegant restaurant in San Francisco's
Embarcadero Center, I sat across from Henry, who was
wearing a royal blue silk tie and a brown tweed jacket. We
shared "this old thing?" stories and had a good laugh.

We ended the evening with some coffee back at my
house.

Things were looking up more than I'd hoped for.

My plan was to take Maddie's felt witches and glue
ghosts, with a note, to the Fergusons on Wednesday afternoon. If no one was home (or if the whole family was already in jail, I mused), I'd leave the package at the door. I
wasn't anxious to see any of the E&E Parts owners, except
possibly mild-mannered Sam, too soon.

I rummaged through the Halloween items and supplies
on my crafts table to find Maddie's creations amid the rub-
ble of half-finished items, scraps that hadn't been swept
into the wastebasket yet, and oddments that needed to be
sorted and put into the proper bins. The life of a crafter.

Maddie and Taylor had been busier than I thought. Besides the witches and ghosts, they'd finished several miniature masks and a couple of scarecrows.

I picked up one of the scarecrows. About five inches long, with a tiny plaid shirt and a red felt smile, it would be perfect for a miniature fall centerpiece. I rolled the scarecrow between my fingers, checking the glue job Maddie had done. She was getting better at not overgluing, one of the giveaways of an amateur crafter.

Something struck a chord. The figure looked like most traditional scarecrows. Like the one the Fergusons set on their porch every year. Like the one that must have been on the porch before it was replaced by Oliver Halbert's lifeless body.

Where was that scarecrow now?

Had the killer taken it with him? I pictured him running down the street, a floppy, life-size scarecrow over his shoulder. Not likely. Had he broken in to the Fergusons' house and dumped it in the hallway? The police had searched the immediate area while I'd been there with Maddie and the teenagers. If they'd found the scarecrow on the grounds, they would have taken it as evidence, I'd think. It might have Oliver's blood on it. I would have remembered if they'd carried out a scarecrow.

My mind raced with the question and unlikely answers.

Another scarecrow came to my mind. The one I'd seen in pieces during my tour of the factory, stuffed behind the mops and brooms and Lillian's costume. Had that been the original scarecrow? Why would the killer cross town to plant the real scarecrow at E&E Parts?

Unless . . .

I replaced Maddie's mini scarecrow on the table and went to get my notepad from my bag. I hadn't taken the time to clean out my tote from the long weekend's activities. (And last night I'd used my dressy, beaded purse, crafted by Mabel at one of our meetings.)

Pleasant memories of last night would have to wait, however.

My spiral notepad was still open to the pages I'd used at the crime scene on Friday afternoon. I read through the names of the flustered teenagers, and found the one I wanted.

Ashley Gordon, Two-two-one Lee Street.

I held my breath waiting for directory assistance to find her telephone number, then let it out when I was connected to her.

"Hello?" Another sigh of relief at the sound of the young voice.

I explained who I was, regretting having to remind Ashley of the dreadful scene on Sangamon River Road.

"I didn't see anything else," she said, before I could ask her my crucial question. I was used to teenagers feeling guilty whether they were or not.

"I just need to clarify something you said already, Ashley. I won't keep you long. Can you take just one minute? It's very important."

"I guess."

"You told me that you'd been at the Fergusons' house earlier that day. Is that correct?"

"Yeah, but honest, it was lunchtime. It wasn't anywhere near the time we saw—"

Did she honestly think she was a suspect? I cherished moments like this when I was teaching—it gave me such power over their young psyches.

"I believe you, Ashley. I just want to know, are you sure you saw the real scarecrow on the porch that same day?"

"Totally. Me and my boyfriend—well, my ex-boyfriend—

Noah were there. He'd never seen it jump up and scream, so he was, like, totally freaked."

"Thanks very much, Ashley. I hope you can go back to what you were doing and have a good evening."

"Okay, 'bye. Me and my friends are watching *Scary Movie 4*."

I should have known.

Where was Skip when I needed him? He wasn't answering his phone. Could my nephew have taken my advice and decided to take time off for further recuperation? Why did he choose this time to obey me?

I left a message for Skip: "Did you ever find the original scarecrow? What happened to the real Ferguson scarecrow?" Neither of these questions seemed to be the right phrasing. I tried again. "I think the original scarecrow, the one that was on the porch before Oliver's body appeared, is at the Fergusons' factory. How could it have gotten off the property unless one of the Fergusons . . . ?" Should I say the word over the phone? I had the silly thought that I'd better leave it at that.

Furthermore, where was Henry when I needed him? I left a message for him, also. "I have to deliver the Halloween decorations to the Fergusons' factory. If you're free and want to take a ride, call me."

Was everyone on a long lunch break?

I knew the wise course would be to wait for one of them to call me back. It probably wasn't the best idea to go to the factory by myself.

While I was waiting (pacing) I called Susan. No answer there, either. I left a message apologizing for not being available lately and told her to call me whenever she wanted company bearing fresh ginger cookies.

Ten minutes had passed since my call to Skip.

It was broad daylight. It wasn't as if I planned to challenge the twins or aggravate Lillian or Sam. I just wanted to check out the scarecrow in the corner and delivering the Halloween decorations provided the perfect cover. No one would be the wiser. What if the scarecrow had Oliver's blood on it and one of the Fergusons was removing the evidence right now? Or was it already gone?

If I were the killer, I thought, I'd display that figure in full view of the partygoers, with all the other decorations. Hide it in plain sight. A popular trick in mystery fiction.

I'd waited long enough.

I called the factory.

"Good afternoon. E&E Parts." Lillian's voice.

"This is Geraldine Porter, Lillian. I wondered if I could stop by with some decorations. My granddaughter made them but she's not feeling well and she insisted I give them to you in plenty of time for your party."

"Your lovely little granddaughter. Yes, please do stop by. I'll be here until six."

Lillian had a unique way of mismatching her words to her tone, so that when she said "lovely little granddaughter" I wanted to protect Maddie from even a moment in Lillian's thoughts. I could have asked how her "wonderful grown-up boys," were, but thought that would be rude. I'd try to find out another way.

Remembering the strong breezes that usually swept over the outskirts of town, I put on a (beige) windbreaker and took one more look at the silent phone.

I gathered the ghosts and the witches and headed for the factory.

Chapter 21

The treeless industrial neighborhood didn't look much different than it had on Monday morning. I saw very few vehicles and no people at all as I drove through the streets that were named to honor aviation history.

I turned from Neil Armstrong Lane to Hangar Way and stopped about a block from the factory. I took out my cell and tried Skip and Henry again.

No answer.

No problem. I continued on to the entrance of E&E Parts. I wished the neighborhood weren't so deserted. Hadn't Lillian mentioned what a good thing it was that they had no residential neighbors, since factory grounds tended to be noisy? Not this one.

I grabbed my tote and the bag with Maddie's Halloween crafts plus a few of my own and walked up the path, with a neat lawn on either side, to the glass double front doors.

I didn't see a doorbell or another way to announce my presence and figured most visitors were delivery people who arrived at the dock on the side of the building. I peered through the glass and immediately jumped back.

A witch was walking toward me.

Lillian, in full costume, opened the door.

I'd have been frightened if she hadn't looked so absurd. Witches should be tall and thin as a broomstick, I mused, not short and chubby like Lillian. Her outfit was voluminous and shapeless, as if she'd cut a hole in a bolt of black polyester and stuck her head into it, letting the fabric fall where it would. The hemline was several inches too long, making Lillian look even stubbier. Her hat was lop-sided; her grin comical.

"I know. It's pretty funny-looking, isn't it?" Lillian remarked. "You're handy with a needle, I'll bet. Maybe you can help me with this."

"I'd be happy to try," I said.

She took the plastic bag of decorations I offered. "More treats," she said. "You're too kind."

Why didn't I believe she was sincere? In fact, she handled the bag with a slight hesitancy, using only two fingers at one corner to raise it to her eye level and examine the contents. She might have thought I'd handed her a poisonous apple, but that would have been backwards.

Lillian ushered me into one of several offices in an area that was to the front of the workshop. I wished she'd have led me back to where the mops and brooms were, but there was plenty of time for that.

We discussed the best way for me to help her with the costume. I ended up kneeling on the floor next to a desk that held Lillian's nameplate while she stood on a small stepstool. I longed to open the desk drawers and search through the credenzas along the wall—not to find the scarecrow, but who knew what other clues might be filed away? I wondered if the police had confiscated the files as part of a follow-up on Oliver's investigation.

For now, I simply used the supplies in my ever-handy sewing kit and pinned up the dress.

"I think this will be better," I said, standing. I folded some of the fabric around her arms to make sleeves. "I can take this home and sew it up for you on my machine, or I can just baste it in place right now."

"Just baste it, if you would. I'm never going to wear it again, after all."

I was glad to hear that.

The twins' mother didn't show any signs of the distress I would have felt if my sons had been accused of fraud that led to a man's death. It seemed like just another normal day at E&E Parts. Except for the witch's costume.

Lillian asked for privacy to change into her regular clothes. I took advantage of the opportunity by grabbing my tote and the plastic bag of decorations from the desk where Lillian had deposited it and walking toward the work area. I knew it wouldn't take long for her to throw off the black fabric, so I moved quickly.

I pushed open the swinging doors to the workshop. There were no lights on and I wondered if the production end of the factory was officially closed. I hadn't thought to ask Skip where exactly all the Fergusons were. Maybe the twins were already in jail and work had stopped. If so, Lillian was certainly putting up a good party front in spite of it.

It had turned overcast outside and the hulking gray machines scattered throughout the concrete floor took on the specter of tombstones. I wondered where Sam was. Or anyone. I was glad swinging doors didn't have locks.

I passed oversize tools that had plugs thicker than

I'd ever seen. The plug for my reading light would have seemed miniature in comparison. Were there more volts in a factory? What were volts anyway? My brain was clearly overloaded.

The brooms and maintenance equipment were on the right wall as I remembered. I headed over, carrying the bag of decorations as my cover. "I was just going to put these with the other decorations," I planned to say, if caught back here.

I found the gray barrel-shaped container with cleaning supplies. The golf clubs were gone, which might have explained where Sam was.

And the scarecrow was gone, which definitely explained why I felt a sharp poke in my back, from a hard object.

"I'm sorry it had to come to this, Geraldine. Turn around."

I turned to see Lillian, still in her costume, pointing a gun at me.

She'd set me up, the crafty old witch. She wanted to find out the real reason for my visit, and she did.

"Sam said you might be trouble. He said you noticed the scarecrow when you were here the other day. I destroyed it that night, but I knew the damage was done."

"I—what do you mean?" Sam had given me too much credit. I'd had no idea what I was looking at the other day.

"What am I going to do with you, Geraldine? I knew you were bad news as soon as I heard you were out there taking notes the day the kids found Oliver's body. I sent one of the boys to find the notebook but they botched the mission."

"One of the twins was after my notebook?" I thought about the way my desk drawers had been tampered with.

Lillian didn't answer. She was now holding the gun with two hands. Was this a good sign or a bad one? Dare I hope that she might drop it?

I moved inch by inch. *Inch by Inch, It's a Cinch*, the Pier Thirty-nine souvenir T-shirt read. I wondered if I'd ever see it again. I tried to close in on the brooms and mops sticking out of the barrel, potential weapons, but Lillian moved with me, keeping the gun trained on me and her witch's body between me and anything I might use to defend myself. Not that a broomstick was any match for a gun.

Lillian in a flowered housedress was scary. Lillian at the head of a conference table at a board meeting was scarier. Lillian in a witch's outfit, holding a gun, was scariest.

Every nerve in my body was on edge. Lillian must have known she couldn't get away with killing me, but I didn't think it mattered to her. She seemed like a woman who had nothing to lose.

This was not the way I'd pictured it playing out. I was younger, taller, and infinitely more fit than Lillian. I'd been worried about running into Sam or one of the boys, who might have been able to best me in a physical conflict. I hadn't counted on being done in by a squat old lady with a lethal weapon. There was nothing like a loaded gun to gain an upper hand, no matter what your age or size.

"I've lived in this town a long time, Geraldine. I hear things. I know you were asking questions in the coffee shop and pretty much making a nuisance of yourself around town. I knew it was only a matter of time before you'd figure it all out."

"Lillian, your sons are going to have to answer for their business practices, no matter what you do to me."

"You sound like Oliver Halbert. Who was he and who are you to tell me what I can and can not do for my sons?"

"Did Oliver confront you with what he found out about the fire?"

"Oliver came to the house when the boys and Sam were at the factory. I was home alone. I often go home and cook something and take it back for lunch. I take care of my family. He threatened to expose the twins' little error, leaving them liable for everything—inspection irregularities, the fire, the janitor's death. Shooting him was self-defense on my part, when you think about it."

I thought about it and it was not self-defense. Maybe I should make it self-defense in my case by at least trying to attack Lillian. I looked around for something I could use. Any of the machines would have done the job, if I could have lifted them. I saw grinders, blades, heavy blunt objects, and a myriad of things that would do for a stabbing. Nothing within my reach, however.

"This could be over, Lillian, if you just put the gun down."

Apparently I didn't have decent words, either, just lame platitudes. I felt a stream of perspiration roll down my back. I knew my hair was as wet as if I'd been out trick-or-treating in the rain.

"It's already over," Lillian said. "I shot Oliver." Lillian's eyes glazed over. Should I make a move? Before I could decide, her gaze met mine again. "If I could only figure out what to do with you."

I knew she meant not all of me, but my body.

"I'm sorry we had to give up one of our guns, and now another," she continued. "We have a number of them that aren't registered. Do you know why?"

There was only one correct response. "Why, Lillian?"

"Because there's evil in the world." This from a woman in a costume that could have passed as the devil's own. "We've been robbed over and over. Kids break in and smash things just to steal a screwdriver. Or they tip over every machine just to hear the noise. It costs us thousands of dollars for their entertainment. But if you shoot one of them, the police are harder on you than they are on the thieves. So we take care of ourselves."

I wondered if Lillian were confessing to a rash of killing petty thieves. One more wouldn't matter. She could always say I was an intruder. It was looking worse and worse for me.

"It was already dusk and I didn't know what to do with Oliver." Lillian had gone back in time. I shuffled my feet to relieve the pressure of standing still for so long. She jerked the gun. I stopped shuffling. "I dragged the scarecrow into the house and out the back door, then I managed to push Oliver into place on my porch. It's a good thing there are no stay-at-home moms on my street."

"And you drove it over here to be part of the decorations." I wanted to tell her how brilliant she was, perhaps recommend Edgar Allan Poe's "The Purloined Letter." I did neither.

I'd closed in a little on Lillian. My best shot was to overpower her in a surprise move. If I could catch her off guard, she might not think to pull the trigger.

Thunk. Thunk. A noise from the office area.

"Geraldine?" Henry's voice? Why so formal?

Lillian turned toward the sound. It was now or never. In another two seconds, Henry's life would also be at stake.

I swung my heavy tote down from my shoulder and against Lillian's hand with full force. The gun fell to the floor and I kicked it as hard as I could into a pile of wood shavings that reminded me of Henry's workshop, and ran back toward the office area where his voice had come from.

But it wasn't Henry.

"Geraldine? Is that your car out there?" Sam asked.

I ran past Sam, who was nonplussed, clearly not part of Lillian's plan for today.

I burst through the double doors and—this time it was real—into Henry's chest.

Skip pulled up at the same time. Which was my signal that I no longer had to be in charge. I could allow myself to collapse.

As I slipped to the ground, my head ending up at Henry's feet, I heard the howling of a witch.

Chapter 22

"We hauled them all in," Skip said. "All the Fergusons. For one reason or another."

Nine hours later, my adventure at E&E Parts seemed like a bad trick someone had played on me because I didn't have enough treats to hand out.

At midnight, Skip, Henry, Beverly, and I sat in my living room, trying to make sense of a monstrous Halloween season.

"Did the twins know that their mother was a killer? Did Sam know?" I asked.

Skip shrugged. "I've never seen such a family. It's a very complicated dynamic. Everyone in the Ferguson family was covering for everyone else. Lillian gathered her clan around her and, without revealing that she had killed Oliver, got them all to swear that everyone was at the factory all day on that Friday. Sam might have figured it out when you pointed out the scarecrow."

"But I had no idea it was the real scarecrow the first time I saw it."

"It happens," Skip said. "Sam might have had a feeling about it and then interpreted your innocent remark accordingly."

Henry had had his arm around my shoulders since right after I'd been checked out of the ER, it seemed. "Is Lillian Ferguson the oldest female killer? Or the oldest killer, period?" he asked.

"Not at all," Beverly, our criminal justice student, answered. "You should look up this case of a woman in Minnesota who shot a man who was her caregiver. She was eighty-eight and he was in his sixties. I think it was because she was jealous of the attention he was paying to another woman."

"I guess you're never too old to start a new life," Henry said.

We all cheered the idea, if not the Minnesota woman's, or Lillian's, choices.

"If you men don't mind, I need a final word with Gerry tonight," Beverly said.

"I don't mind, but—" Skip began, looking at Henry.

"Enough, Skip," I said. "I'll see you tomorrow. And don't forget you promised to go to Maddie's Halloween party this weekend."

The men trudged off in mock poutiness.

Once we were alone, Beverly wasted no time.

"I was so scared for you, Gerry, even though Skip didn't call until they knew you were fine."

"I really am fine." I spread my arms to indicate: no bruises.

"The worst of it was that I thought you were upset with

me, and if anything had ever happened, I'd never have for-
given myself."

I might have known Beverly wouldn't let me get away
with simply returning to normal. "I know I've been a little
distracted, but why would I be upset with you, Beverly?"

She shrugged and looked at me with a guilty expression.
"Maybe because I've been spending too much time with
Nick? But we're at that stage where we're still getting to
know each other, and—"

"There's no need to explain. I don't begrudge you one
minute of time with Nick, or anything or anyone else who
makes you happy. I feel terrible that you'd think otherwise."

"What is it, then?" she persisted.

"I had something on my mind that doesn't matter at all
now, really," I said.

"Okay, but I'm here if you want to hash it out."

"I'm fine, thanks. Sorry I let it get to me. Why don't we
move to the atrium and I'll get more tea."

"And more cookies?"

"And more cookies."

I felt cheery enough to sing, if I were the singing type.
Things were back to normal on all counts.

The feeling lasted all of five minutes, the time it took for
me to gather cookies and tea and head back to the atrium.

Where Beverly was standing with a pad of paper in her
hand.

"What's this, Gerry?"

The name and number of Sunaqua Estates was what
it was.

I couldn't believe how careless I'd been. It must have
been only in my dreams that I'd torn that paper to shreds
and tossed it in my recycling bin with empty detergent
bottles and crinkled foil.

I took the small pad from her. "It's nothing," I said.

Beverly's expression was as sober as I'd ever seen it. "You found out? After all these years."

I cleared my throat. "You knew?"

Beverly gave me a strange look. "How could I not know?"

Why did this remind me of an Abbott and Costello routine? There was nothing funny about it.

"Did it happen when you were both living at home?"

She pointed to the notepad. "Are we talking about the same thing here, Gerry? Sunaqua Estates?"

"The . . . the baby."

"Angela. My daughter. When did you think she was born?"

Beverly's daughter? Was Beverly trying to cover for her brother?

I could tell by her face that she wasn't. I looked down at the tray of tea and cookies on the atrium table and wondered how it got there. Surely I hadn't managed to set it down in just the right place, without spills or the crashing sound of breaking china.

"Angela was your daughter?"

My atrium took on an otherworldly glow. Beverly and I sat down together, slowly, as if we were practicing a part in a play.

Beverly stared over my shoulder; her voice seemed to come from the past.

"I was fifteen years old. That's four years older than Maddie. I was still using my yellow phone that was shaped like a banana, but I thought I was so grown up. Grown up enough to date a senior. My mother was against it, but I was so flattered." Beverly ran her sleeve across her teary eyes, the way children sometimes do. "I went upstate to Sunaqua to have the baby. The plan—my mother's plan—was to leave her for adoption, but the baby was premature and had a lot of problems, so my mother let me stay with her for a while."

"And the father?"

"Huh. He never gave me the time of day again. How foolish I was."

"You were a child, Beverly. He took advantage of you."

I heard every word Beverly spoke, at the same time trying to adjust to a whole new awareness. Not Ken's baby. Beverly's little girl. I wondered how long it would take for me to absorb the facts. Angela was Ken's niece, not his daughter.

Beverly looked over my shoulder, focusing on a high point on the wall, as if a photo of her baby were projected there.

"Angela was jaundiced, with a high fever all the time, and she didn't know how to feed. The doctors thought it was a flu. After a couple of months she seemed okay, but then she contracted delayed-onset meningitis." Beverly paused. Remembering. "There were . . . complications. She . . . died."

Beverly took a sip of tea. She looked at me as if I'd just arrived at the table.

"I can't imagine how painful that was, Beverly. I can't imagine."

With no prompting, but out of her own reflections, Beverly seemed finally to grasp the nature of the misunderstanding. "Gerry. You thought Ken had a baby, didn't you?"

"I saw some photographs."

She shook her head. "I told Ken to destroy every one of them."

"He didn't. In fact, he sent money to the Estates on a regular basis. I had no idea until last weekend."

"I had a feeling he was doing that but I didn't want to know. When Angela died, it was so painful I couldn't bear it. My mother saw it as a good thing, believe it or not. She let me stay upstate until it was over. Didn't you ever wonder why I was graduating from high school a year older than most kids?"

"I never thought about it. Kids start at different ages; a year plus or minus wouldn't seem odd."

"It did to me," Beverly said. "I made Ken promise he would tell absolutely no one. When he met you, when I met you, I came very close to telling you, but I couldn't. Ken begged me to. It hurt him to keep it from you, but I was adamant. The longer I waited, the more impossible it became. Now I realize how wrong and selfish I was to pressure him that way."

"You were a kid and in a lot of turmoil."

"I thought you'd think less of me."

"That would never happen, Beverly."

"Once I knew that, it was too late. What was done—"

"Couldn't be undone."

My world seemed to have changed shape. In the first, dark, angular world Ken had a child he never told me about. A new light, round world took its place and in it Ken was the big brother, protecting his sister and keeping a promise he made to her.

"You've never told anyone?"

"Not even my husband. When Skip was born and he was all there, you know, and bright and healthy, I was so grateful. I thought surely there would be something wrong with him. Because there was something wrong with me."

"What an awful burden, Beverly."

"Can you ever forgive me? If I ever dreamed you'd find photographs and that you'd think—"

I reached out and took her hands.

"Can you forgive me, for not going to you when I found them?"

We sat for a long time, holding hands, each reconciling a different part of our past.

Chapter 23

Angelican Hills School went all out for its Halloween party. A small stage play, with our haunted dollhouse as an outstanding prop, was a big hit. Maddie got accolades not only for her performance as one of Shakespeare's witches but also for doing such a wonderful job on the house.

I was very proud of her. She'd finally figured out all on her own how to make the flimsy white ghost stick out from an upstairs window. She'd attached a white pipe cleaner to the ghost's body and glued one end to the edge of the windowsill in such a way that the support didn't show. The ghost appeared to be emerging outward and upward into the night.

In a predictable move, we headed for ice cream after the play, at Palo Alto's equivalent of Sadie's.

Everyone acted true to form.

Richard questioned the use of the school's tuition money on such an extravaganza.

Mary Lou explained how the arts in all forms were an important part of a child's education.

Maddie said, "The sundaes here are wicked."

Skip said, "I'll have two."

Henry said, "My treat."

The ice cream parlor was located in an upscale strip mall where every store handed out treats to anyone who was in a costume. While we enjoyed our sundaes and shakes, we greeted the usual ballerinas, pirates, vampires, clowns, and assorted Disney characters. This year there seemed to be many more high-tech costumes, too, like the toddler with a racing car, complete with running lights and a loud horn, protruding from his stomach, as if he were the driver. A teenage girl with the right side of her hair bleached blond and the left side a dull dark brown reminded me of my favorite cookie in the windows of New York delis: the "half-moon" or "black and white."

If we'd been asked to vote, mine would have gone to a miniature nun, about six years old, pushing a baby carriage. I wondered what the message was.

Dorothy from Oz appeared in a blue pinafore and red slippers. I was happy to see she hadn't brought the scarecrow.

Skip's costume was a big hit: a T-shirt with stencils of bees all over it, some with thick red marks through them.

"To bee or not to bee," Maddie had squealed.

One highlight of the evening was when Beverly leaned over to me from my left.

"I'm going to renew the endowment to Sunaqua Estates," she said.

The other highlight was when I decided to lean over to Henry on my right.

I gave him my best smile. "I've been thinking about that trip to Chicago."

Gerry's Miniature Tips

MINIATURE TIP FOR HALLOWEEN WITCH

This fun witch can be as detailed or as simple as you like. Adjust the pattern to make it simpler for younger children by eliminating smaller accessories such as the belt buckle and the necklace. Older children will want to add accessories of their own choosing.

Materials:

- Plastic spoon
- Standard pieces of lime green, white, purple, black, and light brown felt
- Pipe cleaners: one lime green, one gold
- 2 small wiggle eyes (available with doll parts in crafts stores)
- About 12 miniature light purple pom poms

- Scissors
- Tacky glue

Instructions:

1. Cut a square of lime green felt large enough to fold over and completely cover the top portion of the spoon.

2. Place the spoon on top of the green felt. Only the top (the part that holds the food) section of the spoon will be wrapped, not the handle. Place a dot of glue onto the back of the spoon to tack the felt in place. Wrap the felt completely around the spoon top, gluing as you go, tucking and gluing ends of the felt onto the back side of the spoon.

3. Cut out two identical dresses from the black felt. You can make a pattern first by laying the spoon on a piece of paper and drawing a dress around it. Lay one dress on your work surface and place the spoon on top, positioning it so the top of the handle lines up with the neck of the dress. Place the other dress directly on top and glue the assembly in place at the shoulders and neck area, being sure to leave the arm areas free.

4. Cut the lime green pipe cleaner into four equal pieces, which will be the witch's arms and legs. Fold each piece in half. Insert each piece so that the loops are sticking out and glue the pipe cleaner arms, legs, and dress in place. Glue the rest of the dress together along the sides.

5. Cut a strip of purple felt for the belt, wide enough to cover the waist area. Glue the piece together in the back. Optional: cut a square from the black felt for

the buckle, and glue to the front of the belt. Add beads or other ornaments to the belt, as long as they are "witchy" and not too cute!

6. To make the witch's hair, cut a 4-inch-by-3-inch rectangle from purple felt. Use scissors to fringe one of the long sides. Arrange the "hair" around the witch's head and trim where needed. Glue in place.

7. Cut two identical hats from the black felt. Just as you did with the dress, you can make a pattern first, being sure the hat pieces are pointy at the top and wide-brimmed on the bottom. Arrange the pieces of the black hat on the purple felt hair and glue in place.

8. Optional: cut a skinny strip of purple felt to use for a hatband and glue in place as you did with the dress belt. Add an ornament if desired.

9. Add a necklace by applying glue around the neckline of the dress and arranging miniature purple pom-poms in place.

10. Cut a small pointy nose from the lime green felt and glue the large end of it to the center of the witch's face so that the pointy end sticks out.

11. Glue the two wiggle eyes in place.

12. Make a mouth from a thin strip of white felt.

13. The broomstick: cut an 8-inch-by-3-inch rectangle from the light brown felt. Use scissors to fringe the 3-inch end, about 2 inches inward. Roll up the felt to create the broom bristles and glue together as you roll. Insert the gold pipe cleaner into the bottom end of the bristles and glue in place. Glue a thin strip of the light brown felt around the base of the broom

and trim the ends. Insert the bottom of the broom handle through one of the green pipe cleaner hands and glue in place.

14. Fly away to the moon!

MINIATURE TIP FOR SPRAY OF FLOWERS

You'll need flowers for that Halloween trip to a cemetery. Here are some ideas.

Materials:

- Pots of colored foam, shredded (A good brand for ready-made foam is Flower Soft, which comes in many different colors and combinations of colors.)
- Thin, flexible wire, white or green (If your design doesn't require the flower stem to be bent, a toothpick will do.)
- Scissors
- High-tack glue
- Medium-size beads (Look for beads to serve as vases. Beads with relatively large-diameter holes work best.)
- Thin tissue paper
- Narrow ribbon (1/16-inch) ribbon to wrap as a bouquet, if desired
- Scrap piece of Styrofoam or nursery foam

Instructions:

1. Spread out paper to make a work area. (The foam pieces are tiny and tend to fly around. You'll be glad you have a way to scoop them up and pour them back into the pot for later use.)

2. Cut the wire into sections about 2 inches long.

3. Dip a wire piece into a glob of glue, or use your finger to spread glue over the tip of the wire.

4. Add foam pieces. You can either roll the glued end of the wire around in the foam or grab a small amount of the colored foam bits and sprinkle them on the gluey tip. Use your fingers to work the arrangement as you wish: into a solid spherelike pattern to look like a bulb (e.g., yellow foam can be fashioned to resemble daffodils) or a long, thin stem of flowers (e.g, purple foam can be fashioned to resemble lilacs).

5. Stick completed flower stems upright in a piece of Styrofoam and let dry, approximately 30 minutes.

6. Gather stems as desired into a bouquet. Cut the stems to the same length, and add a dab of glue to hold together. Use tissue to wrap the bottoms in bouquet style. Add a small ribbon (2-millimeter silk ribbon works best).

Or:

7. Gather stems and insert into the hole of a medium-size bead. Bead can be crystal, wood, or any shape or material, as desired.

MINIATURE TIP FOR GLUE GHOSTS

Materials:

- White school glue
- Waxed paper

- Wiggle eyes
- Felt, buttons, pom-poms, and other optional accessories

Instructions:

1. Place a piece of waxed paper on a flat surface.

2. Squeeze glue from the bottle into the shape of a ghost.

3. Place wiggle eyes into the glue at "eye level."

4. If you would like to decorate your ghost, use felt, buttons, pom-poms, or whatever you like to add character. Ideas: Make a bow tie from felt, use pom-poms or beads for buttons, fabric for a scarf. Use your ghostly imagination!

5. Set aside to dry overnight. Note: It might take up to 12 hours to dry completely, depending on the thickness of the glue.

The glue should dry almost clear. Peel the ghosts off the paper and decorate the house or a party table or use as party favors.

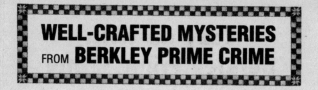